ARYA MATTHEWS

UNREASONABLE

RELUCTANT HEARTBREAKERS & SWEET TROUBLEMAKERS

INKED
KEYBOARD
PUBLISHING

unREASONable

Reluctant Heartbreakers & Sweet Troublemakers vol. 1

Published by Inked Keyboard Publishing.

hello@inkedkeyboard.com

ISBN 978-1-7332386-4-9 (ebook)
ISBN 978-1-7332386-6-3 (paperback)

Book, cover, and additional graphic design by Varvara Jones @ Inked Keyboard Publishing.

Fearlessness

Inspiration

Freedom

Inner Strength

Loyalty

⦿ Track 1
A Doomed Deal

Marshall

I kick the green room door closed to shut out the squealing fangirls at the far end of the hallway. I love them. I really do. They're my bread and butter, but after a three-hour show, I'm sweaty and sticky and dying for a second of silence, which I know I won't have until we're back home in a couple of days.

"The next gig is the last time I'm on the bass. I swear. The last time." CJ flops onto a worn leather sofa and drops his head back. He loves the guitar. Bass is just okay. It's his job—his second choice—not his dream.

"Yeah, yeah. Heard that before." Shane, our lead guitarist, tosses a towel at CJ and snickers when it hits him in the face.

"I mean it," CJ gripes at Shane as he covers his face with the towel.

Our manager barges in without knocking. "Boys, boys."

She always does that. Kiera is excellent at promoting us and awful at respecting boundaries.

"That was amazing. Amazing!" She clasps her hands together, making me wonder, for the hundredth time, whether she isn't our biggest fan. She probably is. When we signed with The Label, we had a hard time finding a manager that shared our vision. Kiera, inexperienced but super enthusiastic and in the middle of redefining her life's career, jumped right in, and cried from every corner just how great we are.

CJ starts from the sofa, "I am not playing the—"

"Bass anymore. I know. I know, my darling." Kiera sits next to him and lifts the corner of his towel tent. "I hope you can endure through one more show though."

"I can't exactly bail on the last gig of the tour, especially since we're playing it at our home base."

Kiera pats his cheek. "I'm glad to hear it. You've always had the best work ethic, Cristian. Because of that, I have a surprise for you."

CJ sits up, the towel sliding onto his lap. "We're getting another player?"

The exhaustion in the room melts away, replaced by a charged, anxious silence. Everyone exchanges glances. I peel off my sweaty T-shirt and pull on a dry one, but I keep my eyes on Kiera. She lounges on the sofa with her arms up on the backrest, a cunning smile on her made-up lips. I don't like that smile one bit. When Kiera smiles like that, mad schemes follow.

"Well?" Zach asks from the corner while he changes his socks and shoes.

Kiera continues, "The Label is willing to let you add another member to your band, but there are conditions."

I sit on the edge of a small coffee table. Of course there are conditions. Hopefully, they are too much for CJ to accept, and things will stay as they already are—perfect.

"Such as?" CJ asks when Kiera extends her pause for longer than necessary. She wields dramatic tension like she's the one who invented it.

Her smile broadens. "You can be the lead guitarist, but Shane will probably need to be on rhythm—"

"We'll rearrange as needed. If needed," I mutter. The Label will let us add someone? They have no say in how we handle the band roster. Not as much as they like to believe anyway.

"Done," CJ blurts out before anyone else can weigh in on the matter.

I look over at Shane, who would be giving up a lot of his spotlight if this happens, but he shrugs like he doesn't care one bit.

Kiera laughs. "Ever so eager. But wait for the rest of it."

CJ waves her off, and I get an uneasy feeling in my gut that the rest of the conditions won't be so simple.

"The Label will pick the bass replacement on their own, without an audition or you having a say in who that is. You'll have to stick with their choice for six months, long enough to record a single or two. And at the end of the probation period, you'll be able to decide whether to keep your new bassist or not. It's really not that bad if you think about it. Call it a music experiment."

I open my mouth to protest, but the rest of the band launches into the fray first, CJ being the loudest. "No way! That is not fair."

"How can you expect us to agree to this?" Shane adds. "Without an audition? Never."

"Seconded," Graham chimes in while he packs his favorite pair of drumsticks in his duffel bag.

"No audition, no new bassist," I say. "Sorry, CJ."

Before either Kiera or CJ can respond, our phones chime with a text from our driver telling us he's ready when we are and that the venue staff have cleared our path.

I grab my jacket. "Let's go."

Our driver's got great timing. Everyone's eager to get some rest, and hopefully, this talk of the new bassist will expire on its own now.

At least for tonight. I can bet my Telecaster, though, that CJ won't leave it alone altogether. He's desperate to ditch the bass.

"Do you know who The Label wants to give us?" Zach asks Kiera once we pile into the minibus. I could punch him for stirring the pot again. "What if it's Adam Jarvis? There's been talk he's been wanting to split from Random Ravens. Or Sam Kingsman? He's just finished a record with Gabriela Mendoza, so he'd be available for new projects."

I shake my head and crack open a cold bottle of Diet Coke. "Theoretically. He's always in high demand. We may be too late already. If we chose to do this."

Zach's got more speculations up his sleeve, as usual. "I know! We should ask them to poach Tristan Bailey from Acid Churro Dreams."

Shane joins in. "His temper is legendary, though, so maybe not. We already have Marshall."

He laughs and ducks behind his seat, ready for me to throw something at him. The only thing I've got is my caffeinated potion, but I need it. Besides, if I threw the bottle at him, it'd prove his point about my temper, which I may or may not have issues with.

Kiera's scheming smile is back. "I can't give you anything right now, guys, but I promise you, the g—the addition would be amazing. Honestly, you should agree to it."

Sitting next to CJ, I insert myself into Kiera's line of sight. "No. Not without meeting him and having him play with us. Absolutely not."

Kiera shrugs, still eyeing CJ. "I guess you don't want to play guitar as much as you say you do."

He fidgets with a key pendant hanging from his neck. "It's tempting," he says to me.

"I know that you're really, really sick of the bass, but this insane idea will come back to bite us. Big time."

"Just six months, Marshall. And if it flops, I'll play bass again."

Hope. That's all that I see in CJ's eyes.

I sip the soda and try to ignore my friend, but Project Viper is his baby. He conceived the idea, harassed the rest of us into joining, and worked his fingers to the bone until we signed with a reputable recording label. If anyone has the right to negotiate the matter, it's CJ. He gave up everything for the band. Even picked up an instrument that he didn't really like to fill in the spot when we kept failing to find a bassist early on. Maybe it's time for CJ to have something go his way.

"We want it all on paper with a signature from The Label's president, especially the part about kicking the new bassist out in six months if he sucks," I say to Kiera.

"Of course, Marshall, darling." Our manager rubs her hands. "This is going to be the best. You think you're popular now? Oooh, boys. You haven't seen anything yet!"

CJ and I exchange looks. CJ seems curious, but I'm doubtful it'll go according to Kiera's plans. Her enthusiasm is way too suspicious.

"This is going to bite us," I repeat because I know we've just signed up for certain doom.

⏵ Track 2
Meet the Band

Alexandra

My eyes won't stop burning like they're full of sand. After twenty-six hours on planes and in airports, jet lag from a ten-hour time difference, a crash course on local slang, a full wallet of new ID, credit, and insurance cards, it's finally time to meet the band.

Kind of.

"Alexandra, stay close," my guide urges as we weave through a thick crowd of diehard Project Viper fans.

"Okay." I'm trying to.

The show hasn't started yet, but the audience buzzes with excitement, which rubs off on me from packed, black T-shirted bodies. I've never seen Project Viper perform live. When I could afford it, my parents refused to let me go. Too crowded, they'd said, too dangerous, and the music was too mass-produced. When my parents no longer objected, Project Viper had moved on with their tour, and I had more pressing concerns than chasing after my favorite band.

Fiona, the assistant to the band's manager who doubles as my helper for the time being, flashes her pass at two tall, barrels-for-biceps men guarding the perimeter of the stage. One of them checks his smartphone then nods for us to proceed.

"We should have a great view from here." Fiona takes me to a small section of the arena floor barricaded from the rest of the crowd with chest-high metal barriers.

I have to say, I like her a lot. Fiona Knight is one of the first people I've met in the United States. She had waited for me at the airport along with Kiera Denver. When I saw her, I wondered why Kiera brought along a runway model. Fiona's got a slim, confident physique, dark skin, a short crop of curly hair, and eyes marked with golden eyeliner. I feel like an ugly duckling without a chance of ever becoming a swan next to her. Appearances aside, Fiona kindly answers all of my questions, no matter how mundane or dumb, and it feels like we've been friends our whole lives.

I spot a young woman and an older man with cameras and clutch the pass that swings like a dead weight around my neck. These people have a reason to be here. They are professionals. I'm just a fan brought to witness my idols in action through a set of circumstances that still eludes my comprehension. I shouldn't be here. I don't deserve this fantasy treatment. But maybe I do. Maybe it's fate paying me back for the absolute nightmare the last six months have been. I've barely breathed through them.

The girl with the camera darts past us, dropping a quick, "Hi, Fiona."

"Hey, Jules," Fiona responds. "Working with your dad tonight?"

But the girl's already gone to the other end of the stage.

Raucous laughter accompanied by chants for the Vipers bursts from behind the rows of barriers, followed by curses and some liquid splashing on my arm. Beer. Gross. I wipe it off on my shirt.

Fiona does the same. "I hate crowds. And I hate beer. Smells like urine. I can't believe people drink it."

"You wouldn't believe the kind of stuff people drink."

"I suppose you'd know. You come from a place that's infamous for its drinking habits." Fiona eyes the rowdy group with a freezing scowl before turning her attention to the stage. "Have you seen Project Viper live before? They came to your hometown at the beginning of this tour."

"No. And I've never been this close to any other performers either." I wave at the nearly non-existent space between me and the stage. Excited goosebumps run up my arms.

"I suppose if all goes well, being close to them will become a regular thing. How do you feel about that?" Fiona shoots me a curious glance. "Do you want it to go well?"

What kind of question is that? "I'm here, aren't I?"

The opening band spills onto the stage. They raise a swarm of excited cheers. Project Viper always has someone cool open for them. This time it's Acid Churro Dreams. The mosh pit crowd dances, and their passion is contagious. My feet move too. The arena continues filling with attendees. The music threatens to pop my eardrums. Fiona gave me a pair of fancy electronic earplugs, but I wait to use them. First, I have to soak in the throbbing mass of sound around me.

Smoke swirls above me, so much like my mood. Hazy but on edge. Uncertain but entranced. Music drags me to the bottom of the ocean of my hopes and dreams and my simmering misery. Does anyone else ever feel this way about music? Does it steal their souls as well?

I'm standing really close to an enormous amp, and my ribcage aches. It feels like I'm breathing for the first time. I lean back onto the barrier, out of the way of people wielding expensive cameras, close my eyes, and listen. I've imagined this all wrong. I thought concerts like these were fun and exciting, like a party, and they are, but just standing here hurts in the best kind of way. This is a warning. If I do this, music will take my life and my sanity. It will take my all.

Fiona's question comes back again. *Do you want it to go well?*

I open my eyes and stuff the earplugs in my ears. A million times yes. I *need* it to go well, not just *want*. Project Viper is the promise of a new life, a prospect that sends my heart beating faster as the taste of hope and something new teases my tongue.

The opening act wraps up their performance. My blood's on fire with anxiety. The stagehands swap equipment, but my feet itch to run. What if The Label's crazy scheme works?

Fiona taps my shoulder and leans in to shout, "Are you all right?"

I don't want to shout back, so I just nod. I'm as all right as I can be because I don't even know what all right is anymore. Is there anyone who does?

The stage lights flicker out. Darkness envelops the stadium. All around me, phone screens become thousands of bluish-white stars. A countdown appears on an enormous screen in the middle of the stage and two smaller ones to the sides of it. I hold my breath, suddenly wishing we were watching the concert from some less obvious spot. I'll be noticed, and remembered, and my new life will be over before it even starts.

When the countdown reaches zero, the air vibrates with soul-shattering guitar chords and hypnotizing drumming. I know these chords and this beat. I've listened to this song thousands of times. *Thousands.* Hearing it live makes me want to squeal with the rest of the girls, but I clamp a hand over my mouth.

Marshall Jones runs onto the stage. Swinging a microphone on its cord, old-school style, he waves to the crowd. He's only twenty-two, but his confidence is through the roof. Black jeans, an orange leather jacket with his customary gray T-shirt underneath, and…

That voice.

I bite my lip hard and remind my heart to beat. Come on lungs, breathe. I've seen countless videos of the Vipers on the Tube, who hasn't? But Project Viper and Marshall Jones in the flesh are a miracle to behold.

The crowd sings along. I want to as well, but I won't. I'm not here for the show. Well, I am, but I shouldn't go crazy like the girls in the front rows of the mosh pit who convulse in hysterics and worshipping tears. I can't judge them though. Marshall has a reputation among fellow musicians for being an intolerable show-off when it comes to his vocal range, the strength of his "pipes," and being a maniac on stage. And rightfully so. His energy gives him a glow, like he's a nuclear core ready to blow, like if he doesn't sing, dance, jump into near-perfect splits, and run through the crowds with reckless abandon, he will go off.

And I'm to stand on stage next to him and be the Vipers' new bassist and backup vocals.

I've agreed to attempt the impossible. The world loves Project Viper with their unfathomable Marshall Jones and his enthralling voice. Who am I to intrude on their hard-earned fame? I'm just a nobody off the street. They'll hate me. They'll shun me and toss me out.

And they'll be right to do so.

(Not) Nice to Meet You

Alexandra

Four days after the concert, Kiera, Fiona, and I drive to the Viper
Nest, the band's residence and practice facility. Of course they'd have
a lair and a name to go with it. I won't admit it out loud, but I think
it's awesome, if a bit odd, that they live together. Don't they have
girlfriends? If I remember correctly, at least one of them does.

Mid-September Portland obliges and dishes out a string of sunny
days. It feels like the middle of summer, so warm compared to good
old Saint Petersburg this time of year. So different with its boxy,
simplified American architecture, yet so familiar with an abundance
of banners and business signs.

"The Nest is on the edge of Arlington Heights," Kiera says from
behind the wheel. "It belongs to the Tang family—"

"The keyboardist's?"

"Correct," Fiona confirms from the passenger seat.

Kiera continues, "You'll notice that houses are kind of one on top
of the other in this neighborhood, but the Tangs managed to snag
a large parcel of land there back in the day and built two houses—"

I have to interrupt again. "Two houses?" How can anyone afford one enormous house, such as the ones passing by outside, let alone two?

Fiona laughs. "The Tangs are very wealthy. Think hundreds of millions. Zach doesn't broadcast it, but his grandparents in South Korea own a highly successful corporation. Or five."

Kiera jumps in once more. "Fiona's right, but anyway, the Tangs moved to Utah, and since they treat all Vipers like their sons, they let them use the house. Plus, it's nice and private."

Kiera keeps talking, Fiona adds in her comments here and there, but their words float right past my ears. I don't care that much where the Vipers live. I just hope they'll like me.

The road winds left and right, then loops around. At the end of that loop, we pass through a tall wrought-iron gate and park next to an impressive two-level manor with a wraparound deck and pristine landscaping of different shrubs and rose bushes.

"You'll stay in the guest house." Kiera points at a smaller house at the opposite end of the vast driveway.

My mouth drops. I know I've been gawking a lot since my arrival in the US of A, but that is quite some guest house. Also two-level, the guest house is finished with spotless white siding and more rose bushes, all of it set against a background of freshly mowed lawns. There's also a three-car garage on the side. Not that I'll need it. I don't know how to drive, and with only six months to mesh with the band, I doubt driving lessons will be on my agenda.

Right as we climb out of Kiera's black Tesla, my new phone buzzes in my pocket. Not many people text me here. The majority of them are already with me, so I'm all the more curious as to who's reaching out.

CE: Good luck tonight.

Connor Eaton. He's the one who brought me here. Even though none of our previous conversations made it seem like what I'm about to do will be impossible, his text reminds me that I'll need a whole lot of luck to pull this off.

"Ready?" Kiera asks.

Fiona's already headed straight for the main doors.

I shoot a quick thanks to Connor then haul my bass out of the car. The sharp scent of cut grass still hangs in the air and grounds my nervousness a bit. "Ready."

What else does she expect me to say? Can't she tell I'm all nerves and jitters? On second thought, maybe it's a good thing she can't tell. If I can keep my poker face without even trying, I'll take it.

I've been looking forward to this since the moment I heard of the opportunity, but after the show, my anticipation has been different. It's no longer the typical fangirl excitement or dreams of a flashy career (although there's some of that as well), and it's no longer fueled by my hunger for a chance to earn legitimate money and, hopefully, get a new start. My anticipation now carries hints of desire to prove myself. To prove to the Vipers that they won't be ashamed of me. That I won't be a burden. That I will do everything in my power to keep the flame of their fame burning bright. All I have to do is survive half a year with five of the best alternative rock musicians in the world. And pretend I know something about playing bass.

"Wait." Kiera taps my forearm. "You know what your role will be with the band—play bass, assist with vocals as necessary. However, the band isn't expecting you."

I stop staring at the enormous house and raise an eyebrow. "They don't know I'm coming? Or they don't know they're getting a new bassist?" Neither sounds good. She realizes that, right?

Kiera cringes. "Oh, they know all that. They're just not expecting you." She motions with her hands up and down, encompassing all of me. "So be ready for anything, okay? And remember, they can't kick you out. As long as you don't commit any crimes or tarnish the band's reputation, you're staying for at least six months. I've heard you play and sing. You're easily on the same level as them, so make quick work of them. Stun them with your talent and claim your place. They will resist, but I know you can do it. I see a fighter underneath the surface of a cute girl."

Easy for her to say. Besides, she's completely wrong. I don't have a place with them. I'm an outsider and an intruder regardless of my musical abilities. We'll see about the fighter part.

Kiera's half-warning, half-encouragement plants a foreboding tightness in my chest. I square my shoulders, refusing to let it settle in. "Let's do this."

Fiona opens the door for us. "No fear."

I expect the house to be loud with music, the band practicing or something, but the white walls with several family photos and abstract paintings echo only the faint sounds of a television and Kiera's high heels clicking against the gray marble floor.

We enter a wide room with tall ceilings and a massive screen on one of the walls. Four of the Vipers stand around a long sectional, chatting quietly, but my focus is on the one who sits on the couch, his eyes glued to the screen.

Shoulder-length black hair, high cheekbones with hints of fuzz, and the ever-traditional gray T-shirt. Marshall. He's so quiet, so ordinary. Catching a glimpse of him like this feels almost intimate.

"Afternoon, everybody," Kiera greets in a confident voice, all "boss" at that moment. "This is Alexandra Lermontova."

"New assistant?" one of the guys asks. Buzzed, warm blond hair, a muscular build, hands in his jeans pockets—Shane O'Neal, twenty years old, the current guitarist and the youngest member of the band. Which still makes him a year older than me.

Realizing that I'm the youngest person in the room makes me feel like a baby. It's the worst. I'm not a baby. I won't act like one. I'll be diligent and responsible.

Kiera flashes him an icy smile. "You're funny, Shane, sweetie. Alexandra is your new bass player."

The shock on their faces is priceless, but I can't shake off the feeling that I've stepped into a snake pit.

Ha. Project Viper? Snake pit?

Now is not the time to entertain myself with puns though. Back to being nervous. My hands tighten around the handle of the case that holds my shiny new bass. Fiona's no fear echoes in my ears, but it grows dimmer and dimmer under the evaluating looks of the Vipers.

"No way." CJ Sanchez is the first one to break the silence.

Lean and naturally tan, the rumored flirt of the band sports dark hair with bleached tips. He's smiling. From the photos of him online, I know that he smiles a lot in general. This time it looks more like, "Ha ha. Good joke. Where's the real bassist?"

Fiona pushes me in the back, forcing me to stand next to Kiera instead of slightly behind her. The Vipers continue staring at me in disbelief. It's dang awkward.

Zach Tang steps forward and offers me his hand while his dark, almost black eyes evaluate me in a quick glance from my feet to the top of my head. "Nice to meet you. I'm Zach. I play the piano. I'm also the effects wizard, as I'm sure you know."

"I do know that, and it's nice to meet you too." I shake his hand. His friendly attitude relaxes me somewhat.

"Where are you from?" Zach stands next to me while the rest of the guys continue staring. "Your accent is awesome."

"Lermontova? She must be Russian," Marshall says. He's still on the couch, arms crossed, frowning at the football game on the screen.

I'm shocked by his crisp pronunciation of my last name. He said it just like a Russian would, and his guess about my origins is spot on too. I would've been more impressed if not for his apprehensive tone though.

"Alexandra is indeed from Russia. From Saint Petersburg," Kiera replies. I swear she's more excited about me being Russian than about my skills.

Marshall finally deigns to face me. To glare at me.

My long black bangs are my only defense against him and the alarming electricity that crackles between us. He's going to be a problem. While the rest of the band still hangs suspended in surprise, Marshall's tense posture sends a strong message that I'm unwelcome. It's fine. I expected at least one of the Vipers to react this way. But even as we continue our glaring match, I know with an undeniable surety, once and for all, why he's the face of the band. Why their popularity grows stronger and more widespread every year. Marshall's green eyes arrest with their intensity, and his mouth is nothing short of a magnet for kisses, even while it's pressed into a thin, clearly disapproving line.

"No." Marshall strikes without mercy deep into my soul, then continues watching the game.

One word, just one syllable is enough to crush my resolve to stand firm. I blink and shrink behind Kiera again. Irresistible on the outside, Marshall is a true viper. Did he somehow sense that one of my deepest fears since boarding the plane to the States was them rejecting me? They have every right to. They need someone experienced, charismatic, and probably a little older. Someone who knows how to deal with the press and the online community, how to handle a tour, how to use a recording studio, not a barely nineteen-year-old with quaking knees.

"Now Marshall, darling, be a gentleman and abide by the deal," Kiera chides him.

With impressive speed, he hops over the side of the sectional and joins the rest of the group. "We agreed to no audition. We agreed to all the insane secrecy. But what's this?" He waves at me with derision. "Where did you find this matryoshka? How old is she anyway, fourteen? Are we a teen music boot camp now?"

I take another step backward under that onslaught of questions. Okay, okay. Be done now. I get it. You're disappointed.

"She's older than you were when you started the band." Kiera stands next to Marshall, and now the two of them look at me together—one with disapproval, the other with an odd kind of pride. If not for Fiona, whose sole presence keeps me from turning and running outside, I would've crawled out of my skin from embarrassment.

Marshall shakes his head. "Take her back."

The thought of returning home squeezes my whole body with panic. There is no home. This is it. The small suitcase in the trunk of Kiera's car is all that's left of my life. There is nothing to go back to. Not anymore. No family. No safety. No future.

I swallow, set my bass on the floor, and engage Marshall in yet another round of glaring. "I'm not here for you. I'm here for him." I point at CJ.

Sanchez laughs at the top of his lungs, then comes over and wraps his arm around my shoulders. "I'm sorry, Marsh. The matryoshka stays. I like her."

Kiera gives me a covert thumbs-up. The Vipers' drummer and Shane's older brother, Graham O'Neal, pats Marshall on the back but says nothing.

My heart finally slows down to a more reasonable pace, which is quite a feat given CJ's proximity and his strong, clean cologne, or body spray, or whatever it is that assaults my senses. Marshall may be the face of the band, but CJ can give him a run for his money. So can Zach, and the O'Neals. Sizzling hot musicians. It's going to be my new cuss phrase from now on.

Marshall clicks his tongue and looks away. Have I won?

"Don't say I didn't warn you. She'll ruin us."

I haven't won anything. He just thinks I'm not worth the bother.

"All right, all right, everyone. I ordered dinner. It should be here any minute." Kiera motions for us to move to a large table in the adjacent dining area. "Let's have pizza and introduce Alexandra to our chaos."

"Pizza! Pizza!" Zach and Shane chant together, arms pumping like they're twelve, not twenty and some.

"Come on now, Matryoshka," CJ says. His arm is still around me, and I don't mind. It's been a long time since anyone held me. He leans in and whispers, "And please don't say you don't like pizza. Otherwise, I'll have to join forces with Marshall and boot you out."

It looks like I've acquired a nickname, and a cliché one at that. Oh, well. It'll have to do for now. It could be worse than being called a traditional Russian nesting doll. And I'm starving. I haven't had any food today because when I'm nervous, I can't eat. It all comes right back up. Puking in front of Project Viper hasn't been on the list of my goals for the day, but I think I'm calm enough to stomach a bite or two now. "I love pizza."

"Great. And if Marshall gives you any trouble, you tell me. We've been friends since seventh grade. I know how to deal with him." He winks at me.

"You two lovebirds coming or what?" Shane yells from the table. When we join the rest of the group, he adds, "Careful, Alexandra. You're his favorite person in the world now. I'm actually worried that if you can play bass in any kind of a decent way, he's gonna propose."

Everyone laughs.

CJ picks up a placemat and tosses it at Shane's face, although he's also smiling. "Shut your yap."

"CJ, sweetie, manners," Kiera scolds him gently. Her phone rings.

She checks the screen and heads out of the room. "I've got to take this. Fiona, I'm leaving you in charge."

Fiona issues the smallest of sighs, making me wonder whether she's just as on edge about this whole thing as I am.

The doorbell chimes. CJ pulls out his phone. "Pizza's here."

They must have an app or something that shows their gate security camera.

"I'll get it." Fiona goes to deal with the order.

He follows her. "I'll help you."

Zach rushes to the cabinets in the kitchen that sits right next to the dining room and piles a bunch of cups, plates, and napkins onto the shiny marble countertop. When I try to help him bring the dishes to the table, he stacks everything into one tall tower and angles it away from me. "You're the guest of honor. Today, at least. I got this. You enjoy yourself."

Enjoy, he says. Right.

Fiona and CJ return right after we settle around the table and place several cardboard boxes in the middle, causing the guys to inhale with their eyes closed. Particles of baked dough and melted cheese hit my nose as well when Shane flips the box closest to him open. The pizza inside is a simple pepperoni, but my mouth waters like it hasn't had food in a decade.

Everyone fills their plates and cups. I expect alcohol, at least beer, but no. They either drink soda that came with the pizza or plain water. Is someone recovering from an addiction and the rest are showing their support?

"Do you have any questions?" Shane says to me after everyone's gone through a slice. "We've been together for a few years now, but you don't know us at all yet."

I only have a million questions, but where do I start?

Marshall reaches for a slice with mushrooms and onions, but his hard green eyes are on me. "She's the one who needs to convince us to keep her, not the other way around. So I say, we ask questions first."

Fiona shoots him a tight-lipped look, and butterflies resume their death match in my stomach. What if someone asks something I don't feel like sharing? What if they laugh at me? I guess I'll just have to suck it up and roll with it. No fear.

"You all get one question each," I say.

"Here's an easy one," Zach starts. "Tell us about your family. Do you have any brothers or sisters?"

The keyboardist chooses the most dangerous questions of all.

"I'm an only child. And the rest of my family... It's complicated." I take a long sip of root beer and set the cup a good distance away. It tastes too much like cough syrup. Disgusting.

"That's a common thing around here," CJ responds and reminds me that all Vipers but Zach come from troubled families. I'm dying to know more about how they overcame their difficult upbringings, but it's not a good time. I'll have to wait until I'm on closer terms with them to pry about that.

CJ continues, "Do you play any sports?" CJ continues. "You're Russian. Hockey? Figure skating? Skiing?"

Oooh, stereotypes. I love stereotypes. "No. I don't do any of those things just because I'm Russian. And I'm really sorry, but I couldn't bring my pet bear with me." I bite my lip hard, regretting my sarcasm. I can't be flippant with them. Not yet.

Graham snorts, and Zach bursts out laughing.

"Well played." Shane toasts me with his water cup. Instead of asking a question, he says, "How about you get a turn? What do you want to know about us?"

Hmmm.

Asking Marshall if he's always such sunshine in a bottle to people he doesn't know isn't going to help me win any points with him. How about something simple then? "What instruments does everyone play? I mean, other than what the media says?"

Marshall turns to Fiona with an are-you-kidding-me look. I have a feeling he's going to think that everything I say is dumb.

Zach humors me. "I'm not hiding any secret talents. My parents have dedicated their lives and my childhood to raising a prodigy pianist, but I joined a rock band instead. Epic fail."

He and Shane high five, both of them chortling.

"Drums," says Graham O'Neal, who until then hasn't uttered a word. At that, his explanation is over.

CJ plays bass and guitar. Marshall plays guitar as well but admits he isn't as good as CJ or Shane. That explains why I've never seen him with a guitar, but I still can't believe he said it. He's so full of himself, it's hard to accept he can reveal his shortcomings in such a casual way.

When it's my turn to answer, I keep my voice low. "I also play guitar and—"

"Bass. You're a total pro, right?" Marshall leans back in his seat and, draping his arm over the back of the chair, smiles at me.

He's painfully handsome when he smiles, but there is a certain menace lurking in his eyes. He's baiting me.

"Oh, Alexandra will be a great bassist," Fiona says before my neurons even start firing in a consideration of a response. "And you should hear her sing. She's got the loveliest voice I've ever heard."

Her praise is wonderful and all, but Marshall's eyes grow colder. "Will be a great bassist?"

CJ intervenes. "Next question."

Marshall picks that right up. "What are you afraid of?"

My heart slams against my ribs with a painful thud and comes to a screeching halt. Scorching hot memories don't bring with them the heat they should. My hands become cold and sweaty and slide right off the shiny table when I grip its edge.

Everyone waits, all eyes on me, but all I see is dancing flames.

"Remember, we're asking all these silly things just to get to know you a little," Fiona says. "No one will judge you. Perhaps some of us even share your fears."

I blink away the flames. My panicking brain scrambles to figure out a way to skip out on answering. Maybe I can go to the bathroom or something, but under Marshall's scrutinizing gaze, I can't come up with anything short of running out of the room.

"I don't like fire," I wrestle out at last.

"Could be worse," CJ says. "Shane's afraid of heights."

Marshall tosses a wadded napkin at him. "And so are you."

"And so am I," the former bassist confesses. "But not as much as Shane."

Everyone laughs, even Shane, who doesn't seem offended at their fun at his expense. They engage in a quick exchange about their own phobias and ignore me for a moment. I use the distraction to slip away to the deck outside and breathe some cool air. My hands shake, and I clutch them tightly as I lean on the railing with my eyes closed.

Why did Marshall have to bring up fears? In and of itself an innocent topic, it stirred up emotions and mental images I've been struggling to keep at bay for the last six months. It's not a childhood accident that instills the fear of fire in me, and it's impossible to talk about what does, but it's vitally important that no one talks about or even mentions fire ever again. I know I have to talk about it in order to heal and all, but healing isn't happening right now, only survival.

The door slides open, releasing a clamor of cheerful voices. CJ joins me at the edge of the deck. "Are you okay?"

I rub away the tears that prickle my eyes with my fingers. "You guys live in a cool house."

CJ gives me a soft smile. "Hey, it's fine to be overwhelmed, especially with Marshall's warm welcome. You are welcome here, though, no matter the circumstances. And if you ever have trouble with anything or just need to talk, I'm here for you. Ask anyone. I'm a great sounding board."

I can't help but laugh a little, although his words make me want to cry all the more. I don't have any siblings, but I've always wanted one. It seems a bit too cruel for life to give me one now. "Thanks. I promise I'll do my best."

CJ taps my nose with his fingertip. "I know you will."

House Rules

Marshall

Shortly after dinner, Kiera finishes her phone call and comes back to the living room. She's smiling like she has finally achieved the biggest triumph of her life. I really hate that smile.

Kiera hands Fiona a set of keys. "Alexandra, Fiona will show you your new home. I hope you like it."

I shoot a questioning look at Zach when I recognize the chibi sushi keychain—the keys to the guest house. The pianist shrugs. That is so not an answer as to why he allowed the tiny Russian to stay on our property.

After Alexandra and Fiona take off, Kiera turns to me with a much more somber expression. "Now, stop glaring at everyone, Marshall. You signed the contract, so suck it up."

The whole band stares at her with astonishment, not just me. We've never heard Kiera speak like that. She's the ever-peppy Fairy Queen of Land Neverfrown, even when she means business.

Hands in the pockets of her long cardigan, she pins each of us with a look. "We've got to talk about some house rules in terms of

Alexandra. One, she will live in the guest house. I thought it'd be best to give her some privacy."

Everyone nods, but I have to address something that's been gnawing at me since I first saw the girl.

"How old is she?"

Kiera shrugs. "She's nineteen."

"She looks younger." Zach flops on the couch and starts a video game.

She does look younger. Just about five feet tall, a thick braid over her shoulder, long bangs over her eyes. Curvy hips but somewhat modest on the "front lines."

"She's nineteen." Kiera's tone hardens. "But even though she's technically an adult, consider me her guardian. So, if either one of you gives her so much as a papercut—"

"Please, Kiera." Her insinuations aren't lost on me. "As though anyone would want to get that close to her."

"You know the saying, Marsh, about protesting too much?" Smirking, Shane waggles his eyebrows at me.

"Stuff it."

He shrugs, but his dumb smirk remains. "Just saying."

"Enough." Kiera throws us all another warning look, and a chill crawls over my skin. Apparently, I've been underestimating this woman.

"Did she come to the States alone? No parents, no siblings?" CJ asks.

"Yes, alone. She'll tell you more later. Now, I know you expected some famous bass virtuoso, but give her a chance." She turns to me. "She'll be amazing for you. Think of all the social media hype we'll gain with her appearance. A cute Russian girl with vocals worthy of an opera performance?"

"We need a bass player." My surliness returns in earnest. "We

25

need someone to take CJ's place, not a singer. I can handle the mic just fine on my own."

"She'll be your bass player, don't worry. But we'll milk all of her talents to promote you. She'll make us lots of cash."

Now everything makes sense. It's about the money. The Label owed someone a favor, so the president brought in a daughter of some rich big cheese to play band. My guess is she can play zilch and sings even worse, no matter how much Kiera sugarcoats it. From rock stars to babysitters in one day, all because CJ couldn't stand playing bass anymore. We should have never said a word of this to Kiera and just quietly auditioned someone on our own.

The front door creaks. The Russian returns.

"That house is so…" She notices that I'm watching her and sidelines straight to Kiera. "Am I really going to live in that house all by myself?"

Kiera smiles, all warmth and sunshine again. "You'll get used to it. And you won't be alone. You'll have Fiona. Just call her, and she'll come whenever you need her."

"*Ya ne nuzhdayus' v prisluge*," Alexandra mutters.

I don't need a servant.

I'm never telling her I understand Russian. It's not public knowledge, but I'm trying to finish an art history degree I started when I was eighteen. It takes forever when you're more than full-time employed in a band and can't attend anything in person. That's how I speak Russian. That's how I'll support myself when I'm old and can't handle the stage anymore. I'll teach art history. In the meantime, if she has a tendency to blurt things out to herself, I'm going to hear some rather entertaining comments.

"You want to show the boys what you can do with that bass?" Kiera asks.

Finally, something useful.

Alexandra's eyes widen in unmistakable fear, and I suspect she's going to fail so spectacularly that Kiera will have to oust her out before the end of the hour, contract or not. Our manager can be a maniac at times, but she doesn't want us to flop on stage. She's probably never heard the little Russian girl play before and agreed only because The Label told her to.

Alexandra picks up her bass. Its hardshell case hides most of her frame. "Not here, right?"

"Right. Rehearsal room has the amps and much better acoustics." CJ takes her bass and leads the way.

Alexandra follows him like a grateful puppy. Pathetic.

I enter the rehearsal room last. She opens the case and pulls out a beautiful Fender Precision Bass in a candy-apple red finish.

"That's a sweet P Bass," CJ says. "I used to have one like that until we sold it at a charity auction about a year ago."

"What do you want me to plug it into?" Alexandra asks as she puts her shoulder strap on.

CJ and Shane dive toward the bass amps, but I'm already there.

"Don't trip over yourselves," I say to those two, then grab the coiled cable, fling it loose, and walk to our newest member to plug it into her bass.

Alexandra's hand tightens around her shoulder strap, and she takes a step back from me. I pretend that I don't notice, but it's amusing that I make her nervous. Good. She should be.

I go back to my original spot. Observation works best from a distance. Alexandra looks positively dwarfed by her P Bass. I shake my head when she fidgets with the settings on the knobs for volume and tone. She's a kid with a battle-axe.

"What's your favorite song?" Shane asks with his usual enthusiasm.

"Um. Any song or one of yours?"

"They're yours too now," CJ says with a playful smile.

Is he flirting with her? He'd better not be. She's here to work, not waste time on who knows what.

Alexandra says nothing in response. She strums the strings with all of her fingers, softly, like it's a six-string guitar.

Arms folded on my chest, I wait. She's going to make such a mess of things.

CJ plugs in an electric guitar. "How do you feel about giving *Court of Fools* a go? If you don't know it, I can pull up the tabs for you on my phone."

"I definitely know that one. Although, it's the vocals that make that song." Biting her lip, but only on one side, Alexandra steals a glance at me. "The instrument parts are quite simple."

"How about *I Don't Want to Answer That* then?" I suggest.

That song made us visible on the international charts. It's easily in our top five most popular songs, and it's one of our top five most complicated songs as well. Aspiring guitarists cover it on homemade videos all the time. She's bound to fail.

"Okay." She circles around the room, the cable dragging after her. "No, wait."

She stops at the window and looks at us. Her gaze pauses on me again. I stare right back. What is happening in that head of hers? What was she thinking when she agreed to this?

Either way, she doesn't back down, and I have to give her credit for that. But she doesn't look too excited about it either. One little girl out of my awesome band in three, two, one...

► Track 5
Slightly Unexpected

Alexandra

Marshall is glaring again. He can be my guest because he can't ruin this moment for me. They're ready to hear me play, but I need to pause and relish playing with Project Viper for the first time. World-class musicians have their attention on me while I stand in the room where chart-smashing songs have been written and rehearsed and brought to life. If I close my eyes, I can hear them. Only there's no need to imagine anything. Soon enough, these songs will become my day-to-day reality. The Vipers will play them for me. They'll play them *with* me. Hot-blooded Marshall, flirty CJ, easy-going Zach, curious Shane, quiet Graham. I am so, so, *so* lucky. They're all mine to learn from and to hang out with for six whole months. Longer than that if I manage to win them over. If I can stop fangirling and play.

I take one more fortifying breath, my nerves less fraying now, and tell Graham, "Go ahead."

Already at the drums, Graham counts us in. I practiced *I Don't Want to Answer That* for hours before I came to the States and more after. I thought I had it, but when I'm put on the spot, my fingers do their own thing while my mind screams at me to drop the bass and beg forgiveness for imagining I'm on the same level with them.

"A little softer." CJ's encouraging smile gives me hope that I don't sound as bad as I think I do.

Playing bass on its own is quite amazing, but playing it with other instruments, through a robust amp? I dissolve in the dark, rich sound that fills the room.

Marshall doesn't sing along, and the song is empty without him. In the slower bridge, I steal a peek at him and regret it immediately. He leans his back against the wall, thumbs stuffed in the front pockets of his jeans, a brooding expression on his face. He will definitely cause me trouble. He will be my worst nightmare. I will never come out of these six months with Project Viper alive.

"That wasn't too bad," Shane says after we wrap up the song.

I exhale. Adrenaline still crackles in my middle, sweetening the idea that at least not all of them are set on banishing me right away.

"Not too bad?" Zach pipes from his spot. "She's got pretty darn good rhythm and emotion. Marsh?"

Marshall leaves the rehearsal room without saying anything.

Zach goes to Utah to spend some time with his family and takes the O'Neals with him. Marshall and CJ stay. So do I, of course. Where am I going to go? We sleep in until unholy hours. They're exhausted from the tour, and I'm still battling the effects of relocation and the time difference, although that's finally starting to diminish.

I follow the checklist I made before I came here that consists of all the songs I need to memorize, including learning the musical jargon in English and a whole lot more. In the mornings, I practice bass for hours on my own then play more with CJ. Even though the band should enjoy a rightfully earned vacation, he spends hours with me, explaining more intricate bass techniques and streamlining my practice routines. All with utmost patience and without any complaints. Oftentimes, he's the first to suggest we should practice together. He is the perfect tutor. I take every bit of advice he's willing to impart and practice more after dinner. The more I practice, the better I get. The better I get, the less reason Marshall has to scowl at me.

"You're sounding better every day," CJ comments one afternoon as we come to the kitchen for some lunch.

It warms my heart to hear him say that. He has no idea how much it means to me. I have to succeed with them not only because Project Viper is my new start, but also because of all the help I've received to get here. I can't squander this opportunity.

He rummages in the fridge. "What are you in the mood for?"

"Surprise me."

The fridge is always stocked with soups, salads, fruit slices, and high-protein snacks. The Vipers employ a nutritionist and a cook who prepare all of the food to keep us in shape. To help with that, the guys typically abide by an exercise routine as well. I'm required to take part in the fitness regimen, but I'm still enjoying the insane variety of food. In my three weeks with the Vipers I've eaten more kinds of fruits and vegetables than in all of my nineteen years before coming here.

CJ smashes two sandwiches in the panini grill then brings over two bowls of salad made with cubed feta, tomatoes, and cucumbers.

The front door swings open. Animated conversation floats from the entryway into the kitchen, growing louder as the visitors approach. Fiona and three other girls enter the kitchen, each rolling a wheeled suitcase.

One of the girls, a curvaceous blonde with lush hair that swoops over her shoulders in perfect, loose curls, gives CJ an eyebrow-raised look. "Bringing a girl to the Nest? Are you finally getting serious about someone?"

He frowns. "What do you mean?"

"Everyone, this is Alexandra, Project Viper's new bassist," Fiona announces with a calm tone, like my addition to the Vipers is nothing special.

Mouths open, the three other girls stare at me. Why does it matter to them who I am?

The golden-haired bombshell turns to Fiona. "You're serious? The new bassist is a girl? Now, that explains why Shane said I'm in for a surprise. I know why he'd keep mum about her—he's a complete troll, but why didn't you tell us?"

Fiona smirks. "Where's the fun in that?"

Her friend, the only one who's said anything so far, replies with, "That is fantastic. I'm Elise, by the way. The Vipers' stylist and Shane's girlfriend." She sits across from me and dazzles me with a warm smile.

"The numbers are finally evening out," says another girl. Tall and slender, she rocks bright red lipstick and a tight bun of snow-white hair.

"Well, that depends, Charlie," says the third girl, her voice quiet. I almost gasp when I recognize her. She's one of the photographers from the concert. "Elise, you, and I are just the support, and Alexandra's the one who'll have to deal with—"

Charlie rebuffs with, "She won't have to deal with them alone."

The girls engage in a round of banter as though CJ and I aren't even there.

He returns with our paninis and sits next to me. "Why are you all here?"

Charlie tucks a lock of her platinum blonde hair behind her ear. "We're here to take a few pictures. However, this is slightly unexpected."

Her eyes take me in, and her lips fold into an unsatisfied pout. I take a quick bite of my salad. Why is she looking at me like that?

"What's wrong, Charlie?" CJ asks.

She shakes her head once. "It seems like we've got a little more work to do than anticipated. Alexandra needs to look a little less like a baby. I'm glad I asked Elise to come."

I bristle at that. Is it because I don't bother wearing makeup right now? The new climate set my hair and skin on the fritz, so I'm giving it a few weeks to adjust before I figure out a new makeup routine. The tomatoes now taste a bit sour at the idea of having to cake my eyes with mascara every day again, but I will do it to get them to stop thinking I look like a child.

CJ wraps one arm around me. "Don't laugh at my *Matryoshka*, Charlie. She's still learning the ropes."

My cheeks burn, and I push him away. The girls laugh.

"CJ, I thought only Shane had a problem with touching everyone left and right. Maybe not." Elise gives him a meaningful smile.

"I promise I'll behave from now on," he says to me.

Charlie rolls her eyes and waves to Juliette. "We'd best start setting up for the photos."

Juliette nods.

"Go ahead and finish eating," Fiona says. "We'll be upstairs."

The girls head out of the kitchen, just in time for Marshall to walk in and block the passage to their posse.

"Oh, hi. I love seeing you all and whatnot, but what's up?"

"We're here for a small shoot for Alexandra. Even though you're waiting until March to see whether she's going to be a permanent addition to the band, The Label wants us to prepare the media assets," Charlie explains. "Just doing my job, promoting your band. You hired me, remember?"

Marshall smiles, wide and not at all genuine. "Juliette's the one who does the photos. And I didn't hire you. The Label did. It's the only reason I listen to your ridiculous ideas."

"My ridiculous ideas turn you into eye candy for all the girls who spend cash on your songs and the Viper merch. You're welcome." Charlie sidesteps him and continues on her way, and Marshall joins me and CJ at the dining table.

"I love how Kiera forgets to tell us about things like this. Good thing we didn't go anywhere today," he grumbles.

I take one more bite and focus on the flavors of my salad rather than the disappointment Marshall's words bring me. I can't go anywhere. I have no driver's license. I never had a chance to learn how to drive back in Russia. I was too young to do so before my life unraveled, and later there was no money. I'll have to find some way to get out of the house now and then. Maybe with Fiona?

Marshall returns me to reality. "You'd better eat fast before the social media harpy swoops back."

"Nice to know I'm not the only person you hate," I respond as I pick up the still hot sandwich. My fingertips are sore and peeling from all the bass practice, and the heat stings more than usual. I have no choice but to drop the sandwich back on the plate.

"Marsh really does hate Charlie. They get on each other's nerves something awful." CJ is almost done with his panini. "He doesn't hate you though."

I check to see if Marshall agrees with that statement. He's resting his chin in his palm, elbow propped against the tabletop, eyes on me. He's always watching me, judging my every move. I know I don't measure up to his standard. Not yet.

"I'm still undecided on that," he says with a completely straight face. "I'm giving you until our first gig."

CJ lets out a loud sigh. "Geez, Marsh. Relax a little, will you? Eat something."

Marshall rises from his seat with that devious and irresistible smile of his that harvests thousands of likes on social media. "Nah.

I've got to see what Charlie has in mind for your *Matryoshka*." He goes to the fridge and takes out a can of Diet Coke.

I chide myself for getting caught in the sticky web of his smile and push away from the table. "Don't you dare come along."

"Thanks for the invitation. I wouldn't miss it for the world." He cracks the can open and takes a long, relaxed swig.

I want to toss the rest of my salad at Marshall, but that will only make him laugh. So I choose to not waste my energy on him any further. He's obviously one of those people who enjoys riling others up. He will not get that pleasure from me.

Destroy It

Marshall

I don't resent Charlie nearly as much as everyone thinks I do, but my hostility toward her keeps the girl at bay. Otherwise she acts like I'm one of her dolls to dress and pose for her perfect online posts. As for Alexandra, I see that she's putting forth a lot of effort to mesh with us. I'm not blind. But we were good before her. Nothing had to change. Now everything is upside down. We're supposed to be resting and writing new songs, but CJ spends all of his time with her, supposedly teaching her the ways of the band.

What else are they doing together?

I dismiss that thought as soon as it manifests. Nothing. They are doing nothing but jamming on their basses. Right now CJ seems too invested in his new mentor role to notice anything or anyone else, even though typically his calendar would be filled with dates three months in advance.

I can't remember the last time I went on a date. It's been years. It'll probably be that much more before I'll even consider dating again. We mocked Shane for his fear of heights the day Alexandra had arrived, but I wish my fear was that simple. I'm not afraid of snakes, spiders, heights, or darkness. I'd be a happy camper if I was afraid of any of those little things. You can usually avoid nasty creatures and most other unpleasant things. I hate change. Change is unavoidable and constant. It waits around every corner and leaves me feeling vulnerable and unprepared no matter what I do. I hate that feeling. There's nothing but change and chaos now that Alexandra is here.

While Juliette sets up photography gear, I settle into an enormous bean bag chair next to a tall, potted mandarin tree and drink my Diet Coke. Fiona and Charlie push Alexandra into a padded swivel chair in front of a wide mirror in the corner and unbraid her hair. Elise swipes through images on Pinterest, suggesting different styles. Alexandra shakes her head at each and every single one of them.

"I don't want a new style. I like everything exactly the way it is." Her voice rings unbending, her accent strong.

For whatever reason, I approve. She does have claws after all. I wondered when they would come out because so far she has been accepting of everything. Her hair, apparently, is a different story.

Elise taps a finger against her lips. "Flat iron and some smoothing product then?"

Alexandra accepts. Only the trouble doesn't end there.

When it's time to pick out an outfit, she flat out refuses to wear anything sleeveless or with a deep collar.

"But look at you!" Elise never relents after only one try. "You're a doll with those hips."

Alexandra glances at me, and her cheeks turn deep red as she says, "Then show off the hips. Why do I have to be naked up top?"

"You haven't been here a month yet, but you're already acting like a diva?" I tease Alexandra. "Not this hair, not these clothes."

Clutching her outfit to her chest, Alexandra first shoots me a glare, then looks away, eyes downcast in a guilty way. Hm.

Fiona takes Alexandra to another room to change, and Charlie waves me over. "Stop being a smirking creep and come here. We'll do some shots of Alexandra with you and CJ. I already texted him."

As proof of her words, CJ materializes at the top of the stairs that lead to the loft, Alexandra's bass in his hands. He has changed into a pair of black jeans with his favorite white leather belt and a black tee.

I heave myself out of the bean bag chair with a growl. When the girls get something into their heads, there's no weaseling out of it. Especially if they're sent by Kiera. One way or another, they'll get their way. I'm better off letting them annihilate my afternoon. Maybe that way I'll have an evening all to myself. "I'm not changing."

Elise points to the chair in front of the mirror. "Sleek or messy?"

At least I get to choose my hairstyle. "Messy."

Elise works on my hair while Charlie poses for Juliette so that the assistant photographer can make sure the lighting works. Juliette's father is our usual photographer, but recently Juliette started doing quick shoots like today all on her own.

The sweet, citrusy scent of hair product hits my nose. I squirm in the chair.

"It's just a shoot." CJ stands next to me, watching Elise organize my hair into a controlled chaos before applying several dabs of whatever skin potions she likes to use to make us presentable for the photos.

I'm about to snipe something back when Elise pats me on the cheek. "All done. You get your beauty sleep these days, don't you? I barely had to do anything."

No, Elise. I don't sleep very well at all, thank you for asking. There's this girl that's invaded my life and my family and stole my best friend. And I can't get rid of her because of the contract we all signed.

I vacate the chair, keeping my sarcasm to myself. They don't need to hear it.

Alexandra returns to the loft and surveys the scene. She's changed into a pair of skin-tight black pants and a long silver top with lace on the back. A set of chain necklaces and a pair of knee-high black boots complete the look. She's the same girl, yet so different. The same hair, but her dark, outlined eyes and sheer lip gloss add a bit of a wow factor to her appearance.

"That's a cool outfit," Juliette comments with a wide smile.

"Do I look like a proper rock star?" Alexandra rests her hands on her hips and upturns her nose.

She might be facing Juliette, but her eyes dart my way. What does she hope my reaction will be? Interesting that she wants me to react at all. I won't.

CJ escapes from Elise and takes a turn around Alexandra. "Very nice. Marsh and I are going to be pretty much useless now." He presses a fist to his chest, feigning heartbreak.

Alexandra laughs, and I realize that this is the first time I've witnessed it. When we practice, she speaks little and only asks music-related questions. When we don't practice, I make sure to steer clear of her and all the reminders of how she has upended my perfect life. Still, when she smiles, her face lights up. Tiny dimples form in her cheeks. Her laughter is comfortable and easy on the ears.

"Let's get a few shots of you and your bass without the boys first," Charlie suggests as she sits on a couch opposite to the wall they designate for the backdrop.

"Just remember, you said 'a small shoot.' We don't have all day for this," I tell her. I have no plans whatsoever, but she doesn't need to know that.

Charlie ignores me and continues firing pose suggestions to Alexandra and Juliette.

When it's time to have me and CJ in the photos, I switch into performance mode. As much as I despise Charlie's tactics, my smolders make us money.

"Stand as close to each other as comfortable," Charlie says. "Your fans need to believe that you feel like Alexandra is the best thing that has ever happened to you. That she is a welcome addition to the band."

Will do. Even if her presence is my worst nightmare.

"She certainly is." CJ wraps his arm around her shoulders and pulls her close.

He's always touching her. She never stops him. Something's definitely brewing between them.

"Aw, this is almost cute." Charlie rises from the couch and comes to shove me closer to my bandmates. "Get in there."

"CJ's the one who's handing over his reins with the bass. Why do you need me?"

"Because you're the frontman. Your approval is just as important."

"Well, I don't approve." I place my arm around Alexandra's back, careful to touch her as little as possible. Even then she stiffens.

"Arm around Marshall, Alexandra," Charlie orders. "Don't worry. He won't bite."

"What if *she* does?" I joke. It's stupid, but I need to do something to shake off the tension.

CJ chuckles and throws me a look I can't decipher over Alexandra's head.

"I just might." Alexandra places her arm around my waist and squeezes with surprising firmness.

The camera shutter snaps. Flashes go off and cut through the tension. Charlie claps her hands as she studies Juliette's screen. "This is gonna be the best."

The room darkens, and a roll of thunder rattles the glass in the windowpanes. An inexplicable feeling of walking into a disaster claws through me.

"I need to adjust the light a little, so have a tiny break," Juliette says.

"I have another idea for a photo with the bass." CJ leaves his spot.

I'm used to being touched, but Alexandra's forced embrace doesn't sit right with me. Her spitefulness is fine. I can handle it. What I can't seem to deal with is the regret that enters my chest when she follows CJ.

In her hurry to move away, Alexandra stumbles and pitches toward me, and my hands fly to her forearms out of a reflex.

An uncomfortable laugh slips off her lips. "Sorry." Hands on my chest, she adjusts her stance and looks up at me. Embarrassed blue eyes meet mine.

I'm trying to compute what's happening. All of my thoughts blend together into one fuzzy mess while I fight to free myself from the grip Alexandra's gaze has on me. Nothing's happening. She does nothing, says nothing, but I feel threatened somehow. Let go. I have to let go of her. I must stop touching her. How do I do that again?

With effort, I manage to order my hands to release her and take several long steps to the window.

Later, a few minutes after midnight and before I'm finally sleeping, a phone notification pings in the darkness of my bedroom—an email from Juliette with a link to the photo session. She and her dad always work late to let us see the photos before Kiera and Charlie so that we can have our pick and not have anything we hate posted online.

I follow the link to the folder on cloud storage and scroll through the images. I kind of hate to admit it, but Alexandra photographs well. Dozens of stylish photos in, I spot one of that moment when she grabbed onto me. At least in that photograph, it looks like I'm holding her with much more care than I actually did. Juliette has tweaked the photo with some filters and overlays and added a soft, dream-like haze to it. We look like two lovers in a tender embrace.

I tap the photo and add a comment.

Destroy it.

Not Fed to the Wolves. Yet.

Alexandra

I stand on the path that leads from the guest house to the Nest's main residence and breathe in. Portland autumn air is cold and crisp and quite humid, same as back home, yet so different. Portland smells different. Less pollution, less cigarette smoke, less garbage.

Everything is different. My house, the food, the way I spend my time. My new home is definitely an improvement, as is the food. There's no denying that joining the Vipers opened the doors to a lot of things. I have money in my bank account again—five thousand dollars that Connor referred to as pocket change—a fancy bass, and everything I can think of available at my beck and call.

Everything but family or friends. The Beatles were right. Money can't buy you love.

It's been a little over a month since my arrival. Marshall still gives me a stink eye and acts apprehensive. No. He's not apprehensive. He just plain hates me. When Kiera described the guys before I met them, she always praised his perseverance and good attitude. I've seen none of that.

Well, Marshall perseveres. In his disdain for me. And his constant remarks on how I'm not a good fit for the band.

I can be. If only he had a little patience and gave me a chance. I'll prove it to him. I want to succeed with the Vipers, but I also admire them as the band they were before I came. Energetic, overwhelming, and awe-inspiring. I want to be a part of that. Despite what Marshall believes, I'm not here to destroy them. I have no clue as to how I can convince him of that. He's unapproachable.

Unapproachable yet cool. I watch him any time I feel safe doing so, trying to reconcile how his immense personality and soul-baring voice fit inside one human being.

A breeze runs over my bare arms. I shiver with pleasure. That's different too. Wearing a T-shirt outside in Saint Petersburg at the beginning of October is madness. Here I can still bounce around in summer clothes. That's worth smiling about.

When I make it to the main house and into the kitchen, the whole band's already there for breakfast. Shane, Graham, and Zach have come back from Utah, and the guys are busy talking shop.

"Phew, you're still here." Zach hugs me. "When I didn't see you last night at dinner, I was worried Marshall fed you to the wolves."

"There's an idea," the disgruntled singer says before eating a spoonful of oatmeal.

He frowns at the bowl, full of delicious looking oats, berries, and seeds. Judging by the resigned sigh that precedes the next spoonful, he'd rather eat something else. Anything else. But the Vipers are usually diligent in sticking to their diet plan, so Marshall continues eating without complaints. If only he could do the same during our rehearsals. A girl can dream.

"I didn't feel very well." I hide my hands behind my back.

Playing hours upon hours for weeks after months of barely touching strings comes at a skin-splitting price. Never mind that my back is murdering me from the weight of my bass guitar. It's awesome and all, but it's monstrously heavy. It's probably no big deal for someone as tall as CJ, but I'm in the lightweight category. It takes some serious effort to wield that axe. Add to that my fingertips that throb and peel. They're ugly, but it's a small price to pay for Marshall to stop glaring at me, a tiny pain compared to what my life will be like if I fail.

"Feeling better today?" CJ points to an empty seat next to him and moves a fresh bowl of oatmeal across the counter when I sit down.

"Yes."

Fiona gave my hands a salt bath with a bunch of essential oils and a hand massage last night, so yes, my hands feel better. I'm not any less exhausted though. I eat my food and daydream of a nap.

Marshall ignores me. I should feel relieved, but his coldness stings. Everyone else talks to me and acknowledges my existence. They're nice guys, if a little quirky in their own ways here and there. Like Graham. He's not a talker. He's a shrugger. How's it going? A shrug. Want some food? A shrug. Does your thumb hurt? A shrug again even though he dislocated it during his trip to Utah and ended up needing a brace. I like him though. I like them all. Even Marshall. I'm curious to get to know the nicer version of him that he presents to everyone else but me. Again, a girl can dream.

After I'm done with my oatmeal, I relocate to an armchair in the living room. Once alone, I fish my old phone from Russia out of my shorts pocket and find the most recent video I have of my family. It was taken on Mama's birthday.

We celebrated at home. Mama took half a day off, I skipped a whole day of school, and we baked and made a big meal with salads, roast chicken, and a tall cake. Papa came home from work with an armful of roses and a kiss for her. I was always embarrassed when my parents kissed in front of me. Now, of course, I wish I had watched them more and embedded into my heart just how much they loved each other.

In the video, Papa notices me filming and gives me a hug, sending the focus of the video to the corner of the entryway. I bite my lip and take slow breaths. I miss home. I miss my parents. I miss belonging and having someone to go back to instead of sleeping in an enormous house all by myself, with a constant, invisible reminder of how all of this can go away in five months.

"Marsh, remember that dumb trick you tried to do?" Shane's chipper voice cuts through my cocoon of sadness, and I'm so grateful for him saving me from bursting into tears.

I look over my shoulder. Shane and Marshall sit next to each other at the kitchen island, shoulders touching as they hunch over Shane's phone.

Squeals drift from the screen. Marshall laughs, his whole face aglow with delight. "Yeah. That was in Rome, wasn't it? I was going for a backflip off that amp, but CJ stood right behind me."

"That really hurt actually," CJ says through a mouthful of food. "You almost broke my nose."

Marshall laughs again. The tabloids like to write that CJ and Marshall are best friends. Watching them over the course of the past few weeks, I know it's true. CJ treats Marshall with the same level of flippancy and camaraderie as he would a brother. Also with the same respect. They can be squabbling all day over a passage in the song, then eat dinner and watch basketball as they sit on the same couch and cheer for the same team.

Marshall's eyebrow rises when he catches me staring.

I love watching the Vipers. Love sharing that sense of belonging even if from a distance. There's no belonging with Marshall though.

He bites at the slightest provocation, like a snake. The name of the band suits him well.

I turn away and play the video again and again, and I realize that no matter how many times I watch it, it won't fix anything. I can never go back. No one can bring their loved ones from the dead. My life's here now, doing what I've never imagined in my wildest dreams.

✳

"Come on, Alex! When are you going to get that bit?"

Marshall's exasperated tone cuts the song short. Again.

Graham trails off his drumming with a rattlesnake hiss over the snare drum.

I glare at the belligerent singer. I've been doing my best to not engage, but I'm too exhausted today to control my temper. "I got it right."

"No."

"Yes."

"No." Marshall strides over to me.

CJ rises from his bar stool. "Marsh, dial it down."

I take Marshall's glare straight on. "I got it right."

"No! The emotion is all whack. Dead. Are you asleep or something? Do you even like playing bass, Alex?"

"Alex is a boy's name. My name is Alexandra."

I swing the bass strap over my shoulder and thrust the instrument into his hands.

Not good. Even though I want to kick him in the kneecap, I shouldn't. If I start fighting with him, I'll put the band in an uncomfortable situation of having to choose sides. It's not fair to them or Marshall. They've been together forever.

Marshall tilts his head, brandishing that annoying smile of his. "Finally giving up?"

He'll never quit trying to make me leave the band, will he? Why would he? He doesn't know, can never know what's at stake for me here.

"I need a drink," I say through clenched teeth. "And I *will* be right back."

I march out of the rehearsal room. When the door closes behind me, voices murmur, but I can't figure out any of the words. Not that I care to. If I'm being honest with myself, Marshall had it right. My playing is barely there today, but not because I don't like what we're doing. My hands are on fire, every single joint groaning, and my back muscles hate me.

My phone buzzes in my back pocket. I jump in surprise. The screen displays *CE* as the caller ID. It's only Connor. Although, I suppose, I shouldn't say *only*. If not for him, I wouldn't be here.

My papa met Connor when he went on a student exchange for a semester and stayed with Connor's family. They became good friends. Connor even visited us in Russia several times when I was younger. When my parents died and I posted announcements on their social media accounts, he reached out to me asking if I was doing okay, if I had my school plans or my bills under control.

After I graduated high school, my parents asked me to research schools I wanted to attend a little more and give them another year to save up for the expenses, so I wasn't enrolled anywhere and tuition payments weren't a problem. I kept somewhat afloat working multiple part-time jobs. Delivery, sitting at cash registers in supermarkets, mopping floors. I was an eighteen-year-old in need of a full-time job with no work experience or any prospect of schooling, and my only real skill was singing. It was getting me nowhere. In fact, every day I was falling behind on my rent. My parents had left me nothing. At least no one could make me pay their debts.

The phone keeps buzzing in my hand, and I remember to answer. "Hello, Connor."

I keep my voice low because the Vipers are not supposed to know about his involvement. Connor called me four months ago, checking up on me again, and I finally gave in and told him how desperate I had become. His response? No problem. He had heard from my papa that I was a talented musician, and he had a really close, really influential friend in the music industry he could talk to on my behalf and kickstart my music career. If it was something I'd be interested in.

I had plenty of interest, but trust this person I'd only met a handful of times with my future, my dreams, and my life? Go to the United States and leave everything behind?

I thought long and hard about it. All of two minutes as I stared at my empty wallet and thought of how my measly paychecks from my measly jobs were coming in a week, and said yes. I was one step from rock bottom anyway.

"Good afternoon, Alexandra." He sounds busy but in a good mood. Someone asks him an unintelligible question, and Connor says, "Just a second."

He goes quiet, and I hurry to the kitchen, where I fling open a cabinet door, pull out two cloth bags filled with rice, toss them in the microwave, and punch in two minutes. I've seen the guys use the bags when they have an ache somewhere after a workout. I can definitely use some warm relief right now.

"Still there?" Connor asks.

"Yes."

I look in the direction of the rehearsal room, holding my breath for one of the Vipers to come out. People always interrupt at the least convenient time. Kind of like Connor is right now. It's not a good time to talk at all.

"Could I call you back in the evening?"

"I won't take long," he says. "I just wanted to check how you're doing. Kiera tells me you've been holding your ground."

Kiera's been a liaison of sorts in this whole ordeal. I really don't envy her.

"Oh, yes. It's all great."

Connor chuckles, and I can't help feeling he doesn't believe me.

The microwave beeps, and I jump again. Every little noise startles me. That's because I'm keeping secrets from the Vipers. I'm not allowed to tell them how I got to be with them. I bet they have their suspicions. I bet they'll ask me questions eventually, but even if they do, I shouldn't confirm anything. It's part of their deal when it comes to the new bassist—no questions asked. I wonder how much influence Connor's friend has over Project Viper or The Label.

"Just remember, if you have any trouble with your new friends at all, you tell me. I'll handle it."

"I will. Thanks." I will never tell anyone anything. I don't need to give Marshall another reason to hate me.

"You're going to stick around then?"

"Definitely."

"Good. You should. I hear those five can be stubborn, but Kiera has no doubt you'll tame them."

I wish I had her confidence in the matter. "I bet I will," I say instead.

We say goodbye, and I start the microwave over to make sure the bags are as hot as they can get. While I wait, I down a small bottle of green smoothie. Once the microwave beeps, I pull out the bags and sit on the floor behind the island, out of sight should anyone come looking for me.

Wrapping my hands into the soft bags full of rice and heat, I sigh in relief and rest my head against the island side. If only I could wrap the warm bags around my soul. The heat chases the pain out of my hands, and my mind clings to that lightweight bliss. My eyes grow heavy. To shake off the sleepiness, I fish out my list of tasks from my shorts pocket.

"Getting a drink, huh?"

Startled, I chuck one of the of rice bags at the intruder's face. At Marshall's face. Great.

He's crouching next to me, lips tight, and a part of me freaks out that I've just made him even madder than before. A bigger part of me wants to send the other bag to join its twin.

"What do you want?" I snatch both rice bags and push them around the corner of the island, out of his sight.

"What's wrong with your hands?" Marshall takes my left hand, my fretting hand, and turns it palm side up, seemingly concerned.

His touch feels hotter than the heat bags straight out of the microwave. The worst thing is that I can't decide whether I hate it or like it. Something deep inside of me won't shake off that idiotic excitement I've had since the photo shoot when Marshall Jones deigned to touch me. It doesn't help anything. It does the opposite, in fact.

"You push the strings too hard," he says, rubbing my peeling index fingertip with his thumb.

Concerned, right.

I yank my hand out of his grip and press it to my chest. "You're one to talk. You can't use your own voice right. Don't think no one notices how you can't get enough breath for that long line in *Don't Set Me Free*. You cheat with the guitars to cover it up."

He's a fantastic singer, but face-to-face practice reveals what the recordings don't. He's prone to tearing through his vocal cords in certain situations, perhaps without even realizing it.

I expect him to start arguing with me, but he doesn't even blink. It's like I've said nothing at all.

"Maybe we should stop for today." He sounds suspiciously sincere, but I know better. He's just trying to find any proof he can that I'm a quitter and don't belong with them.

I glare at him. "I'll be right there."

"You'll make it worse."

"Then get me a Band-Aid."

Marshall chuckles. "You're so stubborn."

"Takes one to know one?" I use his shoulder to help myself get up, then hook a foot behind his ankle and send him toppling from his comfortable crouching position onto his behind. Forget you, Jones. I'm not giving up.

"Alexandra," he calls after me in a calm, even amused voice. His dark, warm, temptations-manifested-through-sound-waves voice. My body turns around even though I'm determined to ignore him.

Marshall's on his feet, holding up a white square of folded paper between two fingers. "You dropped something."

My list. Ice grips my shoulders. Did he see what it is? I don't dare to go to him to take it back. Marshall has an unfair advantage over me when I have no power over him other than to be an irritation.

I approach him only close enough to be able to stretch out my hand. "Thanks."

Marshall waits to return my list. I stand in front of him, like a beggar, cracking on the inside. Give me my list!

But also…also…

Give me your trust?

He places the paper into my hand, his fingers brushing my skin and sending lightning through my arm. Then he walks away. I squeeze the list in my palm. Darn you, goals. I'm never carrying you around with me again. Forget visual reminders of my progress.

I refuse to eat dinner with the Vipers that night as well. Another look at Marshall may just snap all of my restraint, and I'll stab him with a fork or something. Or worse—I'll cry. As angry as I feel about his constant nitpicking, the feeling of helplessness is starting to gain a strong hold of me. What if he never relents and never accepts me?

In the guest house family room, Fiona places a mug of thick hot chocolate on the coffee table in front of me. She brought over some immigration paperwork to sign, but I wonder if I'll need it. The way things are going, I'll be put on the first plane back to Russia the moment my six-month contract is up.

"Thanks for the cocoa." I take a few sips then warm my hands on the mug. "Marshall always acts like I'm slaughtering their music. You've heard me play. Do I really sound that bad?"

Fiona has sat through a couple of rehearsals. Probably to inform The Label of our progress. She's always straightforward with me, and I hope she'll tell the truth this time as well, no matter how painful. CJ says I'm getting better on the bass, but I can't help wondering if he's being nice.

Fiona takes a long sip of her own hot chocolate. "You sound a little rough now and then, but not enough for Marshall to snap at you as often as he does. Why do you never tell him to shove it?"

"Shove it? I don't understand."

Fiona smiles. "Buzz off. Scram. Lay off. Leave you alone."

I laugh at the list of synonyms she fires off without a moment's thought. "I don't tell him to leave me alone because I don't want to add any more conflict to the mess." Not that I'm succeeding.

Fiona shrugs. "I sort of understand it and sort of don't. Still, it's your choice, and I'll respect it. But girl, you need to find a way to show him that he can't intimidate you. You're part of the band. You'll be on the posters, tabloids, and social media posts. You're not a faceless substitute bassist."

"I know, I know. But how?"

Please tell me. You can have all of my money if you reveal to me how to conquer Marshall's ire.

"That's up to you to figure out. Just remember, your opinion is also important."

I nod even though she's wrong, of course.

Who on earth needs my opinion?

Just a Lonely Kid

Alexandra

In the morning, I come downstairs to a cheerful clamor of dishes in the kitchen and several voices singing along with the peppy pop song streaming through the speakers. Fiona, Charlie, Juliette, and Elise sit around the table crowded with cardboard containers, plates, and a pitcher of orange juice.

"Good morning." Fiona hands one of the containers to Charlie, who then passes it to Elise. "We get together like this a lot and thought you might like to join us. I hope it's okay we intruded on you like this."

"I don't mind."

I sit with them at the table and stare at the containers filled with all kinds of breakfast foods: hash brown patties and sausages, mini Danishes, and fruit salad. I don't mind the girls inviting themselves over at all. For one thing, the Vipers are strictly prohibited from eating the foods strewn across the table in front of me, apart from the fruit salad. Healthy diet and nutritionist and all.

For another, no one here has included me in anything yet. Everyone's busy and already has their friends. Being considered one of the group without actually doing anything to earn it feels good enough to make my eyes sting.

"You should try some of the Danishes." Charlie picks up a tiny pastry topped with gooey cherries and drops it on a plate in front of me. Her usual high-strung attitude is completely gone, and a pleasant smile dances on her lips, so different from what she shows around Marshall. That guy's amazing at bringing out the worst in people.

"Thanks." I take a bite and almost groan. My mouth is full of pure bliss—flaky, buttery pastry and tender, sweet fruit. I've not eaten anything of the sort for weeks at this point. "More, please!"

The girls laugh and eat and ask me mountains of questions. About Russia, about my family, about how I like being in the States. I do my best to dodge anything that brings on painful memories or redirect their attention to different topics. They don't need to know about my grief. I'm not here for compassion. They can't help me anyway. They don't know me. I don't know them. It's complicated, and I know I'm the one to blame for making it so, but for now it's easier this way.

I still have a fantastic time with the girls. It's easy to share their jokes and gossip even though I haven't known them for long. I even lower my guard enough to ask, "Is it true then that Shane, Graham, CJ, and Marshall are orphans?"

"Not orphans," Juliette says. "They don't have families, and it's a bit of a mess. How do I explain it well?"

Fiona helps her. "Zach, as you know, has a full family, and all's well there. The O'Neals only landed in foster care after their dad completely went off the rails with drugs when Graham was thirteen and Shane was eleven. CJ was also thirteen when his parents lost their parental rights. We don't actually know the full story there. And Marshall's been tossed about in the system since he was three or so. Even though he was really young, he didn't get lucky. No one adopted him."

I'm dying to keep talking about this. I don't fully understand how foster care works. Back in Russia, there isn't a reasonable equivalent. Or if there is, not many people enroll in it. At least I don't know anybody who did this. But I'll have to look into it later on my own. I don't want to bog down everyone else's easy morning with my questions about the American culture. The Internet is my best friend, and talking about this particular side of the guys' lives suddenly doesn't feel right. If I want to know something this personal about them, I'd better ask them myself.

Still, as we finish our breakfast, I can't stop thinking about the guys' parentless pasts, especially Marshall's. He's been an orphan most of his life. No mama to tuck him in at night. No papa to watch TV with him and take him out for treats. Maybe he's not my enemy. Maybe he's just protective of the family he has made for himself with the guys. Maybe he's just a lonely kid who simply needs a hug.

He's not going to get it from me. I'm a lonely kid who needs a hug too, but I don't terrorize others just because they play with my friends.

Bested by a Fan

Marshall

The girls kidnap Alexandra for a day of fun and give me a break from our tedious rehearsals. I exercise, play video games, catch up with my financial accounts, and even check on the state of a couple of startups I invested in last year. More importantly, I try to compose. It's been several months since I cranked out a song. CJ's usually the one who takes charge of that aspect of our band. He's fantastic, but I also have a trick or two in my arsenal. I'm not just the face and the voice of Project Viper. And I'm not as bad at singing as Alexandra says. I know what I'm doing.

The problem with the songwriting today is that the lyrics have an image that accompanies them—a petite, black-haired Russian girl with ice-blue eyes. The song centers on the refusal to allow a person to destroy one's hard-earned peace, and I know I veer into the *proper* emo rock territory, but I have no choice. The song is devouring my mind. I want it out, I want it dark, and I can't finish it.

Thoughts of Alexandra wreak havoc on my sanity. I think about her all the time, swinging between anger and curiosity. Why did The

Label pick her? What's her background? What's the extent of her talents? Kiera praised her to the skies, but so far Alexandra hasn't shown anything extraordinary.

When I wonder about what she likes, hates, or what her favorite show is, I strike those thoughts out with viciousness. No, no, and no. I will not be friends with her. I will not get to know her. She hasn't earned my friendship or my interest. And I will never accept her.

When I see Alexandra the next morning, she's already with CJ. The two of them jam with abandon in the rehearsal room.

I watch them from around the doorway. CJ sounds good, as always, and I wish I could say Alexandra sounds dead awful, but she's good too. Precise and relaxed. Is it because she's only with CJ and no one else is watching her? That does not instill any confidence in her abilities to perform. Or is it because she is *with CJ*? Is she interested in my best friend? Does CJ feel anything back? He's been spending an inordinate amount of time with her. They do everything together. He even takes her out on shopping trips, and I'm no longer relevant, his best friend.

"Good. Have you ever heard me play the bass part in syncopation during a live show? It's different from what's on the recording," CJ asks Alexandra.

"Not well."

His mouth drops. "Not well? Are you going to show me how it's done then?"

Alexandra laughs. "Yeah."

He starts the song over, and Alexandra performs a perfect accompaniment in syncopated rhythm. "Like this," she says after they go through the section.

"You're such a show-off." CJ ruffles her hair.

She smiles with delight. "Only because you've been the best teacher."

My chest burns, and I step away from the doorway to breathe the heat out. I'm jealous. I admit it. Sue me. I never expected to lose my best friend to someone we've barely met.

Zach walks down the hallway, finishing off a high-protein chocolate popsicle. Judging by his scrunched up nose, it's not that fantastic.

"Alexandra's found her groove, it seems." Zach licks the popsicle stick one last time and stuffs it in his jeans pocket.

I have to agree no matter how much it pains me. "Yeah. She's definitely not as bad as I expected."

Zach claps me on the shoulder. "I think she just needed a bit of time to get used to us."

Graham and Shane join us.

"We're practicing in the hallway today?" Shane asks.

I chuckle at his half-baked joke, but this is exactly why I resist Alexandra's addition so much. We are already a team. More than that. We are a family. And we allowed Kiera to bring a stranger into our midst. Someone who has no clue what it took us to get where we are today.

Memories flood my vision. Meeting CJ in seventh grade as we both trudged around the track behind the rest of our classmates. Nobody, not even the gym teacher, cared that we could barely drag our feet. All we got was a handful of mocking comments and a warning that if we didn't hustle, we'd get a fail. We exchanged wordless glances, and by the end of that year CJ and I were always the first ones around the track, just out of sheer spite, and after some training. Once we realized we had similar backgrounds, it was more than a desire to prove others wrong that glued us together. We lived every day to show each other that we could thrive despite the circumstances.

Shane, Graham, and Zach go into the rehearsal room, diffusing my flashbacks, and I follow them.

"Morning, Zach!" Alexandra throws her arms out for a hug.

Zach squeezes her tight. I'm six feet, but he's taller and has to lean down quite a bit for her. "I get the first greeting. *Matryoshka* likes me the best today! Hey, teach me some Russian so I can pick up cute girls like you."

Alexandra pushes him away. "You'd best stick to music. Play them some Tchaikovsky. Don't try to talk."

Zach strides to his keyboard setup with a laugh. CJ watches the pianist with narrowed eyes, and I wonder again whether my best friend has feelings for Alexandra.

She greets the O'Neals one by one as well. I take my spot at the microphone and pull it out of the stand to check if it's on.

Alexandra turns to me with a beaming smile. "Good morning, Marshall. What song should we start with?"

I drop the microphone at that smile and her eyes piercing right into my soul. I have no weapon against *that*. How can I stay mad at her when she looks at me with such… I can't even decipher her expression. Joy? But when has Alexandra looked at me with anything but a silent prayer to gods that I'd disappear?

"You pick," I say.

Her eyes sparkle with even more excitement. "*All Your Broken Promises*."

Zach plays the intro and garbles it. "Hmph. Haven't played this in a while. What brought it up? We never play it at any of the shows."

"You should! It's my favorite. Do I get to pick a song for the next setlist? If so, I want that one."

I put my brains together enough to replace the microphone. It's a little surprising that she likes that song. While it's reasonably popular with our fanbase, it's not too prominent. And it's one of the songs I wrote, not CJ. And it's her favorite. I've got to stop dwelling on that. "It's usually fan favorites and a couple of our choosing—"

"Well, I'm a fan and *us* all at once. Convenient, isn't it?" She starts playing the bridge from *All Your Broken Promises*. Confident, fluid, perfect. Impossible.

"You're so sneaky," CJ says with a pleased note to his tone.

Alexandra pauses to look at him over her shoulder. "I am Russian. Can we at least warm up with it?"

I clear my throat. "Sure."

Alexandra does a little jump on the spot, like an excited kid, and I can't help thinking again that her bass is too big for her.

She has no trouble playing at all this time. It probably helps that we're playing her favorite song. She must have practiced it a lot.

I, on the other hand, feel rusty. After we finish the song, Graham re-drums the chorus once more, then another time, each time using a slightly different sequence. "Which one is it?"

"The first one," Alexandra replies without hesitation then turns to me. "Also, it's not 'everything consumed by dust,' it's 'everything consumed by rust.'"

"It's dust," I object. "Dust."

"Rust," she insists.

We argue, but it doesn't feel like we're fighting. She's still smiling.

"What do you want to bet that it isn't?" I ask.

Alexandra takes off the bass and puts it on the stand, then pulls out her phone. "If I'm right, you'll sign my bass. If I'm wrong, you pick."

I like her confidence, but I won't lose. "Deal."

Alexandra swipes through her phone, long dark hair hanging over her shoulders, its ends brushing her hands. I want to reach out and push it out of her way.

What in the…?

A moment later, my voice fills the room.

I hate listening to myself on recordings, and this particular time I hate it more. She was right. It's rust. What's more, she shows me her phone screen with a Google result of *my* lyrics. Rust again. I forgot my own song.

Graham chuckles from behind the drums. "Good job, Marshall. Bested by a fan."

The rest of the rehearsal is full of jokes, all at my expense. I let them have their fun. I've earned the mockery.

Alexandra waits until after dinner to claim her reward. She finds me in my room, carrying her P Bass and a Sharpie. "Don't think you can hide from me here."

"I'm not hiding." I just need to catch up on some assignments for college.

She comes in and places the bass on my bed. I tuck the iPad with my reading under my pillows before she sees anything.

"What were you reading?"

"A bit of Tolstoy." She's not going to believe it.

Alexandra rolls her eyes. "Right, Tolstoy."

Called it.

"You don't think I'd enjoy Tolstoy?" I don't actually, but I have to read him for my Russian Literature class. I only have this one class this semester, thank everything. We've been so busy with Alexandra, I've had no time for homework. I'm going to have to pass to register for the spring semester.

"I really don't think he's up your alley," she says.

"What else do you think about me?"

Alexandra grins. "You don't want to know."

This conversation is odd. Not the words themselves, but the fact that she's talking to me at all. I've caught Alexandra watching me many times, but as soon as she realizes I'm onto her, she retreats. Shy? Or maybe she hates me. I wouldn't be surprised if she did.

"Do you want to know what I think about you?" Will she retreat this time too?

"I already do." Alexandra looks around my room.

I can't help wondering what she makes out of my shelves stuffed with art books, a massive collection of CDs I've procured from every musician I've met over the years, and the black bedding, black curtains, and black rug. Black is a good color. Constant and soothing.

"So, what do I think about you?"

Alexandra's eyes snap back to me. "*Ty dumaesh', chto ty slishkom prityagatel'nyi i krutoi, chtoby delit' stsenu s kem-to kak ya.*"

You think you're too hot and awesome to share a stage with someone like me.

"You would've never said that if you thought I could understand you, would you?" I barely manage to keep laughter out of my voice.

"Maybe I would, maybe I wouldn't." Alexandra smiles, pleased with herself, assuming I have no clue.

I chuckle. "Wow."

Hot and awesome? Does Alexandra feel attracted to me? No way. She's just mocking me. And if she isn't—

No, she is. She definitely is.

"A thought for a thought," Alexandra says. "What do I think about you?"

"You're crazy pleased you beat me at my own song, that's what. Don't deny it." I take her bass and flip it over so that the strings rest on my lap.

"Guilty as charged." She looks at the foot of my bed and shakes her head as if she's considered sitting down but thought better of it. "You have a lot of art books."

It seems she does want to talk to me after all. I'm still unsure how I feel about that, but maybe it wouldn't be such a bad thing for us to get to know each other. A little.

"Do you miss Russia?" This is the most neutral question I manage to come up with.

"Yes." Alexandra's voice is calm and even, but she hugs herself with one arm and crosses the room to stand at the window. .

I try to imagine what it would be like to miss home. I never really had a place I could call my own, not until the Tangs took me in. Even six years later, I feel like a guest here now and then.

"Do you get to talk to your parents often? How do they feel about what you're doing here?"

Alexandra grips the windowsill and looks out the window. "We don't talk. If we did, if we could…" She draws a heavy breath before forcing out a smile. "They'd say I'm crazy."

I always thought explaining my family situation to others was a pain, but Alexandra's life back home also sounds complicated. She wouldn't be here, halfway across the globe from her home if things were peachy.

"You are crazy." I give her a warm smile, making sure she knows I'm joking.

"Probably."

She turns around and taps the marker against her palm. My neck prickles with the knowledge that I should say something comforting or encouraging to her, but my tongue refuses to move, and I don't force it. Alexandra couldn't have expected us to wait for her with our arms wide open. Except maybe Zach.

"Do you remember your parents at all?" Alexandra asks.

The marker keeps bouncing against her hand, and she won't look at me. I wait until she does to answer. "No. Do you want to sit down?" I nod at the edge of my bed.

She reluctantly sits on the corner.

"Remember, Charlie told you I don't bite."

Alexandra falls onto her back and stares at the ceiling. "She lied."

"You're not going to make it easy for me, are you?"

"Will you make it easy for me?" She keeps avoiding eye contact, making me wonder if that's how she finds strength to tell me things she otherwise wouldn't.

"Easy has no value." The dry wisdom rings hollow on my tongue. I might as well not have said anything.

Alexandra rolls onto her side, props her head on her hand, and finally looks at me. Knees bent, her other hand resting on the quilt, she appears comfortable and relaxed, the way a girlfriend would.

"What happened to your parents? Why did you end up, as you guys say, in the system?"

A dig for a dig. I see. I made her uncomfortable, so she'll return the favor.

"I don't know what happened to them, and I don't remember. I was three. One night they just disappeared." I wrap my fist in my shirt sleeve and rub the dull spot on Alexandra's bass. "The neighbor found me sitting in the apartment door, crying and calling for them. Or something like that. I don't even know if that's the real story. How do they explain to a three-year-old where their parents went off to? Maybe they were involved in something criminal and were snatched and murdered, or they ran, or they fell off the bridge into the river. Who knows?"

"You don't have any grandparents? Aunts? Uncles forty-five times removed?"

I laugh. "No. The fun thing about my parents is Dean and Kelly Jones never existed. I have an authentic birth certificate, but all information about them is false. Their work records were also full of lies, so the government couldn't find their next of kin."

To my surprise, Alexandra smiles. "They were spies. And I'm sure they didn't want to leave you."

"It doesn't matter anymore," I say with a shrug. I hate thinking about them, giving all the whys and what-ifs space in my brain and power over my heart. In the end, I survived.

"Now, what do you want me to write?"

A minute later, Alexandra heads out, holding her bass like it's the biggest treasure she has ever had.

"Goodnight, Marshall," she sings from the doorway.

I've heard her sing, of course, but this time her voice is not overshadowed by mine. Smooth. My name's like velvet when she sings it.

"Sing something else," I blurt out.

Alexandra narrows her eyes at me. Everything I say and do plants suspicions in her, it seems.

"No."

"Then leave already. I've got to finish my Tolstoy." I do my best to glower at her, but she giggles.

"Enjoy."

Once she's gone, I take out the iPad but can't focus anymore. I rest my head on the pillows. She made me write, "Alexandra is the bass goddess," and sign underneath. She is a goddess, all right. Of mischief and torture, sent to plague me.

Nobody's Matryoshka

Alexandra

In the guest house, Fiona twists the bass this way and that, eyebrows raised high, appraising its back and Marshall's signature. "You made him do it after all." She came by to check on me right as I returned with my now signed bass.

I smile and stick my tongue out, all warm on the inside. Marshall chicken scratched that signature in a hurry, as though the marker was burning his fingers, but he did it nonetheless. "I guess he's a stickler when it comes to keeping his promises."

Fiona hands back the bass. "Well done. You showed him that you're to be reckoned with without causing any conflict."

"I guess I did. Such a lucky thing too. I couldn't believe he messed up. I wasn't even going to say anything at first, but I couldn't help it. He always points out my mistakes."

"Good for you." Fiona pats me on the shoulder. "Good night."

"Good night."

I take the bass guitar to my room and spend a long while caressing Marshall's signature with my fingertips. For one thing, I got him to admit that he was wrong. For another, my first attempt to build a better relationship with him worked better than expected.

After the girls confirmed that Marshall and three of the other Vipers had troubled upbringings, I resolved to try and be patient with Marshall despite his grouchiness. My thinking was that maybe if I were the first one to show him that I want to be friends anyway, he'd soften up. It seems to have worked. We had our first normal conversation. Sure, I annoyed him by pointing out his mistake earlier, but he didn't throw me out of his room and didn't refuse to sign the bass. Now, if I have to leave the band, I'll have this perfect memento from him. One of a kind. Just for me. A compliment, however reluctant, from Marshall Jones himself.

The next morning, I get further proof that Marshall's still a work in progress. I arrive late for breakfast, but I smile and make eye contact with him. Marshall continues eating with a stone-cold expression as his eyes follow me around the dining area. I check my clothes. Red, vegan leather leggings and a white, long-sleeve thermal tee. All new and clean. I smooth out my hair. What's wrong then?

Shane takes his dishes to the sink and pats my shoulder on the way there. "You look good," he says, leaning low so only I would hear him.

"I know," I mutter back, not entirely sure why he's said that.

In the afternoon, while I hide in the guest house for a few minutes of quiet, CJ texts me and tells me to come to the main house upstairs loft. Hmmm. It's been a few weeks, but I haven't been upstairs very often. It's the Viper bedroom territory. Even when I went to claim my autograph from Marshall, I came uninvited. I work on ignoring the lonely thoughts that creep up on me. The guys aren't shutting me out by not inviting me to hang out with them upstairs. They spend plenty of time with me in other areas of the house. The inner voice reminds me it's either meals, fitness, or practice. It's never a time with friends like I have with the girls.

I comb my hair and go back to the main house. No need to dwell on things that are out of my control. I can't force the Vipers to like me, Marshall being daily proof of that. I can only give it my best shot and hope it works out.

On the staircase that leads to the loft, I pause and listen to the Vipers bantering. Marshall's laughter is loud, and he sings every other sentence, using well-known tunes for his replies. I've never heard him do this before. My feet glue themselves to the stairs, and I absorb every little bit of his voice. I was determined to not let all these feelings of loneliness get to me, but I can't help regretting being here when Marshall is so full of joy and humor with his friends and so clammed up with me.

"So, how do you guys feel about Alexandra so far?" CJ asks.

"I'm already here!" I shout from the stairs and climb the rest of the way. I may be dying to know what they think, but I won't eavesdrop.

The Vipers sit in a circle on the floor, surrounding six huge plastic containers, one of which is black with a red skull and crossbones.

"You made it." Looking ashen with discomfort, CJ pats a space on the floor between him and Zach.

"An honest evaluation wouldn't hurt." I sit next to him. "I'd rather not wonder if I'm wasting your time."

"Sorry," he groans.

"Okay, sure. Let's talk about it." Zach scoots closer to me. "If we had to vote on whether or not you could stay permanently with the band today, I'd say yes."

"You would," Marshall says.

"That makes a no from you." I refuse to crumble in front of him. "CJ?"

"Yes," he says, a little too quickly. Then again, he wouldn't give a different answer. I'm here to save him after all.

I look at Graham. He shrugs, as always.

A whatever grade is not helpful right now.

That leaves Shane. I face him.

"No," Shane says but hurries to add, "for now. I think you're awesome, but I need to see you in action. How you handle shows, public appearances, and other stressful events."

Shane's not apologizing, and that's a relief. It's his band and livelihood after all, but two out of five after a month is not a good result. However, it's only been one month. I have five more to prove I can do it.

"What's all this?" I do my best to look at the containers and not Marshall, who's quiet now. Of course.

"Fan mail." CJ flashes me a huge, sinister smile and wiggles his eyebrows.

Zach leans closer. "You're gonna love it."

"Or she's going to get scared," Marshall says as he opens the first container.

Upon closer examination, I see that it's got his name on the lid. The other containers are also labeled.

"I seriously doubt there's anything scarier than you." I hold his probing gaze. "And if I can handle you, then I can handle anything."

"Nice!" Zach lifts his hand for a high five. I hit his palm.

"Handle me?" Marshall grins. "You wish you could."

CJ slips the lid off his container, distracting me from the sudden turn my thoughts take at the idea of handling Marshall Jones. I'm not going to go there. I will totally not think of messing his black curls or tracing his hard bicep with my fingers. Nope. Admiring Marshall is off limits, from a distance or otherwise. That's not what I'm here for. I'm here to learn from CJ.

Who, actually, is more trouble than Marshall. The singer keeps his distance, but the former bassist crosses personal space boundaries without thinking.

"Next time, there will be seven boxes," CJ says as he drapes his arm over my shoulder.

Marshall keeps watching me, so I hug CJ back before I ask, "Seven?"

"Yeah." CJ taps my nose. "One for you too. I bet it'll overflow."

"Or we'll have another black box." Graham starts digging in the Jolly Roger container.

"You be nice," Zach scolds him.

Graham shrugs. "I'm not saying it'll happen, but it's a possibility that Alexandra's addition won't be welcome by the fans."

"True," Marshall says.

CJ holds me tighter and shakes his head. "Don't listen to these two unbelievers, *Matryoshka*."

"I won't." I hug him with both arms and stick my tongue at Graham.

CJ lets me dig in his box of envelopes, cards, and printed emails. He's been great. It's obvious he has a lot to do with the band's overall creative direction. He always bombards the band with new lyrics. Marshall listens to him. All of the Vipers do. Their bond is undeniable and unshakable. There's never any topic off limits, never any real disrespect. They roughhouse and call each other names, but everything is done in good humor. And when it's time to play music, they give it all without reservation. When I first saw them perform, I was afraid this endeavor would take everything from me. I'm not afraid anymore. I know I can give my soul to music. The Vipers have been for years. Giving everything they've got to music helps them thrive.

"Why so thoughtful?" Zach asks while CJ laughs at something Graham has dug up from the black container.

"Why is all mail open?" I ask. "For safety?"

Zach nods. "Charlie's team rips through everything before it gets to us in case there's something dangerous. The rest of the nasty stuff goes in the black box, and we decide whether we read them or not."

"Are there ever any death threats?" I whisper.

Zach chuckles. "Sometimes, but we do well with keeping our lives private, so it's not a big concern. Besides, The Label keeps tabs on the most desperate of crazies. Don't worry."

"How come you're so normal?" I realize it's not something we've been talking about, but the thought jumps from my mind to my tongue in less than a second.

Zach scrunches up his nose. "Come again?"

I love those wrinkles on his nose that make an appearance whenever he's confused or annoyed with something. "How come there's no alcohol, no swearing, no smoking? You stick to a fitness routine, don't party, don't do drugs, don't parade with a new girl on your arm every week. You're not what most people expect rockers to be."

"Ah, that." Zach chortles. "Yeah, well, maybe it's because we're mama's boys."

"You're the only one with a mom," I point out.

"Yes, but Zach's mom is every Viper's mom," Marshall says. He's got good hearing, apparently. "She would destroy us all for stupid behavior. Also, it's in the contract for the Nest. It's the only condition that warrants us the use of the property: no alcohol, smoking, drugs, or raves. Didn't you have to sign something like that as well?"

I had to sign so many papers, I lost track of all the things I wasn't supposed to do. I figured if I sat tight, I'd be okay.

"And that's it? The contract is the only thing that keeps you all so dignified? You're all complete nightmares then when you're on tour? I seriously doubt that. Come on." I elbow Zach in the side. "What's the real reason? You know I won't make fun of you."

Zach drills me with a dubious look. "You? Won't make fun?"

"When have I ever made fun of you?"

"Not yet doesn't mean you never will," Marshall chimes in again, and this time I glare at him.

"He's right, you know." Zach smiles.

His resistance, however teasing, robs me of all excitement at this opportunity to question one of the more chill Vipers about the band. I also lose all interest in fan mail. I know the guys probably didn't mean it this way, but ultimately, it's nothing but another reminder that I don't belong with them.

Zach reads the messages and sorts them into stacks according to what people call him. Hot-n-sexy stack grows much faster than the rest.

"You're full of it." Shane lays waste to Zach's order by mixing all the letters into one big mess.

Zach retaliates by pulling a stack of gift cards from Shane's fist. "Why do you always get the good stuff?"

He's not kidding. Shane's extracted something like thirty restaurant gift cards from his fan mail.

"It's because I'm cute." Shane bats his eyelashes at Zach.

Graham tosses a wadded letter at Shane's forehead. The younger O'Neal hisses and rubs his skull. While he's nursing his superficial injury, CJ sweeps in and collects all of Shane's and Zach's gift cards and stacks them in front of me.

"Enjoy. You deserve it for all the nonsense you get from these two."

"My spoils!" Shane wails from his spot. "You took away the only good thing about fan mail."

I laugh and catch Marshall smiling.

Zach saves me from dwelling on Marshall's unexpected softness by sidling closer and saying, "We don't do drugs or anything because what's the point? We don't want to be *that* band. Why ruin our health or our reputation so early in our lives? Music is enough. Financial freedom is more than enough. We have fun as is."

I take a moment to process this. My face must show some kind of a concerning sign since Zach asks, "Are you disappointed?"

I hold his gaze. Zach watches me as he waits for my answer.

"You guys are so awesome." I feel safe telling him that. Whether he takes it seriously or not, he'll have a funny comment, strike a pose, or laugh.

"We are awesome." Zach tilts his face upward, endlessly proud of himself, although there's a note of relief in his posturing all the same.

Do the Vipers actually care what I think about them? So far I've felt like I'm the only one dying for approval and acceptance. I laugh at the idea but stop when Zach takes my chin with his fingers and examines my face.

"What is it?" I stutter out.

Raven-haired Zach with his dark brown, sharp, bottomless eyes that reveal his Korean heritage is close enough for me to catch the citrusy scent of the hair products Elise uses with the guys. It's easy to ignore his appearance because he jokes around all the time, but he's definitely more than a little attractive.

He glances at something to the side then brushes his thumb against my cheek. "An eyelash. All gone now."

"Next time just tell me." I slap his hand away and grumble in Russian, "A girl can only take so much before it breaks her heart."

Marshall snorts.

Zach's face grows puzzled. "Cussing me out in Russian? I never would've thought my *Matryoshka* has such a foul mouth."

"Don't get too comfortable with *my Matryoshka*." CJ reaches over my shoulder and pushes Zach away.

The pianist crosses his arms on his chest. "Wanna fight me for her?"

CJ mimics his pose. "I'll win too."

At first, I press my hands to my cheeks, then I realize that they're messing with me. I grab them both by the ears and yank nice and hard.

"Listen to me carefully, my darling sweeties." I copy Kiera's manner of speaking in hopes to make sure my message is clear. "I am nobody's *Matryoshka*, so stop it."

"I'll stop, I'll stop," Zach squeaks. When I release him, he rubs his ear, although he's still smiling. "Strong grip."

I focus on CJ. "What about you?"

"Don't you like me? At all?"

I nail him with a scorching look, one to match my burning cheeks. Take me seriously, dang it! "You're just asking for it, aren't you?"

CJ slides his fingers under my hand on his ear, freeing himself from my grip, and says in a low voice, "Let's have a Riot Night after this."

"What's a Riot Night?"

"It's when we break all the diet rules and go out for an evening of junk food," Shane says with a huge grin on his face.

"What do you say?" CJ asks.

Despite my rough handling of him, he has no hurt or offense in his eyes, only expectation. He makes me feel guilty for my outburst. "Okay."

"You done setting up your date?" Marshall glowers at CJ, but when his friend chuckles and gets back to the fan offerings, Marshall's irritation shifts to me. Jaw clenched, he eyes me up and down, probably wishing, again, that I have never been born.

I stifle a sigh. So much for any kind of progress toward gaining his good opinion.

Riot Night

Marshall

For the rest of the afternoon, I work on subduing my outrage at CJ for asking Alexandra to Riot Night with us. It's the thing that only the Vipers do, no girls. Not even Elise gets invited to Riot Night. It's always been this way. Why does Alexandra have to become part of that equation too? I shouldn't be mad at her. CJ's the one who invited her, but she could've refused. She should have refused.

She should've also refused to do fan mail with us. Especially in those atrocious red leather leggings. The moment I heard her coming, I decided I'd pretend like she's not even there, but I haven't been able to ignore her. Her red-clad legs draw my eyes after themselves no matter what I do. What's worse, I catch myself checking her expression. Is she comfortable with what's happening? Are the rest of the band members nice to her? Does CJ continue hovering around her? And Zach, that bleeping punk. He's worse than CJ sometimes because he can be awkward when he tries to flirt, but his sincerity works like a charm.

CJ does stay close to Alexandra. He never leaves her side once. After his invitation to go out, Alexandra seems to be in excellent spirits and smiles, smiles, smiles. She has a pretty smile. Happy and a little shy. No wonder CJ gravitates toward her. She's definitely his type—petite, curvy, long hair. Hangs on CJ's every word.

"Are you coming to Riot Night too?" Alexandra looks at me through her bangs, eyes full of... What is it? What does she want from me?

I refuse. "Nah."

"Why the heck not?" Shane asks.

"Because I don't want to."

"*Nu nikak emu ne ugodit*," Alexandra says, causing me to smile. *There's no pleasing him.*

"He's kidding." CJ smooths out her hair. "Marshall would never miss Riot Night. Right, Marsh?" He shoots me a meaningful look.

I nod. "Right."

After all, if I go, I can watch how things are progressing between CJ and his *Matryoshka*. And stop it.

There's a burger shack on the outskirts of Portland that we have been frequenting since before anyone knew us. The place has lost some popularity with the locals over the years with an abundance of new chain franchises popping up like mushrooms after the rain, but we continue going there to satisfy our cravings for grease burgers and fresh cut fries. We usually call the owner a couple hours before closing, and she prepares us food and lets us linger an hour after she closes the door. She even refuses to take any tips for that, just says she loves seeing us all "grown-up and handsome."

When we arrive, the last of the customers file through the door, a couple of them throwing glances our way. Alexandra pulls her head into her shoulders and hides under the hood of her jacket. If such a small encounter makes her uncomfortable, how is she going to handle interviews and gigs with thousands of people present?

A table waits for us, piled with baskets of fries, onion rings, double-patty cheeseburgers, and dipping sauces. Straws from soda cups stick out like red and white spears. My mouth waters in anticipation of fat, salt, and sugar heaven.

"It's been a while," says the owner as she flips the sign to closed.

"Hello, Jess," I say, the rest of us echoing my greeting. "Thanks for having us."

"Anytime. But who's that with you? You've never brought a girl before." Jess eyes our new bassist with excited curiosity.

The tiny Russian emerges from under her hood. "I'm Alexandra."

"Jess. Nice to meet you. And who's your poison?"

Alexandra's mouth drops open for a second.

"She's CJ's girlfriend," I say with my most winning smile.

"She's totally mine!" Zach yells from the table, through a mouthful of fries.

"What did I tell you earlier?" Alexandra scolds Zach, then turns to Jess. "I'm no one's girlfriend. I'm a co-worker."

Jess laughs. "Girl, you got your hands full then."

"You have no idea." Alexandra chuckles before she stabs me with one last warning look and goes to eat.

Everyone stuffs their faces, but I'm on high alert and just stand there, watching CJ with his girl. He has one arm around Alexandra's back while she looks up at him, chattering away.

His girl. CJ and Alexandra. Together. I'm not in the picture at all.

"Marsh, you're awful weird lately," Shane says around the straw of his soda. "Are you going to eat or what?"

Alexandra slides out an empty chair next to her. "I promise I won't bite. Just this once."

I drop on the indicated chair and karate chop CJ's hand when he reaches for a burger from a basket in front of me. "This one's mine."

Shane hides a laugh behind his fist, feigning a cough. "Are you talking about food or—"

"What else could I be talking about?" I kick his foot under the table.

He leans to look at CJ's arm on Alexandra then waggles his eyebrows at me. I ignore him.

"So, Alexandra, the deal with The Label was that we get who we get and we don't complain. But I must admit, we don't know anything about you." Zach shovels spoonful after spoonful of a thick shake into his mouth. "I tried to look you up online, but there's no one named Alexandra Lermontova who matches your looks on any of the large social media networks. Or newspapers. Or anything. So where did you come from? What does your family do? How did you learn to play music?"

Alexandra dips a fry in ketchup and steals a sideways glance at me. "You looked me up?"

"I didn't. Zach's the one with nothing else to do."

She turns to the pianist again. "You already know I'm from Saint Petersburg. A regular neighborhood with teachers, factory workers, and software engineers. My parents owned a convenience store. Groceries, an assortment of other necessities. It was close to a school, and we had a bunch of kids popping in for snacks. Mama loved them. She loved ordering fun things to sell to them."

"Owned?" Graham asks. He's always the first one to pick up little nuances like this.

"Yeah, they don't anymore. The Russian economy is always challenging. A couple of years ago, my dad borrowed money to keep the shop afloat after he had remodeled it, but it didn't work out." Alexandra's expression grows distant.

Before I can ask what's wrong, she continues, "And I learned music like any other Russian kid. At seven or eight, you enroll in a music school for seven years, take a specialty, solfeggio, choir, music history and literature."

"Seven years?" Zach keeps asking. "Then what?"

"Then you graduate and hope for the best. My best ended up being me coming here to relieve CJ of the bass duty." She flashes our former bassist an enormous smile, and I almost think she's genuinely happy if not for her earlier subdued behavior. "Most people don't do anything. Just play music for their own pleasure. Others attend more school. I was going to try for Saint Petersburg State Conservatory and a few places in Moscow after high school, but hey. This is better, right?"

Alexandra keeps mentioning how all of her plans stopped with Project Viper like she never intended to join us. It's beyond weird.

"What did you study originally?" I ask despite the danger of coming off as confrontational again.

"Vocals." Alexandra's voice is so small, I'm not sure I heard her right.

"Vocals?" Shane sounds as surprised as I feel. "You studied singing? What about bass then?"

Alexandra drags another fry through her ketchup with more precision and deliberation than the task warrants. "I learned how to play guitar with my dad for fun. He was a great guitarist."

Everyone's quiet.

So, she's a singer and not a bassist after all, just like I thought. Finding out that I've been right all along doesn't exactly bring all the satisfaction I thought it would. Also, she's too good for a complete novice. Fine, she played guitar before, but to switch to a bass guitar in such a short time and own it? She's kind of scary.

Alexandra's eyes meet mine, her own full of guilt. Or maybe fear. Guilt I can deal with, but I'd rather not be responsible for any kind of fear from her anymore. I pick up a strawberry milkshake and set it in front of Alexandra, hoping to distract her enough to wipe away the sheepish look on her face. "So you studied vocals. You seem to be handling the bass just fine."

Shane gasps. "Are you feeling alright?"

With an accompaniment of chortles from the other guys, he reaches over the table to feel my forehead.

Smiling, I lean backward in my chair. "I'm fine."

⦿ Track 12
What It's Like to Be an Outsider

Alexandra

I can't believe my ears.

Marshall doesn't jump on me, declaring over and over again that he was right about me being an impostor. He gives me a milkshake instead. Does he finally accept me? Or maybe feels like he could try to?

My eyes are already stinging from talking about my family, so his more pleasant than usual disposition fills them with tears to the brim. I slurp through the straw. I won't cry in front of the Vipers.

And I will never cry in front of Marshall.

Even if I feel weak and fragile through my core, he can never know. He needs someone strong and unbending with the bass, not a crybaby.

CJ and Marshall engage in a discussion of a song CJ's writing and whether it would fit the album theme, then whether they should continue pursuing a theme at all. Giving a whole album a theme can churn out a spectacular work of art, but it can also flop with a bang.

"Maybe not this song then," CJ says in the end. "We have Alexandra now, and I bet The Label has plans for her. We'll have to wait and see exactly what they were thinking about bringing Alexandra on board."

Shane nods. "Good plan."

"You think The Label would have me be a lead on any of the songs?" I toss the idea around my brain. It could be fun in the studio, but I worry I'd chicken out when it was time to perform live.

Marshall sips his soda, one of his feet resting on his knee. "Fat chance, regardless of your vocal abilities."

Dead silence descends on the table. Zach glares at him, and even Graham, who's usually chill no matter what Marshall says, sighs in frustration. Or maybe I'm imagining their disapproval with all the indignance that flows through me. A moment ago Marshall's been nice, now he's impossible again.

"And the jerk returns," Zach mutters.

Marshall drops a fry. "What?"

My phone chimes in my jacket pocket. Grateful for the interruption from the awkwardness, I hurry and check it. "It's Mr. Eaton. I'd better answer." He strikes again with the worst timing possible.

All five Vipers stare at me with wide eyes. Of course they do. They don't know about anyone in my life, so when someone calls me and I drop Connor's name like it's no big deal… Oops. No one's supposed to know about Connor other than Kiera. I slide my thumb across the screen and try my best to push out a happy voice even though my chest still burns with humiliation from Marshall's remarks and I feel like a complete dummy for mentioning Connor. "Hello."

I take our conversation to the farthest table and sit with my back to everyone. Connor takes a while asking me about my day-to-day activities and making sure everything is well. At the moment, even though everything really is well—the majority of the Vipers tolerate me quite well, my practice sessions with them become smoother and smoother, and I'm growing somewhat accustomed to my new life in the States—the world feels bleak. Marshall sits like a poisoned sliver in my heart. With him everything is one step forward and a mile back. He will always hate me. He will not let me stay with the band. He will not share his family with me, I just know it. I endeavor to stay upbeat despite everything, but an already broken heart can only take so much.

When Connor finally hangs up, I keep my new phone pressed to my ear and spend a few moments with my old one, watching my family videos again. No sound. I don't want anyone to hear my parents call me pet names or laugh. I don't want to hear their voices either. I'll definitely cry if I do.

It dawns on me that I'm sitting in complete silence. I glance over my shoulder. Marshall's the only one left at our original table, rocking on the chair, his face unreadable. The rest of the Vipers stand outside, drinking what remains of their shakes and soda and laughing.

I put my phones away and return to Marshall.

"We're already leaving?"

He refuses to look at me as he stands and says, "I'm sorry."

There's plenty he can be apologizing for. I just never expected him to. He doesn't seem like the type to beg forgiveness when he doesn't want to, and it's obvious he's forcing himself to say sorry.

I grab one last fry and go outside without responding. If I can't have a full-on squabble with him, I can certainly be passive-aggressive.

Marshall sighs behind my back.

"All good?" CJ looks between us.

I give him my brightest smile. "Of course." I smile at Marshall too. Let everyone think we're best friends until death.

"Let's go home then." CJ yawns and climbs behind the wheel.

I sit up front with him. I don't get carsick, but this way Marshall can't sit next to me.

CJ drives us all home. I cling to what dignity I have left and keep pretending like everything's fine by gazing out the window and failing at universal proportions to stop thinking about Marshall. I've managed to brush off his criticisms for weeks, but today his attitude hurts. Today I give in to the feeling that no one's on my side. All my hopes for a new future and new family crumble away. I want to give up on everything, especially on Marshall. I can't change his mind about me no matter what I do anyway.

I draw a slow breath. This is just one moment of weakness, one pinch of despair. I'll shake it off by tomorrow, I'm sure.

What if I won't?

We stop at a traffic light, and Marshall leans between the seats to say, "Alexandra, I'm sorry."

I resist the urge to look at him, but I can't resist asking, "Why are you sorry?"

Marshall exhales. "I'm sorry for saying The Label wouldn't let you be the lead singer on any of the songs."

I act like it doesn't matter. "Never mind. I only asked because I don't know anything about The Label's practices. I thought you would." Will he soften up if I defer to him as to a source of authority and knowledge?

"How the heck am I supposed to know?" Marshall grinds through clenched teeth.

And just like that, he's angry at me again. And now I'm angry too.

"You've been with them for years." My voice grows louder. "I thought maybe you'd have a pretty good idea."

"Well, I don't. When The Label decides something, our opinion doesn't matter. So stop asking. I don't know anything. When I do, you will too. And stop trying to be nice to me. It's annoying, and it won't work! The moment your contract's up, you're out, president's pet."

"Marshall!" Zach exclaims from the back of the minivan.

"President's pet?" I demand.

"How else did you get to be with us?"

My mouth drops. "I've never met the man in my life!"

Marshall scoffs. "Please. Don't bother lying. We're not stupid."

"Marsh, what the eff is wrong with you?" CJ snaps.

Is that what he really thinks of me? What they all think of me? I suspected that they might be tolerating me only because The Label hoisted me off on them, but to hear it out loud, no matter how true… My whole body trembles. Whether from rage or offense, I have no clue and don't care to figure it out.

We come to another traffic light, which happens to be the last one before the Nest, and I climb out of the van and start walking. CJ calls after me, but I ignore him. Sorry, CJ and everyone, that you have to be collateral damage tonight, but I need to be alone. Not in that guest house, a few steps away from you, but completely alone. I need to walk for a long time like I used to do back in Saint Petersburg, need the wind to blow my thoughts clean.

CJ pulls over after he passes the intersection, and Marshall climbs out of the van.

"It's dark, and you're not going anywhere alone. Get back in," he orders.

He *orders*. I keep walking.

Marshall growls and slams the van door shut. For a moment I believe they're leaving, but when the van drives off, Marshall jogs up to my side.

"Alexandra," he tries to engage me, and this time his tone is much softer.

I don't respond. Yes, I'm mad at him. Yes, I'm pouting. And no, I don't have to talk to him. He's made his point crystal clear, so I'm going to do exactly what he wants me to do. I'll stop being nice to him.

Marshall gives up talking and walks beside me in silence, robbing me of solitude and fueling my anger.

Residential Portland sleeps under a blanket of darkness and porch lights. When we arrive at home, I'm still wading in that odd state of mind that refuses to be anywhere familiar after a disastrous evening. But where else can I go? It is dark and it is late. As safe as the suburbs might be, I promised Connor and Kiera that I wouldn't go anywhere by myself. I know, I know. I've already broken that promise.

Marshall uses my deliberation to his advantage. "This is not the best walk you've had, is it?"

It's hard to ignore his peacemaking voice, so I finally look at him. I wish I didn't. I don't know what's wrong with me right now, but all I can think of is that he's unforgivably handsome. I thought so before I met him, but in real life Marshall has a pull to him that's impossible to shake off. His dark hair frames his face, shielding his eyes from what little light the porch lanterns cast, but I still discern every line, every long eyelash.

I give myself a mental slap. His charms won't ensnare me. I won't surrender to his allure or my hormones. Marshall hates me. The only reason he's talking to me right now is probably because the other guys made him.

Marshall looks at me, and I quickly avert my eyes. I can't take his penetrating gaze tonight. He'll see right through me and my every insecurity. I still have to respond somehow. Yay or nay. I forgive you. Get lost.

I end up saying, "You of all people should understand what it's like to be an outsider."

Marshall flinches like I've slapped him and stares at me for a full minute. Then his shoulders slump. He rubs his face with both hands. "You're right."

There's nothing more we can say to each other tonight. Hurt is still gnawing on my insides. As much as I can tell, annoyance, or maybe guilt, chisels at Marshall. We need a good, long break from each other, so I go inside the guest house before I say something else and restart our fight.

✳

Two days after the fight, Marshall doesn't talk to me, I pretend he doesn't exist, and the rest of the Vipers flee the rehearsal room as soon as we're done. This is exactly what I've been trying to avoid.

"I'd kill for some Russian candy," I mutter to myself as I come into the living room.

The guys are all heading for the kitchen—it's lunch time. I don't expect anyone to hear me, but CJ turns around and comes back.

"Let's go get you some snacks." He wraps his hand around my elbow and leads me to the garage.

"It's fine. Don't worry about it." I already feel like I impose on every minute of his time.

"I need to get out of the house anyway. You wanna come with me? If not, I'll stop by a store and bring you something." He lets go of my arm and disappears behind the garage door without waiting for me.

It seems I'm not the only one wrung out by the tension that accompanies our rehearsals. I hurry after him and hop on the passenger seat of his dark blue Wrangler.

"Well, if you're going out anyway..." I steal a glance at him.

CJ grins. He waits for me to buckle up then drives us toward downtown.

"So, how do you feel about the band so far?" he asks. "I put you on the spot a few days ago, but how about some bashing in return?"

"I...love it." Some days are harder than others, but I do love being with them.

He catches on the hesitation I've failed to conceal from my voice.

"You love it, but?"

I shrug. "But nothing."

"Alexandra, you're the worst liar I've ever met, and I've spent enough time with you now to know there is a but."

"I don't want to sound ungrateful."

He pulls into a small parking lot and turns off the engine. "Noted. You are full of gratitude. Now, tell me what's wrong. I can't fix or change anything if you keep it to yourself."

"Can you change Marshall?"

The words zip into the air between us with a lot more challenge and even accusation than I intended.

CJ sighs. "Not really, but—"

"Hey, I'm only teasing. I don't have any problems with him." Other than the problems I have with him.

He chuckles. "Did I somehow forget to mention you're a terrible liar?"

"I love the band," I say, unbuckling and trying to redirect the conversation at least a little. I do love the band as a whole. "I am so incredibly lucky to be with you—"

"Don't even start with the self-deprecation," CJ grumbles.

"Self-depre-what?"

"Where you act like you're so much worse than everyone else around you. You're not. You're inexperienced, and that's an easy fix. We're already fixing it."

I check the storefront. He's brought us to a place called *Annushka's*. I would be surprised if it's not a Russian or at least an Eastern European store with a name like that.

"How do you know about this place?" He hasn't been using any map app or anything on the way here.

"I drive by often. Let's go." He opens his door but turns to me once more. "Don't think about anything. You're already doing great."

Tears prickle my eyes. He's too much. When will he wake up and realize I'm not worth the effort?

We get out of the car and enter the store. The first thing that grabs my attention is the smell—a mix of sugar, spices, pickles, and smoked fish.

"Smells like home, all right," I say.

CJ picks up a red plastic basket. "Anything edible here?"

I elbow him in the side. We both laugh and start grabbing things.

"Is it okay for me to be breaking the diet again?" I ask as I add two small bottles of *kvas*, intending to get CJ to drink one of them. I grew up drinking the dark brown fermented bread beverage, but I'm sure he's gonna hate it.

"Diet!" CJ scoffs. "You're homesick. Besides, you're not going to binge on a crate of sweets, are you?"

I give him a "maybe" look.

CJ laughs and ruffles my hair. *That* I don't like. "Stop ruining my hair!"

He points at a shelf full of bags of different grains. Roasted buckwheat, sunshine yellow millet, and sturdy barley. "So, you grew up eating stuff like this?"

"Yeah. It may look odd, but if you cook it right, it's delicious." I poke the bag with buckwheat. "My mom would always steam this then fry it with carrots and ground beef."

Mama will never make another meal for me again. I shove the thought aside because I don't want to risk falling apart in front of CJ, but it clings to me like a hair to a charged balloon.

"My mom never bothered cooking anything. I grew up on dry toast and dollar microwave meals—" CJ jerks to face away, every motion sharp and embarrassed. "Sorry. I didn't mean to rain on your parade. We're here to get you a taste of home, not listen to my complaints about my past."

I want to hug him, but I worry that if I do, it'll embarrass him even more. So I settle for stuffing a *pryanik* into his hand. "Here. This is one of my favorites."

CJ faces me again, his gaze soft. I think he understands what I'm trying to do. He reads the translated label on the back of the *pryanik.* "Ginger flavored cookie in sweet glaze. I love ginger cookies." He throws the *pryanik* I gave him into the basket and picks up a more fancily stamped one. "Now you're talking."

"It's the size of your face." I laugh.

"You're right. It might not be enough. Let's get more."

For the rest of our time at the store, the mood is light and cheerful, but I hold on to the reminder that I'm not the only one with inner demons and buried pain.

Halloween

Marshall

I park in the Nest's driveway and force myself out of my ancient BMW. Piles of glowing pumpkins of all shapes and sizes crowd the porch, along with bales of hay and festive black and orange garlands. Elise's work. She *loves* Halloween. Correction: Elise loves all holidays. She will be home tonight with her siblings, nieces, nephews, and cousins, but that doesn't prevent her from decorating our porch.

I stop being distracted by the pumpkins.

I can do it.

I can give Alexandra an I'm-ever-so-sorry-for-being-a-jerk present.

This morning's rehearsal was a nightmare, same as yesterday's, and it's got to stop. I can take the first step and restore the shaky peace we've had. As soon as I stop feeling like someone's made me swallow a handful of nails.

I used to be able to shower all kinds of trinkets on girls the one year I attended college in person. Is it the increased popularity that makes me think twice before displaying attention to anyone or just Alexandra who has a knack for making me say all the wrong things?

And holy everything, she does have that knack. Even when I'm not particularly mad at her, I manage to blurt out something absurd and insensitive.

Not tonight.

Tonight I will control my temper and be a gentleman, like Kiera always tells me to be. I will apologize one more time and make sure Alexandra believes me. And I'll stop aggravating her and the rest of the band with my inability to handle change. I hope.

Inside, the smell of hot peppers assaults me. Zach didn't forget. Looks like we're going to have a proper Halloween night with *tteokbokki*—rice cakes in burn-your-face-off sauce. Zach's parents are full-fledged Korean, and the first Halloween we were officially listed as the Tangs' charges, Zach's mom made us the spicy rice cakes. It was the best night of our teenage lives, and we've made it a tradition since then, tours or gigs notwithstanding. No costumes, no trick-or-treaters. A stay-in night with self-proclaimed brothers and a date with pain.

I sneak down the hallway, carrying a new Taylor mini bass behind me. First, I'm going to scope the scene, then I'll decide whether to hide the Taylor until later or give it to Alexandra in front of everyone. I probably should do it with everyone present. I sure haven't been their favorite person since the busted Riot Night.

The air in the kitchen shimmers with spiciness. Plates of rice cakes swimming in red sauce, bowls of sliced pears, soda cans and glasses of chocolate milk cover the wide marble-top island. Zach plays shaman at the stove, and the rest of the band, including Alexandra, sit around the island and chat. Her words about feeling like an outsider won't stop haunting me.

As a kid, for years I fought with bullies and other types who shunned me for being a foster care kid with cheap clothes and explosive personality. Everyone in Project Viper struggled with being ostracized in one way or another during our early teenage years. That's how we got together in the first place—a bunch of outcasts at school. Even Zach had trouble finding friends. He went to a regular school with us despite his family's riches because his parents didn't want to spoil him, but he's a piano prodigy. That in and of itself comes with an interesting set of character traits. The Tangs got custody rights of me, the O'Neals, and CJ when I was sixteen, and things had become a lot different after that, but either way, I've been as mean to Alexandra as some of the people from my past have been to me. I hate myself quite viciously for that. I've become one of the villains without realizing it.

Alexandra's long hair hangs down her back like a pitch-black curtain. Black is my favorite color. I'm full-on mesmerized. How did she grow it out that long? Why do I always want to touch it? What's happening to me? My thoughts about her suddenly center on the physical, almost needy. But I don't need anyone. I have the Vipers. I don't need a girl.

She's almost a Viper too.

I challenge myself to consider this notion a little further.

Do I accept her as one of us?

No. Not really. She's a new teammate, someone we have to teach but also respect for what she brings to the table. Alexandra will never be one of *us* simply because she didn't grow up with us and doesn't share *that* bond. But Alexandra is a Viper, and yet, to me, she isn't. Part of the band, not part of the brotherhood. Part of my life, not part of my heart.

CJ's next to our new bassist, as usual. His eyes shift away from her, and he finally notices me.

"There you are." He waves me over. "I texted you a hundred times. Started thinking you ditched us." Ever so slightly, he tilts his head toward Alexandra while giving me a meaningful look. Unlike the others, he never said anything about my fight with her. That's CJ for you. He guilts you with silence.

Leaving the Taylor around the corner, I check my phone. A handful of notifications hang in the top bar. I shrug. "I was busy."

"Alexandra, are you in?" Zach places the last plate in front of her.

I sit across the corner from her. "She can't take the heat." I make sure to sound as lighthearted as possible and accompany my challenge with a friendly smile.

Alexandra turns her whole body to me. "What are the rules?"

I grin, sensing the best kind of trouble ahead. If she lasts three bites, I might consider thinking about her as one of us.

"The rules are simple," Zach explains as he sets a can of chilled Diet Coke in front of me. "Eat as many as you can. One of us counts the cakes as we eat together. The first one out does all the dishes, and the winner chooses the punishment for the rest. Either way, you're better off either being the last one or the first one for sure. But no cheating. You can't give up early on purpose."

"The winner gets to pick any punishment?" Schemes dance in Alexandra's eyes.

"Any punishment. No matter how stupid." I crank the can open and take several sips so that my gaze wouldn't wander down to her lips and the curves of her neck that tease me from behind the veil of her hair. Somebody win and make me dump a bucket of ice over my head. I really, really need it.

Alexandra cracks her knuckles. "Let's do this."

The guys chuckle, each in his own devious way, and grab their chopsticks.

Graham counts us in, his drummer habit kicking in. "Three, two, one—go!" He counts every rice cake we chew through.

Zach does a number with the heat level of the sauce, and it burns, burns, burns. By the fifth one, Alexandra's whole face is red. She bites her lips, but not a sound escapes her mouth. When Shane sneaks a piece of pear, she does the same.

When we conquer a dozen, Graham pushes away his plate. "Man, what did you put in it today? It's nothing but pain." He downs his chocolate milk in one go.

The rest of us resort to several gulps of the cooling liquid as well. "Keep counting," I say.

"*Ya vizhu prizrakov*," Alexandra whispers to herself.

I'm seeing ghosts.

I don't even try to hide a chuckle invoked by her comment.

"Thirteen?" Graham continues counting.

Alexandra chews on another rice cake and clamps a hand over her mouth.

"Have some milk," Zach says, looking just as red as everyone else.

She takes a huge gulp and sits for a minute. I think she's going to be sick, but Alexandra eventually swallows and says, "Keep going."

After eighteen rice cakes, I start feeling queasy. My nose drips, but so does everyone else's. Shane puts his plate on the counter next to the sink. "Way to summon death, Zach."

"It is Halloween," Zach jokes but joins the younger of the O'Neal brothers in his surrender. "Yeah. A little too much."

"Quick, fish out the rest from the pot," Shane tells him, "before the current sauce settles in too much."

Zach returns to the stove.

CJ, Alexandra, and I stare each other down in turns. Who will give up next? After two more dumplings and an odd look at me, CJ calls it quits.

"One more?" I challenge Alexandra, who has turned pale.

She raises a finger and takes several deep breaths. "You guys do this for fun?"

Zach snickers near the stovetop. "Don't you just love it?"

Alexandra stares at him with raised eyebrows. "Love? No, I wouldn't call it that." She presses a fist to her mouth.

"One more?" I ask again. I can taste the victory.

What should I ask from her?

A kiss.

The thought sends a twitch through my fingers, and I almost drop my chopsticks. Do I actually want to kiss her?

No. Well...

No. Hmm...

No!

"Look at you, Marsh. You lasted longer than usual." CJ munches on pear slices, insinuations all over his face.

"Of course he did." With a determined huff, Alexandra shoves another rice cake into her mouth.

I hurry and do the same, but I know I can't eat many more after that. Four, maybe five.

Graham counts three more for us. I barely swallow the last one and take the smallest sip of water to help it down. Anything more will set me off. As much as I want to win and demand something ridiculous from the stubborn Russian, I much prefer losing to throwing up.

I place my chopsticks on the table. "Fine, you win."

The guys whoop.

"So close." CJ gives me an approving wink.

I press my forehead against the cool marble countertop.

Alexandra does the same. "Never again."

Zach and Shane guffaw. Graham flings the freezer door open, grabs a bag of frozen strawberries, and presses it to his neck. "Ice cream?"

"Only if I can have all of it." Alexandra's fingers crawl for her glass of milk.

Graham hands out pints of ice cream, and for a while there are no sounds other than quiet sniffling and content sighs.

I savor my cookies-and-cream and watch Alexandra's face color return to normal. "So, what do you want us to do for you?"

"It's not exactly a punishment."

Zach leans half of his body across the island. "Do tell," he says in a playful voice.

She sucks on her spoon and looks at me from the corner of her eye. "I want a song on the next album."

Before I can respond, CJ says, "Done." We engage in a staring match. CJ's eyes say, "What are you gonna do about it?"

"A song? We get off that easy? Phew." Zach feigns inordinate relief.

"Well, I don't know. Songs can be tricky, especially duets." Shane's face splits in his customary smirk, challenging and flipping annoying.

"If CJ said you can have a song, then you can have a song," I say and dig up a large piece of chocolate cookie. For now, this conversation is over. Alexandra won fair and square.

As the first person to give up, Graham starts cleaning up. He shoves the plates and cups into the dishwasher, wipes the countertops, washes the pots, and puts everything away, all in less than twenty minutes. I get an unpleasant sting of memories of doing chores while I was still in foster care. Some families were harsh. One foster "dad" was a straight-up nightmare of a drill sergeant. He timed his own kids on everything, and I didn't escape the fate.

Next time I look up from my ice cream, everyone's left the kitchen. When did that happen? Did they leave me in peace, knowing that when I don't talk, I'm deep in thought and need to be alone? I appreciate that they respect that. No matter how long we stay an active band, we will always be a family of our own.

A cough rasps from the living room.

I jerk around but still don't see anyone. All the lights are off.

Leaving my mostly empty ice cream carton on the table, I approach the couch, where I find Alexandra watching something on her phone.

She sits up abruptly and puts the phone away the moment she notices me.

"I was just resting for a minute, but I suppose I can do that at my place. Um, Zach's place, technically. The guest house. Right."

"Wait here." I go to fetch her gift.

When I return, Alexandra eyes me with her familiar suspicion.

I hand her the Taylor. "Happy Halloween."

She unzips the case and runs her fingers across the strings. "An acoustic bass? So small. You got this for me?"

Being asked straight on like that sets me on edge again. I remind myself that the reason I got the Taylor is to try and build a few bridges with Alexandra. Building bridges involves certain materials—concrete and metal, bricks and mortar. I got the bricks—the Taylor. Now it's time to do some talking and put in the mortar.

"Yes, I got this for you. It's a mini edition. Should fit your smaller hands well." I join her on the couch. "And don't get offended. The long scale bass just looks like a challenge for you sometimes. I was only wondering if a short scale would be more comfortable."

She wipes her hands on her jeans and takes out the mini bass. "Not offended. I know I have super short fingers. Oh, wow. The smell." Alexandra takes a deep breath and slowly releases it. "It's the best."

I also catch a whiff of the strong wood scent that wafts from the bass and smile. Some people love the smell of a new car. Peasants. Now, the smell of a new acoustic guitar can make anyone lightheaded with glee.

Alexandra starts playing a song I don't know. I fold my arms and lean back on the couch with my eyes closed, happy to make no comments and listen to her fingers weave through soft notes of several ballads. I was right. Playing a shorter scale bass guitar stitches her somewhat choppy sound into a smoother technique. And now that the mini Taylor feels like a success, maybe she'll consider getting a smaller electric bass. It'll be lighter, and she won't look so dwarfed by her instrument.

"Have you tried this? The strings are butter." Alexandra doesn't speak, she purrs, and a shiver runs down my arms. "I had no idea they made them like this. So light."

The sound of the closing zipper prompts me to open my eyes.

Alexandra caresses her new guitar's case. "You totally lost to me on purpose."

I cross my arms. "You have no proof."

"I don't need any proof. You haven't once let me have the last word in an argument." She looks at me through her long bangs. "Why this time?"

"Another rice cake and I was gonna be sick."

She laughs with both hands pressed to her face. "Had you waited another second, you would've won. I literally opened my mouth to say I was done when you surrendered. What were you going to ask for your prize?" She turns to me and crosses her legs in front of her, yoga style.

I mirror her pose. "We typically do something ridiculous. Shane had to play banjo for one gig. One song, though. Graham took over the band's social media accounts behind Charlie's back once. But this time..." My mind latches onto the fact that our knees are almost touching. What would she do if I moved an inch closer?

Alexandra rests her elbows on her knees and leans closer. "This time what?"

It's a relief to know she holds no grudge against me. Or maybe she does, but for now, at least, she tolerates me. Her blue eyes sparkle with curiosity and mischief, and her thick black hair tempts me to plunge my hands into it.

"I was gonna dare you to kiss CJ."

Yeah, I lie.

We stare at each other in silence for only a second, but it stretches like a bungee cord.

One of Alexandra's eyebrows lifts. "CJ?"

Busted. It doesn't matter what I say now.

"You seem to like him the best of us, but I figured you'd still squirm about it. The punishment's supposed to make you uncomfortable after all."

She doesn't even blink at that. "What about the rest of the guys? What would their punishment be?"

"I'd make them kiss CJ as well. To be fair."

She bursts out laughing. I join her as I imagine that scene. Maybe I should've persevered. It would've been mean but so memorable.

Before I can catch my breath, Alexandra leans in and leaves a lightning-fast kiss on my cheek. "Thank you," she murmurs, "for the bass."

My heartbeat skyrockets. I grab her hand and keep her close. My thoughts scatter like fish from a shark, but I still try to understand what's happening here. I can't. Am I losing my mind? It's simple. Just a kiss on the cheek. But what do I want to do now?

She doesn't speak and doesn't move. Her warm breath, sweet vanilla and cream, tickles my face.

Then she kisses me again.

Anything but Neutral

Alexandra

I move as though attracted by some invisible force. I steal another quick kiss from Marshall, nothing more than a brush of my lips against his. Barely touching. Breaking a barrier. Testing the waters. Saying hello. I swear he'll laugh at me, and serves me right. I've completely lost it. What was I thinking?

Why did I kiss him?

Marshall cups my face with his hands and kisses me once more. This kiss lasts a couple seconds longer, but he's still testing the boundaries. Marshall's hand slides to rest on the side of my neck. His fingers are strong but soft. Heat rushes all over me as though his touch ignites my blood. I can't describe it any other way.

The kiss that follows is all in. Like jet fuel, my emotions—frustration with his hostility, my curiosity about him, my desire to fit with his tribe, my longing for a friend, and my drive to prove him wrong—burn with painful intensity.

He tastes like milk and chocolate.

I grab handfuls of his curls because I have to make sure it's real and not a hallucination induced by an obscene amount of spicy food. No way it's real. I've snapped and gone mental, that's what it is.

We've been fighting so much. He hates me. He's just messing with me. He can't mean it. I won't deny I want him to mean it, but tomorrow I'll walk into the rehearsal room and he'll glare at me as usual, or worse, ignore me. I can just see it.

I'm an idiot.

I pry my fingers away from him and hop off the couch before it goes too far and Marshall annihilates what's left of my heart. He won't have much to begin with after I'm done thrashing it for this betrayal.

"Wait." Marshall jerks me onto his lap.

He presses his face against my back. It feels so tender and good I almost scream at him to stop.

"I know you think that I hate you, but I don't."

I twist to face him. "Impossible."

Marshall runs his hand through my hair and tucks a lock behind my ear. "I thought so too."

My heart liquifies under his caressing gaze and fingertips that travel down my neck to my collarbone to my shoulder. I can barely restrain a pleasant shudder. No one has ever touched me like this before. No one has ever kissed me before, but I'm never telling him that. I won't give him another weapon against me.

I manage to say, "Peace then?"

Marshall falls backward into the couch cushions. "I'm trying."

What an intriguing response.

"Trying?" I lie on my back, legs draped over his lap. "Am I that difficult to be around?"

"Increasingly."

That makes me smile. "How so?"

"With you, everything is different." Marshall shifts his position and plants himself over me, holding his weight on one arm next to my side. "It just is. It all looks and feels different now. Everything sounds different. I have to think about everything I do and say. I have to make sure I respect your boundaries, smile, be totally neutral around you. It is impossible to be neutral around you, Alexandra."

"Trust me, I know that. You've been anything but neutral." I joke with him, but I dissolve in the way he breathes out my name. When our eyes meet, the world is no longer the same. Black and green—colors of Marshall's hair and eyes—is all I see.

Whatever's coursing between us is complicated and dangerous. I'm dying to explore it, but my survival instinct kicks in.

"Good night, Marshall." I slide off the sectional, grab my new bass, and run to the guest house. Thankfully, Marshall doesn't try to stop me.

I've never considered it a possibility, never had a single what-if moment where I imagined Marshall holding me the way he did a minute ago, kissing me, telling me that I've upturned his life in every sense imaginable. I never thought I'd want this. *Him.* When I was offered to join Project Viper, love was the last thing on my mind. It was all about a new life. I worked hard for his approval, not his affection.

And now everything will be different for me as well. Again.

Or maybe it won't be. Maybe we'll burn through our unexpected attraction with a few more kisses and he'll lose interest in me. And it's fine because I finally won. Marshall Jones was nice to me, without any reservations, even if only tonight.

CJ's Song

Marshall

I can't sleep. Surprise! My king bed with the softest jersey sheets has shrunk to a quarter of its size, and I keep flipping between being too cold and too hot, calm and downright panicked.

Alexandra kissed me.

I kissed her back.

Nothing has ever felt more right.

Nothing has ever felt more wrong.

CJ hasn't told me anything outright, but it's been clear as day he's claimed first dibs, figuratively speaking because Alexandra's a person and doesn't belong to anybody. Still, I betrayed my best friend. I've been so worried about damaging the band with my irritation with Alexandra that I completely missed the fact that I could cause more damage by not squabbling with her. By liking her.

I like Alexandra? When did that happen? There's nothing to like about the girl. She's short. She glares daggers at me. She steals all of CJ's time, not that she has to try very hard with those half-concealed, delighted smiles. Delighted and delightful. Crud. If I'm going to allow my thoughts to keel this way, I might as well stop pretending that there's nothing about Alexandra that I like.

Her height is not actually an issue. It just makes her look younger than her age. And I'm impressed by her stubbornness. Despite all of my hostility, she's still here. In terms of music, I know Alexandra's holding back. She studied singing, but we haven't heard her sing yet, not quite. She does some backups, and she's good at that, but what is she truly capable of? How does she refrain from showing us up? If I had someone constantly harassing me about being a crappy musician, I would've taken every opportunity to shut them up. So, she's patient, persevering, determined to succeed, and forgiving. Way too forgiving. I wouldn't have put up with anyone who treated me the way I've treated her, but she still kissed me.

I can't like her. I definitely can't love her. I can't love anybody. Love means being open and vulnerable. I can never be vulnerable. The only way I survived the hardest years was through closing up and never admitting to anyone just how much it hurt or how much I wanted to be loved or, at the very least, not ignored. I was a kid when I came to the realization that opening up could cause pain greater than any beating, and I've avoided vulnerability ever since.

Still, I can't deny the attraction. The sensation of Alexandra's lips on mine and the taste of her mouth overpower every other coherent thought other than the idea that I want more. Our last tour lasted eight months, and none of us had any time for anything. Shane was the only lucky piggy—Elise came along simply because she was doing her job and taking care of our performance outfits and styles. But the rest of us left Portland girlfriendless. I haven't been in a relationship for over three years now. Too insecure. That's what my last girlfriend said when we broke up. She might have been onto something. Alexandra triggers all of my insecurities. That's probably why I couldn't handle being around her at first. She's CJ's type, but now I realize she's my type as well. And now I made it all so much worse. I confused her and confused myself and…

I groan and climb out of bed. The only solution to this torture is music. And caffeine. I stomp downstairs, grab a twelve pack out of the pantry, and head to the rehearsal room.

My good old trusty Fender Telecaster, all black, of course, growls at me with a discord of unloved strings. I usually terrorize my acoustic Martin for songwriting, but right now I want some grit.

"Sorry, bud," I say to the Tele and pat its matte side.

Done with tuning, I plug the guitar into my laptop. I'm going to finish that song I started a while ago. It tingles at the tips of my fingers, and it'll be epic.

"That sounds awesome." CJ walks into the rehearsal room in the morning.

I sit on the floor under the window, surrounded by clumps of paper and empty soda cans. As I stretch, the guitar strap bites into my bare back. I rub the sore spot. "You think it has potential?"

CJ crouches in front of me, pulls over my tattered notepad, and scans the lyrics. "Yeah. *Devastation, Free of Charge*? I like it. It's punchy. What inspired this?"

"I've had a lot on my mind recently."

He looks up at me. "Alexandra?"

My first instinct is to lie, but we never lie to each other. CJ's my safety net, and I'm his. I should tell him about last night. That would be right, but I limit my response to, "Among other things."

CJ continues staring me down. He knows I'm fibbing. "Is this a song for her? She did beat you last night. Again."

"Yes, she can have it, but we'll tell her you wrote it."

CJ scowls at me like I'm a complete lunatic. "What? Why?"

"Because you like her?" I suddenly feel like I'm digging my own grave.

He tosses the notepad on the floor and stands up. "I do like her, but what does it have to do with who wrote this song?"

A bitter sting zings through my chest at his admission. I push it aside. "She won't give it justice if she knows I wrote it. Things haven't been exactly smooth between us."

"I suppose, but you should give her the benefit of the doubt," CJ says. "She would do it justice either way. She's an amazing musician. But she'd do an even better job if you were a little nicer to her."

I rise to my half-asleep feet and hang the Tele on the hook on the wall. "Being nice is your job. She likes you better anyway." Alexandra might have kissed me last night, but she didn't deny it when I said she liked CJ best.

He grins. "That seems to be the case."

I want to punch that grin off his face, but the idea of us throwing fists over a girl quickly dampens the flare in my temper. We've never had girl trouble, and we never will. "Just tell her you wrote it, okay?"

CJ nods. "I will if anyone asks."

That's good enough for me.

We gather for our usual breakfast before rehearsal.

Alexandra comes in last. "What's with all the red containers in the entryway? I almost broke my legs trying to get past them."

"First of November," Shane says. "Elise is decorating for Christmas."

Alexandra gives him a dumbfounded look. "Christmas is two months away."

"Yup," Zach joins. "We always work during the holiday season. Private and corporate parties and such. So, we will have our ornaments and cookies now, thank you very much."

He and Graham set out breakfast. Boiled eggs, ham, cheese, berries, and thin slices of multigrain bread. Could be worse.

"But there's another holiday before Christmas, isn't there?" Alexandra nurses a slight grimace. Looks like she still can't wrap her mind around Elise's tradition. "Giving of thanks something rather?"

CJ pats her head. "Thanksgiving, yes. It's just that Elise loves Christmas most of all, and I promise you, it looks spectacular."

"It sure will once I'm done with it." Elise enters the dining area and plants a loud smooch on the younger O'Neal's lips.

Zach uses a piece of bread as a blinder against them. "Marshall, holler us some carols."

"Hundred bucks." I start making myself an open-faced sandwich from the breakfast offerings.

Zach takes out his wallet. "I got twenty. I can wire you the rest."

"Cash only."

Elise doubles over in a full laughing fit as four five-dollar bills fly in my direction.

CJ adds another twenty. "Alexandra, how much you got?"

"A buck." She pulls out a folded dollar out of her jeans pocket and almost throws it in the pile, then puts it away at the last moment. "But I've heard him sing. It's not worth the money."

Everyone, including Graham, laughs. I try to glare at her but can't. I laugh along.

Zach wipes the tears under his eyes. "Oooh, she got you good, Marsh."

Alexandra won't meet my eyes, but her lips curve in a devilish smile.

"Good job, *Matryoshka*." CJ boops her on the nose.

I almost growl at him to keep his hands to himself, but it's me who should stay away. He's won Alexandra's heart first.

My thoughts dart to last night. I remember her soft skin and warm lips and—

Please, brain, make it stop! That kiss was just a fluke fueled by many difficult days and an exciting evening. Nothing to it.

Alexandra grabs a bowl of berries and sits on the sectional. She does that a lot—excludes herself while we're having fun. I want to kick myself again and again. I'm to blame, of course, but I'll fix it. I'll make sure she's comfortable enough to enjoy everything with us, if she wants to.

In the meantime, I want to know why she won't look at me, so I go over to her. Alexandra is watching videos on her phone again.

"What are you watching?"

She puts her phone screen down. Her eyes travel down my body then snap back up to my face. I check whether I have a problem with my clothes and realize I'm still only in pajama bottoms. It's never been a problem before. The Vipers have seen each other wearing much less than that. Elise too because she's our stylist. I'll have to remember to be more careful about roaming around wearing who knows what. Not that I have anything to be ashamed of. The workouts and the diet have been paying off for years now.

Alexandra bites her lower lip and keeps her eyes locked with mine. Hold on a moment. Is she blushing? Yup. A subtle but definite pinkish hue spreads across the tops of her cheeks. I want to tease her about it, but we're not alone, so I grab a fluffy gray throw off one end of the sectional and wrap it around myself.

"What are you up to?" I ask again.

Alexandra exhales and pulls out a phone out of her pants back pocket. "Did you know about this?"

She shows me our Insta account, which isn't what she was poring over a moment ago. It's also not the same phone. The one she used to watch the videos is smaller, in a dark blue case, still next to her thigh. This one's new, black and covered by a thin, transparent case. Why does she have two phones?

Alexandra must notice my curiosity because she scoots to sit on the smaller phone and waves the new one in my face. "Did you already know or not?"

Last night, Charlie posted an announcement about our participation in a one-day alternative rock festival in the middle of March. The festival marks six months almost to the day since Alexandra joined us. I wonder if The Label is testing her that way. If she pulls off the festival with us, great. If not…

"I saw it this morning. And you'll be fine. You're making mountains of progress."

Her eyes are full of hope and despair all at once. "Really?"

"Of course." I mean it.

"Are you harassing my *Matryoshka* again?" CJ says from the table.

Alexandra smiles and looks at him over her shoulder. He points to the seat next to him, and she leaves me, stashing one phone in the back pocket again and the other in her sweater sleeve. I glare at CJ and can't stop no matter how much I try. I want him to see it and I don't. I want to tell him to stop saying she's his, but I can't. Because she is. Had I been nicer to her from the start, she could've been mine.

The front door chimes, followed by a familiar chatter of voices— Fiona, Charlie, and Juliette. Always together.

"Ready to rock your first concert?" Charlie goes straight to Alexandra like the rest of us don't matter anymore.

"No." Alexandra covers her face with her hands, and CJ rubs her back.

Charlie does the same. "You will be. There's still plenty of time to practice. Now, ready to decorate?"

"Wait. I have a little surprise for the guys," Fiona says.

Everyone looks at her, but just like Kiera, Fiona's a big fan of dramatic tension. She eats a few berries, slowly, savoring every bite, pours herself a drink of water, then drinks it.

"What kind of surprise?" Zach's the first one to lose patience. "Alexandra level of surprise or regular surprise?"

Fiona smiles. "Regular surprise. The Label thought you all were really good boys this year and cleared your schedule from now on until the festival. No gigs, no interviews, no parties. Enjoy yourselves. And work hard in the meantime, of course."

Graham's eyes bulge, and Shane whistles.

"No kidding?" the younger O'Neal says.

Fiona nods. "No kidding."

That's unbelievable. No public engagements for four and a half months? We can chill and write music and do whatever else we want? That kind of freedom ended the day we signed with The Label.

"The president must really, really like you," Shane says to Alexandra.

She throws a half-eaten strawberry at him. "I told you I don't know him!"

"Who do you know then?" Shane continues, obviously teasing her. "Which strings did you pull to get us this luxury treatment? The Russian mafia? KGB?"

Alexandra laughs and rolls her eyes at the same time. "It hasn't been the KGB for more than two decades. It's the Federal Security Service now."

"So it's the Russian government after all," Shane exclaims. "I knew it."

"Leave her be." Elise pushes Shane away, who spins on his bar stool with a chuckle.

"And don't make me print the contract to remind you that you agreed to no questions asked," Fiona adds.

Yes, we did, but that doesn't mean we'll stop being curious.

Why her?

And what's with the two phones?

Exhausted, I slump on the sectional, already snuggled in the plush comfort of the throw. I'd better stay out of the girls' way. They may wrap me in lights and tinsel if they deem me a nuisance.

My phone chimes. I pull it out of my pocket and curse when I see an email from my literature class teacher. I missed two assignments. Great. With all the drama around here lately, the class has been the last thing on my mind. Or, to be more accurate, not on my mind at all.

Juliette sits on the armrest of the sectional and reminds me of something else.

"Did you delete the photo of just me and Alexandra from that little photo session?" I ask.

Juliette shoots me a hesitant glance. "No."

"Why not?"

"You look good together, and I like it." Having whispered that, she scampers away and joins the girls as they start decorating.

I like the idea of me and Alexandra too, but it isn't happening.

Your Phone Is Glitching

Alexandra

Marshall is acting weird again, and I can't help wondering whether last night's kiss was nothing more than a slip in judgment after all. He tried to be nice to me, and as part of the apology, he kissed me. The uncertainty, coupled with the excitement over the festival announcement, threatens to fry my mind.

Halfway through our rowdy breakfast, I decide to stop floating in the ocean of my speculations and ask Marshall about where we stand. It's better if he admits that our kiss was a mistake. If he does, I'll pull myself together and behave like a grown-up woman and squash all expectations. If it wasn't a mistake…

It was. Better not get my hopes up. I can't afford a crumb of hope.

I open my messaging app and copy Marshall's number from the group chat, then stare at the screen. Now what? What should I say? Maybe I can come to the matter at hand in some roundabout way.

> CJ said there's a song for me and
> that we should practice it for that

festival we're going to in March.

MJ: Yes, there is. And get used to
sudden announcements like that. It's
Kiera's favorite thing to do—sign us
up for a gig and tell us at the last
moment.

My heart speeds up with excitement. The Vipers already picked
a song for me! I zero in on that idea. I have a song. I am expected to
perform at a festival. Without warning, things have become so much
more real. Does it mean…? I scan the guys. Helpful CJ, sneaky Shane,
solid Graham, life-hungry Zach, and complicated Marshall, who still
hides on the sectional. Do I have a chance of staying with them after
all, two out of five notwithstanding?

When can I hear the song?

I glance at the sectional again to see if Marshall would decide to
join us. He puts up his feet on the back of the couch and texts me back.

MJ: There are still a couple of rough
spots. Be patient.

I re-read the text. It feels like he's talking about us even though
he's talking about my new song. There are still a couple of rough
spots between me and Marshall, and I sure have to be patient. But
how? How can I be patient after last night? After seeing so much of
his skin this morning. He strutted into the living room in just pajama
pants, flaunting his muscled arms and abs and… I have no siblings.
I've never so much as gone swimming with anyone of the opposite
sex but my dad. Marshall's body has this overwhelming effect on me

that I don't know how to explain. I can't look at him without feeling warm all over, imagining my hands—

"Looks like you found something to cheer you up." CJ plucks me out of my fantasies. "Talking to somebody?"

I hide my phone under the table. "A friend."

Charlie, Elise, and Fiona issue a collective and prying, "Oooh," and Charlie orders, "Spill. Is he from Russia? Do you have his picture?"

The sectional creaks softly. Marshall comes over and sits next to me because it's the only empty seat left. "Can we talk about anything else but Alexandra's countless boyfriends?"

"I don't have *boyfriends*," I sputter in English, and add in Russian, "I never had any."

"What did she say, Marsh?" Shane asks.

Marshall sends him a dagger of a glare. "How am I supposed to know?"

Shane opens his mouth then closes it right back. I can tell he has blundered somehow.

An awful, sinking feeling squirms in my stomach. "Why are you asking him that?"

Shane's face turns red as a beet while the rest of the present company sit quietly with varying degrees of *oops* on their faces.

Shane mumbles, "I thought he heard you better. He's closer to you than I am."

I keep my eyes on the younger O'Neal. "Don't lie. It's not just that."

"Didn't you know Marshall speaks Russian?" Charlie brandishes a conniving grin.

"Charlie, who asked you?" Marshall explodes.

I thought I knew what he looks like when he's angry. I was wrong. I don't ever want to see his slender fingers curled into tight fists again.

Charlie seems completely unaffected by his reaction. "What? I bet she was making comments in her native language, hoping to insult you without you understanding, and you robbed her of that. That's not quite fair now, is it?"

I wish to disappear. I've been grouching at him in Russian without a care in the world. I told him to his face that I found him hot. *You would've never said that if you thought I could understand, would you?* He outright teased me about it! A host of choice swear words hangs on the tip of my tongue, but what's the use now?

CJ attempts to divert everyone's attention to the previous topic. "There must be someone you left behind in Russia."

I'm grateful for his thoughtfulness, but it's like jumping from one slippery stone in the middle of a stream to another. I don't want to share my past with them, however little there is to share. I don't want their pity. I just want to be one of them.

"No one," I say.

"Really?" CJ's voice is laced with doubt.

"Why are you so persistent?" Marshall asks. "Making sure the path is clear?"

Another collective *oooh*, but this time all eyes are on CJ.

He looks at me. "What if I am?"

Tense silence webs around us. Even Zach, for once, doesn't jump in. I search CJ's smiling brown eyes. Is he serious?

He winks. "Just kidding, relax."

"Right, right," Elise teases him across the table.

"I told you before, stop messing around with me," I say to CJ. "And you." I glare at Marshall and make sure he sees it. "Stop goading him into annoying me."

The girls laugh. Marshall does too.

His laughter, lighthearted and pleased, dispels some of my embarrassment. I love his eyes crinkled with joy. Love them. I want to hear him laugh more often, especially at something I say. I want him to think I'm funny and fun to be around.

My phone vibrates in my hand. With everyone returning to their conversations, no one seems to notice our continuing exchange.

```
MJ: Relax. And if CJ asks you out,
go ahead. He always has fun ideas
for dates.
```

I don't understand what he's trying to say at all. That is, I comprehend the words and their meaning, but I fail to glimpse the why behind them. Besides, I'm still not over Marshall speaking Russian.

```
             You go on a date with him if he's
                                      so fun.
```

```
MJ: Don't you like him?
```

I look at Marshall again, trying to see whether he's asking for himself or for CJ. There are no obvious emotions, no hints on his face.

```
                What about last night?
```

Everyone else's words blur into one fuzzy cloud of sound as I wait for his response. My heart cracks a little with every beat. Beat, crack, beat, crack, beat, a message.

```
MJ: Shhh.
```

Marshall's lips form a scheming smile. How am I supposed to understand that?

After breakfast, we decorate the house, then it's business as usual for us. I do my best to play and act unaffected, but my mind bubbles with curiosity. Why does Marshall avoid talking about last night?

In the evening, the guys settle in front of the TV with their salads and grilled chicken to watch an American football game, and I take my dinner to the guest house, needing time to come up with some kind of strategy on how to deal with Marshall. I watch chick flicks, sip inordinate amounts of rooibos with half-n-half, pamper my face with an expensive facial mask, and repaint my toenails. Simple things like that help me relax, and while I still have no clue as to what to do about Marshall, I feel better overall. Sometimes a girl just needs a night at home.

I'm almost asleep when my phone buzzes on the nightstand next to my bed.

MJ: You looked tired tonight. Feeling okay?

You exhaust me. Also, how do you speak Russian?

I still want to kick him for making fun of me for so long. I kept muttering to myself... I forbid the embarrassment to reignite.

MJ: Long story.

He adds a smirking emoji to that. That's all I get? Marshall Jones, world-renowned rock star speaks my language, which isn't common knowledge, and he acts like it's no big deal?

For the record, you aren't cool or good-looking or anything.

MJ: Too late. I know you've got it for me bad.

I will not dignify that with an answer. No matter what I say, he'll use it against me, and I've never been good at comebacks.

MJ: Will we see you tomorrow?

This I can spin to my advantage.

Do you want to see me tomorrow?

MJ: We got your new song all finished
tonight, for the most part.

Do you want to see me tomorrow?

MJ: Your phone is glitching. It's
sending messages twice.

It's not. Do YOU want to see me
tomorrow?

I climb out of my bed, switch on a side lamp, and sit next to the window. I open it, desperate for a breath of fresh, cold air. There is movement in a glowing window of the house across the yard, a silhouette that can only belong to Marshall. I can imagine him glaring at me so clearly that it makes me laugh. The phone buzzes again.

MJ: Go to bed.

I was in bed! You woke me up.

This time I get an emoji with its tongue sticking out. He still doesn't answer though. So I choose to not answer anymore as well.

```
MJ:  I  never  said  it  before,  but
welcome  to  the  band.  And  here's  your
song.
```

Welcome to the band. I wish I could actually hear him say it, but I guess, this way I can print these words and frame them—a solid proof of that once there was a time when Marshall Jones didn't hate my involvement with Project Viper.

He attaches a link to the message. I tap it and listen to the song. My song. *Devastation, Free of Charge.* It's only a demo, nowhere close to being polished, but I love it from the first beat. The song starts out slow and quiet, with a drizzling of the drums, but after the first verse ends, the chorus explodes with rhythm and double guitars and a whole lot more. The music is phenomenal, but Marshall's voice is the highlight, as always. I wanted a song all for myself, but I want him to sing it with me. I listen to it four more times before Marshall texts me again.

```
MJ: Well?
```

```
                    Love  it!  And  I  love  the  title.  Sing
                                        it  with  me?
```

```
MJ:  CJ  will  sing  with  you.  I'd
overpower  you.
```

My excitement snuffs out like a candle in the wind. He sends another text.

```
MJ:  I'm  glad  you  like  the  song.  And
yes,  I  want  to  see  you.
```

The light in his window goes out, but my heart glows. I close the window and return to bed, then listen to the demo over and over again, relishing every note. More than that, I relish his last words. Marshall wants to see me.

I Got You

Alexandra

The next morning Marshall acts like nothing's going on whatsoever. I have violent thoughts because I can't stand this. What is he doing? I'm going to lose my mind.

It doesn't end there. We spend the next three weeks walking around in circles. And maybe he's not walking with me, and I'm the one circling him, but it wears me out either way.

Other than that, everything is great. We write new songs. I learn my way around a recording studio. Project Viper is amazing. I thought they'd be kicking and screaming against writing a new album so soon after the tour, but the songs pour out of them. Even Graham, the ever-quiet drummer, has a lot to contribute to our creative flow.

What's more, they listen to *me*. I'm still hesitant to suggest anything, but when I can't keep my mouth shut, they discuss my ideas on equal footing with their own. I've never dreamed of being in a band, but now I never want to leave. The past two and a half months with them have been the best time of my life.

A couple of days before Christmas, the Vipers pack up to go to

Utah to spend the holidays with Zach's family. I don't feel like I should go. It's still quite possible that I'm here only temporarily, and I don't want to turn this into that one year that girl ruined the holidays.

Everyone is throwing boxes and their bags into the minivan when Kiera video calls us by means of Marshall's phone.

"Oh, you're already heading out? Great," she says. "Alexandra, love, look at you. It's as if you've always belonged with the boys. How are you doing? How are you getting along? Aren't they just the best?"

CJ hugs me with one arm like he always does. Judging by his raised eyebrows, he's curious to hear what I have to say about them. I like CJ a ton. He's reliable, steady, and fun to be around. The other Vipers are great too, of course.

Marshall clears his throat, and I realize I still haven't answered Kiera's question.

I blink and smile. "They're the sweetest creatures ever."

"You know that's right," Zach says with a laugh as he tosses the last bag into the minivan.

Kiera smiles. "Oh, I just knew that you would get along fabulously. Which is perfect because I scheduled you all for a radio interview in downtown Salt Lake. I know, I know. We promised you holiday freedom, but please do this one little thing."

I freeze on the spot. Even though Kiera had us go through a photo shoot and prepare a whole pile of social media materials, an interview is different. I'm not part of the band yet. Not officially. I'm still on probation. Please keep me. Please?

"Fantastic." Marshall beams at Kiera. I can't tell if he's serious or not. I can't decipher him at all lately. "When?"

"Twenty-third, so tomorrow. At four. I'll email you all the details. I'm thinking Marshall, CJ, and Alexandra could go. Alexandra, sunshine, you don't have to if you don't feel ready, but it would be really good practice for you. The rest of you can join if you'd like, but it's up to you. I know how much you all love interviews, especially you, Graham."

The older O'Neal mutters a thanks.

"We could do a couple of songs," CJ says. "Alexandra has the cutest little acoustic bass, and we can definitely work something out by tomorrow night."

I detach from the band. The conversation ends without me, but I'm a ball of fear and don't realize this until Zach appears in front of me and asks, "Where are your bags?"

I remind myself that I don't have to freak out. Kiera gave me a choice. Relief washes over me with such enormous force, I exhale and face the guys. "I didn't pack. I decided it'd be best if I stayed. Fiona invited me to spend Christmas with her—"

"What do you mean with Fiona?" Zach exclaims, sounding genuinely hurt. "You don't want to meet our family?"

Shane crosses his arms and glares at me. "That's bad team spirit, *Matryoshka*. Especially without a warning."

"I didn't think you'd want me to come."

"Why wouldn't we want you to come?"

I turn to CJ for backup, but he lifts his hands and shakes his head. I'll get no support from him. Marshall then. I guarantee he'll be the one to tell them to leave me alone.

He marches over, picks me up, then stuffs me into the back of the minivan. The rest of the guys hop in as fast as they can. Graham's at the wheel and starts driving before the door closes all the way. Marshall buckles me in even though I fight him for it.

"I can't go! Not without my ID." Among other things.

That seems to change his mind.

"Graham, wait." Marshall turns to me. "Where do you keep it?"

I start unbuckling, but Marshall holds my hand. "Where is your ID?"

"I'm in pajama pants!" I yell at him. And if he doesn't cut it out with the manhandling, I swear he'll be singing at a much higher pitch.

"For the last time, where is your ID?"

I glare at him, but Marshall doesn't blink. Stuffed in the back of the van, without an escape route, I can't win this. I cross my arms and turn away. "In the desk drawer in my bedroom. Take my passport too."

Graham pulls up to the guest house.

I'm mad as a wraith. When Marshall hops out of the van, I shout, "And get my jacket!" At least I'm freshly showered and wearing my favorite sneakers.

It takes him all of five minutes to run into the house and come back with my jacket, my mini Taylor, and, surprisingly, a small Project Viper duffel bag I got from Kiera upon my arrival. He tosses the bag onto my lap. I check the contents and find my wallet, passport, toothbrush and toothpaste, hairbrush, two pairs of socks, and lip balm. For crying out loud, he got my lip balm. I seethe a little less when I see no underwear. At least he didn't rifle through all of my belongings.

I zip the bag shut and toss it under the seat. "I'll have to go shopping when we get there. I am not spending the entire trip in pajamas."

"It would serve you right," Zach grumbles from his seat in front of me. "I can't believe you decided to stay behind. I mean, I get why you'd want to ditch Marshall, but what about the rest of us? What about me? What did I do?"

"It's not that." I squeeze his shoulder, more awkward than comforting.

"Sure, sure." He faces me, eyes full of promises that he'll never forgive me for this.

But I've got a trick up my sleeve. If I have figured anything out about Zach at all by this point, it's that he loves attention. "Want a hug?"

"That's the least you can do to atone for your awful behavior." He jumps out of his seat and squeezes between me and Marshall, who chuckles and kicks Zach back the moment he gets his hug.

"As for shopping," Zach continues, smiling now, "I'm sure one of my sisters will be happy to take you. If not, I will."

I point a finger at Marshall. "And you're paying for it. I had no plans to buy new clothes." Then I gasp. "We forgot the presents I got you. They were under the tree. You were putting stuff there, so I put mine too."

CJ waves to grab my attention. "Relax. Graham grabbed everything."

I remember the boxes in the trunk and lean back in the seat. There's nothing more I can say to prevent or even delay our departure.

We're off to Utah.

If all goes according to plan, it's a twelve-hour drive from Portland. But life is life, and traffic can be a woman of ill repute. We leave at nine and hope to make it by midnight.

CJ wastes no time and dives into the discussion about the upcoming interview. Shane, Graham, and Zach refuse to go, but eventually, CJ convinces me to come and play and sing. I do need to practice being in public with Project Viper, and this is an easy interview. No crowd, just the DJ and maybe a couple of other studio people. We'll say I'm a friend of the band, sing a couple of Christmas carols, and CJ and Marshall will sing a Project Viper song. I can do that.

After that, CJ announces it's time to start watching movies. The minivan is equipped with a top-notch entertainment system, of course, so we watch *A Christmas Story*. They say it's a classic. I've never seen it before and can't focus on the show because my thoughts are all about the interview tomorrow.

I don't know any carols. The only thing I could probably play without thinking too hard about it is *Jingle Bells* because I figured it out on my own when I was a kid. That was a long time ago. Maybe I can't even play that anymore.

I get so wound up, I start feeling sick to my stomach. I thought I was getting better, but I'm not ready to perform as a member of Project Viper at all.

After we navigate out of insane Portland traffic, Zach passes a basket of snacks to Marshall. "It's for you two to share."

The basket is loaded with junk food. Chips, candy, fruit leather, long chocolate-covered pretzels. The moment the Vipers are out of Kiera's watchful eyes, they rip off the leash.

Starving, I reach for one of the pretzels, but Marshall shields the basket with his body. He gives me a look that says something along the lines of, "Just wait," and digs through the snacks, then drops a tiny candy cane Hershey's kiss into my open palm.

"That's it?"

"What more do you want?"

There's something in his eyes I can't quite explain. He's not joking or mocking me.

I look at the piece of candy in my hand. I still can't figure it out. "It's just a Hershey's kiss."

He grins and continues watching the movie. "It is a kiss."

I unwrap it carefully because I derive weird pleasure from being able to smooth out a wrapper and stuff the candy drop behind my cheek. It's sweet. It's minty. It's nothing special. I shake my head at Marshall and his cryptic antics.

I thought the Tangs had a big house in Portland. Their residence in Utah is monstrous. It's made to look like a log cabin, but it's enormous. When Zach sees me gaping, he proudly informs me that it has fifteen bedrooms, ten bathrooms, three kitchens, and so on and so forth.

To which I can only say, "Why?"

He laughs and pats me on the shoulder. "You're silly."

His dad, Jung, is happy to see us but asks us to be quiet as we proceed inside because it's five minutes before midnight and everyone's asleep already. He shows us to the bedrooms on the second floor. When the lights go on, I see that the guys get a room with bunk beds. I get a room with a single bed, like a princess. Sweet.

Exhaustion presses me into the soft mattress, but I'm still wound up and worry I won't be able to sleep. The next thing I see though is white light streaming through the gaps around the curtains. It's eight in the morning. I can hear and feel a bustle of activity downstairs. And children's squeals. Lots and lots of squeals. Small feet running back and forth, up and down the stairs. Just how many kids are in this house?

I get a text from CJ asking me to come practice a bit before I go shopping. My nervousness flares up and consumes my whole body with a feverish grip. Once again, I remember what Fiona had told me right before I met the Vipers.

No fear.

I repeat it the whole time I'm taking a shower.

Chaos rages downstairs. I was right about the kids. There are hordes of them running through the house. I stand there in the middle of the living room and watch them spread glitter and glue over every surface while they supposedly make something on a low table in the corner, yelling, giggling, and jumping from couch to couch. There's a movie going on for them on an enormous screen, but no one's watching. This is like nothing I've ever seen back in Russia. I don't know what to make of it.

Zach appears by my side and guides me into the kitchen. Bowls of cereal litter the dining table and the breakfast nook counter. Christmas tunes pour from the radio, but the music is drowned out by the animated chatter. My eyes jump from person to person to person (there's at least a dozen strangers in the room), and I cling to Zach's sleeve.

"Found her," he announces in his usual upbeat voice, and I want to smack him when all eyes turn to me.

CJ motions for me to come sit with him, but I'm intercepted by a group of four women. There is exactly zero doubt they are Zach's mother and sisters. All as one have the same dark hair and the very same smile Zach tends to have.

"Your father said she was a cutie, and she is a cutie," says the oldest of the women, Zach's mom. "Better snatch her quick, Zach."

Even if I can't see my cheeks burning, I can sure feel it.

Zach chuckles, but his tightly pursed lips betray his embarrassment. "I would have to beef it out with CJ and Marsh, and I don't think I'd come out of it alive, *Eomma*."

I want to smack him again, and Zach seems to know it since he beelines to the other end of the kitchen and grabs a bowl.

"Always late to the party," says Zach's mom. "I'm Seo-yun. And these are my daughters Kayla, Hazel, and Nari."

I get introduced to the rest of Zach's family—his paternal grandparents, his sisters' husbands, a couple of uncles and aunts, a cousin or two. It's a lot of people.

I get a suffocating amount of hugs, then Nari grabs my hands. "I'm gonna take you shopping when you're ready."

"Thanks."

When I finally make it to CJ, he whispers, "You okay?"

I breathe out and nod. "This is fun."

I mean it. I've never had so many family members. Mama came from a single-parent household, and even though papa didn't, neither of my parents had any siblings, and both sets of my grandparents died when I was young.

I try to relax while I wait for the guys to finish breakfast, but I don't eat anything—I don't like cereal, and my stomach is touchy because I'm still nervous about the interview. Of course, there's also the usual worry that if I eat anything, I'll throw up, and that's not something I fancy doing at the radio station.

Nari lends me a pair of jeans and a sweater. A second before I step out the door, Marshall sneaks a wad of cash into my palm. I take it without reservations. In fact, I don't even say thank you. He's the one who stuffed me in the minivan without letting me pack.

Nari talks the whole time we drive to the outlets.

"We've been dying to meet you. Zach's been texting about you non-stop for the last few days, worrying we'd overwhelm you."

"Is he allowed to talk about me to anyone outside of Project Viper?" I joke and tuck away the warmth in my chest caused by his concern for later.

Nari grins. "He probably figured that since we'd meet you anyway, there was no point in keeping your existence secret. How do you like the guys so far?"

That is a popular question lately. Kiera asked me that last morning as well. "They're good."

"They are good. CJ seems to have taken you under his wing." Nari shoots me a curious look.

I know what she's trying to pry out of me, so I summon my most casual tone to say, "He's cool."

"And Marshall?"

I'm not going to think of the time he kissed me. And I will definitely not think about how often I wish he'd kiss me again.

I shrug.

Nari laughs, probably guessing what I will never say to anyone as long as I live, and keeps talking the whole time we're out and about. I don't mind. She helps take my mind off my nerves.

When we get back, Marshall grins at the clusters of bags in my hands. "Did you get enough?"

He gave me a thousand. *A thousand* bucks. First the mini bass, now this. Is he made of money? Either way, I did my best to burn through it, but Nari took me to sensible shops, and there are holiday clearances everywhere. I hand him back the remaining four hundred. "I did my best."

"Then hurry up and change. You have a bit of time to eat a snack, but then we'd better go. It looks like it's going to storm, so we're leaving earlier."

I run to my room and sort through the bags. I need to put on makeup too. My outfit consists of a cute sweater dress, silver with sparkling threads, white tights, and knee-high white boots. Not my favorite colors, but I look darn good, and I get further proof of that when I bump into CJ downstairs. His eyes travel down my figure.

"Are we ready to go?" I adjust the strap of the mini bass around my shoulder.

He clears his throat and looks at something above my head. "Did you get anything to eat?"

"I'm okay." Even thinking about food churns my stomach. I'll eat later, once the interview is over.

Jung volunteers to drive us even though Marshall and CJ are more than capable. "I know the area better," he says and sighs with relief after we close the door behind us. I suspect it's because he wants to escape the noise for a while. My anxiety balloons as we drive to downtown Salt Lake City. I keep mentally chanting Fiona's encouragement. *No fear. No fear.* Forehead pressed to the cold window glass, I watch the picturesque canyon landscapes. Utah is beautiful. Very clean. Snowflakes drift down from the darkening skies. There was a moment almost nine months ago when I felt like one of those snowflakes—tossed about by the mercy of the wind.

Where am I now? Another country, but it feels like a whole other world. A new family, but are they really? My wildest dreams have come true, some of which I didn't know I had—joining Project Viper, becoming someone who might be recognized by hundreds of thousands of people in the future, kissing Marshall Jones. Sometimes I pause and wait for this dream to end. It's too good to be true.

I close my eyes when my anxiety morphs into dizziness and take deep breaths.

No fear.

CJ taps me on the shoulder. "Are you okay?"

I force out a smile. "Never better."

The weather does worsen. It starts dumping snow in earnest, congesting the traffic, and we arrive at a tall building with gleaming windows with only minutes to spare. CJ leads the way and checks us in at the reception. The two girls behind a tall, polished wood counter crane their necks to see Project Viper members better. Both of them give me a fleeting look before switching their attention to Marshall and CJ, who flashes them a comfortable smile. "How's it going, ladies?"

They giggle at him, for which he rewards them with Project Viper pictures with his autograph on them. Smooth. He gave them exactly what they wanted before they even asked.

"You're good to go. Seventh floor." One of the receptionists gives us the badges, caressing CJ with her eyes. She slides him a card with a number scribbled in black marker. When did she write it down? That aside, is it what it's like for CJ all the time? Judging by his pleased smile, he doesn't mind. I do. Is that how guys are going to react to me if my status with Project Viper is confirmed? I will never be able to flirt it away as easily as CJ does it.

I think I'm going to throw up after all.

Marshall pulls out his phone on our way to the elevators. "I'll let Kiera know we made it."

My phone buzzes, and even though I know it's probably a group text Marshall has just sent, I still check it.

```
MJ: It'll be great. They'll love
you.
```

He's trying to encourage me. Because he wants to be nice to me or because he wants to make sure I'll do well and won't let them down? The elevator doors slide open, cutting my time to overthink short. Here we go.

The DJ does love me. So does everyone who manages to call in and people online. At least I think they do. The session is a blur. I'm introduced as the band's friend and don't get any particularly tricky questions other than a few about my music career. I practiced those with Kiera when I first arrived from Russia. If anyone asks, I'm an up-and-coming musician partnering with Project Viper for a music experiment. So I say just that. We laugh at some social media comments and play a few songs. My cheeks hurt from smiling. Somewhere in the back of my mind there's a memory of us posing for pictures.

In the elevator again, going down, I'm overwhelmed with relief. My hands feel clammy and my small Taylor mini bass hangs like a hundred-pound boulder on my shoulder. I grip the stainless steel railing inside the elevator to prop myself against the weight of the bass and wipe at my clammy forehead. It's too hot in here.

"Alexandra?" CJ's voice slithers through the fog in my mind. He's right there next to me, but I can barely hear him. Who stuffed cotton balls in my ears?

"I'm fine." All I have to do is get back to our van. "I just need some air."

I make it to the van parked outside, snow blurring my vision. My cheeks are so hot I swear I can hear the snowflakes sizzle as they hit my face. CJ slides the door open while Jung clears the windshield. Marshall waits behind me, I think. He becomes less solid and more of a presence, a shadow, as my vision darkens. My knees start losing feeling in them.

The world tilts to the side. No, it's me.

The Taylor slips off my shoulder. CJ catches it. "Whoa!"

"I got you." Marshall's arms wrap around me before I fall.

My body thinks it's done its job, delivered me to safety, so I black out.

Later

Marshall

Alexandra slumps in my arms. She's out cold, but when I place her on the back seat of the minivan, she stirs and comes to with a slight gasp.

"What's wrong with her?" CJ's face is lined with worry. I've never seen him this freaked out.

"I'm okay," Alexandra says weakly as she pushes my hands away.

Jung starts the car. "Let's get her home. Kayla will be able to tell us more." Kayla, Tangs' oldest daughter, is a nurse practitioner. It wouldn't be the first time the family relied on her in an emergency.

We make a slow way back through the snowstorm. Alexandra falls asleep in CJ's arms, and I sure hope her fainting is nothing serious and Kayla's expertise will be enough.

When we get back, Kayla unleashes a million questions on her. "Do you feel like you have a fever? Did you have any earlier? Headaches? Cough or sore throat?"

"No." Alexandra shrugs off her coat.

"She looked fine the whole time," CJ says. "She played, talked, laughed, then she just passed out."

"Do you have any chronic conditions?" Kayla continues. "Is there any chance you're pregnant?"

That last question makes both me and CJ cringe, and Alexandra finds enough strength to issue a decisive, "No."

Kayla takes our bassist upstairs.

CJ and I go to the kitchen. Everyone else has had dinner already, and there's plenty left, but I don't want any of the salads, fruit, or potatoes au gratin with ham.

Graham sits at the table, glancing at his phone every so often, a half-finished plate of food next to him. "What's with the commotion?"

"Alexandra fainted after the interview," CJ says while I raid the fridge for a bottle of water and prepare a tall glass of apple juice. Who knows if solid food is okay to give to Alexandra right now, but drinks should be safe.

"She did?" Graham looks up from his phone with his eyebrows raised. "I didn't take her for the fainting type. She going to be okay?"

"Yeah. Kayla's with her," CJ responds. He sounds certain, but what if it's something serious? What if she's been ill this whole time and is going to die?

I take the drinks upstairs. Alexandra's door is slightly open. I still knock.

"Come in."

Kayla is gone. Alexandra sits on her bed, under the blanket but still in her clothes.

"Kayla thinks I'm just exhausted."

"Really?"

"Really."

I sit on the edge of her bed and put the drinks on the side table, but Alexandra pulls on my arm that holds the juice.

"I'd like some."

I hand her the juice, and she drinks until not a drop remains. It may be just my hopeful imagination, but her face seems to regain a bit of color.

"Is there any dinner left?" she asks. "I'm so hungry. I haven't eaten anything today."

"You passed out from hunger?" I laugh to stop myself from feeling like a complete idiot. Here I thought she was dying.

"I am sorry," Alexandra says in a small voice, fidgeting with her hands. "I was just so nervous. I know how important it is for me to do everything right. Project Viper's reputation depends on it. I wanted tonight's performance to be perfect."

I'm past feeling like an idiot. I'm not even human at this point. She passed out because of the interview. Alexandra tried her hardest from day one despite my inane comments and attitude. She never wanted to take anything away from me but worked hard to do her part. And I was never of any help.

"You don't have to be perfect." I cover her hands with one of mine to calm their nervous writhing. "Have fun and do your best."

Alexandra's gaze focuses on my hand on top of hers. I hold my breath and wait for her to move. She frees one of her thumbs and clamps it over my hand.

"I'll go get you something to eat."

Her thumb grip shifts to a full hand grab. "*Potom*."

Later.

"Later can be too late. Graham's still in the kitchen. He has no qualms about finishing off holiday dinners."

Seriously, who cares? It's not like he's going to vacuum up every crumb in the house. What I should care about, or shouldn't, depending on which side of insanity I want to dangle from, are Alexandra's questioning look and her soft fingers that slide gently up my wrist.

"Feeling alive again?" CJ's voice floats from the doorway.

I get off the bed. This is CJ's place.

"Yes," Alexandra says. "I'm sorry for making you worry."

CJ comes over and pats her head. "It's okay. You did so well today."

Yeah, I'm out of here. I'm useless. I can't even remember to praise Alexandra for her efforts at the radio station. She doesn't need me.

Zach thwarts my escape by first blocking the doorway then by pushing me in. He carries a white plastic container. "Good. We're all here."

Shane and Graham follow him. We gather around Alexandra's bed. "What's the matter?" she asks in a worried voice.

Zach grins. "Don't worry. Everything's fine. Are you feeling okay? We listened to the interview, and you nailed it. Good job."

He raises his palm for a hi-five, and Alexandra slaps it. "Thanks."

Shane smiles too. "Your first venture into the big, wide world of band business. You should feel good about yourself, and I'm not nervous to bring you along as part of the band anymore."

Alexandra's eyes widen in surprise.

I say, "I told you they would love you."

A shadow crosses her otherwise pleased expression. I don't know how, but I know what she's thinking. The audience loved her, Shane said he's okay with her belonging to the band, but I'm holding back.

"Speaking of business." Zach sets his container on the corner of the bed. "Charlie had this delivered yesterday before we left. She texted me to open this before Christmas morning, so I thought, why not now?"

"Can't wait," I grumble and earn a conspiratorial smirk from Graham.

Zach opens the container. "Interesting." He takes out an envelope and hands it to Alexandra.

She opens it with fumbling fingers. Inside is a Christmas card. I bet Charlie's sent some kind of instructions for Alexandra. Also, I don't think it's presents in the bin. Chunky bundles in white plastic wrap with our names on them give off a sinister vibe. Knowing Charlie, it's something utterly stupid.

Alexandra reads the card to herself first, chuckles, and clears her throat to cover it up. Fantastic.

"Okay, so." She takes another sweeping look over us, then reads out loud.

> Dearest Vipers,
>
> You've had a nice, long break from all things public and social media. We hope you've enjoyed it. Now it's time to do a little work. In the white container you will find…

Alexandra pauses and looks at Graham. "Drumroll, please."

He obliges and taps his palms on her footboard in a rapid beat. She continues to read.

> Christmas pajamas. Be darlings and wear them this Christmas morning. Enclosed is a camera. Alexandra, since you're not quite an official member of the band yet, the job to take the pictures falls on you. It also falls on you to make sure they look as sleepy and disheveled as possible, homey and cute, as they open the presents, eat their breakfast, and goof off. Lots of goofing off, please. CJ knows where to upload the pictures, so please have it done by eleven in the morning.
>
> XO,
> Your Favorite Social Media Harpy

"Pajamas?" Alexandra tosses aside her blanket and grabs the top bundle, which happens to have my name on it. She pulls the plastic apart and shakes out a long-sleeve top and a pair of fleece pants. The fleece pants are fine, just black. But the top...

"Awesome!" Zach picks up my top and holds it up, seriously enjoying the sight of horrid tinsel stripes and ugly kittens in Santa hats.

"You gotta be kidding me. And what happened to the interview being the only thing we had to do?" Graham grabs his set and stalks out of the room.

Shane frees his pajamas from plastic. "No, no, this is great!"

Alexandra yanks my top from Zach's hands, presses it to my chest and shoulders, then falls on her back, laughing.

"I wouldn't cackle so loud if I were you." I lean over the bed for the container, pinning her legs in the process.

As I suspected, there's a pajama set for her too, but when I toss her Charlie's new weapon of torture for years to come—we'll be seeing these pictures every Christmas, I'm sure—Alexandra grabs her bundle and hugs it.

Eyes shining with happiness, she says, "I'm in."

A Purely Physical Reaction

Alexandra

Christmas morning smells like cinnamon rolls and hot chocolate and is filled with rustling of ripping paper and much too much stuff. The kids open their presents first. Toys, clothes, candy, and new gadgets litter the floor. The Vipers wait on one of the couches and on the floor, decked out in their pajamas, which may be as ugly as they come, but my guys pull off wearing them as though the hideous kitten rags are high-end fashion.

What surprises me more is that when I get out the Charlie-provided camera, they don't even blink and keep talking and smiling and teasing each other. There's no scowling from Graham, not a single complaint from Marshall. This is work, a small thing to do that will get them a lot of fan excitement in return, all done with patience.

Unlike the time when Juliette, Charlie, and Elise came to take photos of me a little after I joined the band, I'm not in the pictures with Marshall this morning. Is that why he's so calm about everything?

Fingering my collar, I set the camera down and try to chase away the disappointing thoughts. Kiera told me that Marshall was a hard worker. That must be it. He is working hard right now, and his calm attitude has nothing to do with me.

When the excitement and noise simmer down a notch, the Tangs help the kids gather their new possessions and usher them to the play area in the basement.

After that's done, Zach motions for me to sit next to him.

"You ready for this?" he asks when I join him.

He turned twenty-three a week ago, but his eyes glow with excitement like he's eight. I love that about him. His enjoyment for life fills me with a desire to have more fun any time I'm around him.

I give him a confident, "Yeah," but really, I don't care what I'm getting. More than anything, I worry my gifts to the Vipers will look dumb. And I'm curious about something. "Hey, your family is Korean, but this feels very American."

"I know. We don't do Christmas Korean-style. That's what *Seollal* and *Chuseok* are for, Lunar New Year and harvest days. My sisters are married to an American and a Canadian, so we give them this one *normal* holiday a year. What about you? Do you celebrate Christmas in Russia? Did you call your parents?"

The strap digs into my palm as I hold on to the camera for dear life. "Russia is all about New Year's Eve and New Year's Day. Christmas isn't a big deal in most families. It's a remnant of the *Sovetsky Soyuz* regime when religion was banned." Having to generalize my answer feels like an outright lie, but there's not much else I can do. This would be the most awful time to tell the guys about my family, not that I want to.

"Interesting. Well, I hope you'll enjoy this anyway." He gives me an encouraging smile then starts chanting, "Stockings, stockings!"

Graham shocks me speechless when he joins in. He can be loud when he wants to. I wonder why he chooses to keep quiet most of the time.

Marshall helps pass the stockings and drops a heavy one in my lap. It has curvy stitching of my name on the top.

"Nari, take some pictures, will you?" Zach scoops the camera out of my hands, passes it to his sister, then suffocates me in a tight hug while she snaps a shot of us.

"I can't be in the photos." I reach for the camera, but Nari angles it away from me.

"Relax," she says. "I know what I'm doing. Who do you think took pictures of the guys before they signed with The Label and got a support team?"

Zach nudges my stocking, and I give in. It's crammed with fluffy socks, nail polish, gift cards, bass strings, guitar picks, and candy. Graham's got a set of drumsticks, and Zach a pair of Bluetooth earbuds, but other than that, my stocking contents match those of the other Vipers. Even the fluffy socks and nail polish. Zach's sisters snicker at that. Awww.

Zach cracks open the bright pink nail polish and starts painting his toenails.

"The stench! Did you have to do that?" Graham covers the lower half of his face with his stocking.

"Want me to paint yours?" Zach offers without missing a beat.

Graham glowers at him, then shrugs and outstretches his feet. Tongue sticking out of the corner of his mouth, Zach gets the job done with impressive speed and precision.

Shane laughs from his spot on the couch and sets a foot on Zach's shoulder. "I'll take one for the team."

"Good boy." Zach makes quick work of him.

I laugh at their antics and notice Seo-yun watching me. She's Zach's mom, but she's also Project Viper's mom. That's why we're all here for the holidays. And I got the same stocking stuffers as the other Vipers. At least in the eyes of the Tang family, I'm one of them. This feeling, this unspoken acceptance, is the real Christmas gift to me.

"From my *Matryoshka!*" Zach's the first one to open a gift from me. My hands sweat while he rips off the green paper with golden stripes. When Zach opens the box and pulls out a nesting doll, he smiles and says with a properly fake Russian accent, "Veri naiice."

"You have to take them all out, comrade," I answer with an exaggerated accent as well.

Zach squints at me, then opens the nesting doll and assembles the inner ones on the floor.

"Hold on." He puts the third one together. "That's me!" He brings the doll next to his face to show it off to the others. It bears an uncanny resemblance. The artist that I hired for the job has nothing short of a divine talent.

CJ slides to sit next to him. "The big one is you," he says to me.

He's right. I'm the *matryoshka* that holds them all. They're all a part of me now.

"Then there's me." He lifts the second one. "Why does Zach get one and I don't?"

I exhale, beyond relieved they seem to like the gift. "You all get one."

Zach finishes assembling the dolls and laughs again, hard enough to topple to his side on the floor. "Marsh, that's perfect!" He holds up the smallest one.

"How come I'm the little one?" Marshall protests from the couch with a pointed look directed at me.

"Because you're a whiny baby," Zach manages through his laughing fit.

Marshall shakes his head with a smile he's struggling to suppress. "Well played, sir."

"You're the smallest because you're so precious to me." I bat my eyelashes at him.

I'm joking, but not really. A *matryoshka* without its tiniest doll, its center, is incomplete. It's downright wrong. Just like Project Viper would be wrong without him, and I will be empty without them.

He laughs, for the first time all morning. "I think I'll take the whiny baby."

"Okay, you lot, squish together. You too." Nari points a warning finger at me when I try to slip away. "Everyone in the rip-your-eye-out pajamas has to be in this photo."

"Scoot over," Marshall says to me and slides off the couch, barely giving me any time to make space for him.

Graham flops on his vacated spot, and CJ sits next to Marshall. Nari scolds CJ for blocking Graham, then gets on Graham's case for not conforming, but all I can think of is that my knee is digging into Marshall's thigh.

We still must not fit in the frame because Nari orders, "Closer please," and goes as far away from us as the room allows.

Zach squeezes me on one side, Marshall on the other.

"Shane, climb up on the couch with your brother," Nari says.

Shane obliges by flopping on Graham and driving an elbow into his gut. "Whoops."

"You crappy little brother," Graham wheezes.

Nari takes a few shots while we laugh at them then orders us to look straight at her.

As I turn, I catch Marshall watching me. He's got the crooked end of a candy cane in his mouth, and his face is completely unreadable. I hate it when I can't even guess what's on his mind.

"What?" I ask him.

Marshall shakes his head. Nothing. He's just staring at me, freaking me out with thoughts he'd never share.

I grab the straight end of his candy cane and snap it off.

"Hey!" Marshall reaches for the piece I've plundered, but I stuff it in my mouth.

"Thief." He pinches my arm.

"Grump." I pinch him on the side.

Marshall swats my hand away and squirms with a tickled laugh. My breath catches. He smiled at me. I don't care that it was a purely physical reaction. I made Marshall Jones laugh. Now this Christmas can't possibly get any better.

Whose Fault Do You Think That Is?

Marshall

Charlie texts us around lunch time and approves of our morning effort. A second after I read her text, I change into a pair of jeans and a simple, dark red sweater. I'm not the only one. CJ, Graham, and Shane change too. Zach and Alexandra continue wearing the ugly pajamas throughout the day. I try not to pester them about it, no matter how much the cats in Santa hats dissolve my eyes. Zach craves bonding activities, and Alexandra looks like she enjoys doing anything that makes her part of us, so I won't say a word. I want my friend and my...new friend to be happy.

We spend Christmas Day doing what the Tangs always do—cooking, eating, and tying fleece quilts for kids at a local hospital. I swear I've tied thousands of these things over the past six years. We used to compete to see who could tie the most, and I can do it with my eyes closed. Only this year I keep them open because of Alexandra. She's new to all of this: American Christmas, large families, doing weird things like cutting the edges of enormous sheets of fleece then tying the ends into knots. Now and then she sneaks a look around as though she can't figure out why we bother. It's something Seoyun insists on us doing every Christmas. She says service helps us remember what the holiday is about.

I don't know what anything is about anymore. Like Alice in Wonderland, I've fallen down a rabbit hole. Only I don't expect to come out of it at the other end.

Girly laughter snaps me out of spiraling into madness. Alexandra is laughing with Zach's sisters and their young daughters. Even though everything's so new to her, she does it without fear. She's really something. I wish she was mine.

That's one thought I can't afford if I want to stay friends with CJ. He's been by her side all day. She's been cutting fleece, and he's been tying, and bringing her snacks, and making sure she doesn't overexert herself even though she looks completely fine today. With him hovering around, I can't find a single opening to ask her if she's enjoying herself. I think she is. I hope she is. I wish he'd leave her be for more than three seconds.

It starts snowing again during dinner. It's soft and flaky this time, and the kids crawl out of their skins to play outside. Driven to the edge of sanity, their parents relent and let them. Jung lights the fire pit, and the roasting sticks come out along with marshmallows and the rest of s'more ingredients. I can't resist the temptation of burnt marshmallows and gooey chocolate. It's one of my favorite things.

Alexandra refuses to go, shaking her head like she would rather do absolutely anything than be outside.

CJ tries to persuade her. "Come on, it'll be fun."

She won't bend. "I don't want to do anything with fire."

Good. I can spend at least one moment without her in the same room. I go to our bedroom to grab my jacket and hat and Charlie's gift, and go outside. Graham roasts three marshmallows at once. I toss the cat pajamas in the fire pit and roast my marshmallow over the fire with that much more pleasure.

Graham lets out a single laugh. "Nice. I should go get mine."

"Right? What was Charlie thinking?"

His marshmallows are almost dripping off his stick, but his s'more is perfectly oozy when he sandwiches them between the crackers. "Just you watch. It'll be the most trending post of the year. Internet plus cats plus us?"

I chuckle. He's probably right.

The toasty flavors dance on my tongue as I watch the lights in the valley below. Somehow, eating in the fresh, cold air amplifies the creamy marshmallows and the dark, silky chocolate. We should do this more often, Christmas or not.

CJ manages to convince Alexandra to come outside. I walk away from the fire pit the moment I see them. I won't look or think about *them*.

Alexandra throws my plan under the bus with a snowball she sends at the back of my neck. It soaks through the layers of my scarf, cold and wet and maddening.

I whip around to yell, "I just wanted to eat a s'more!"

Her back to the fire, Alexandra grins and starts making another snowball. I stuff the remnants of my crackers and marshmallows into my mouth and scoop snow with both of my hands. I've taken hits from her all day without her knowing about it, but I won't go down without a fight now.

The kids join in. CJ retreats inside the moment the snowballs start flying. Graham gets hit once in the back and follows CJ. I pelt Alexandra relentlessly. She retaliates and chases me around. Strands of Alexandra's hair have made their escape from under her hat. I've lost mine. My hands burn because I have no gloves, and I feel like a little kid again. It's a good, happy, lightheaded feeling that swallows me whole.

The kids are summoned inside. They've plowed through the sloping backyard with their running and sledding, and it looks like a ravaged battlefield. I allow Alexandra to catch up to me and land a massive lump of snow on top of my head. In exchange, I gain an opportunity to topple her to the ground. She laughs and swats at my hands, but I manage to bury her shoulders under the snow.

"*Ty pokoinik!*" she squeals.

You're a dead man!

I run off.

A snowball whizzes past my ear. As I turn to mock her aim, my foot lands onto one of the plastic sleds the kids have left behind. I tip backward. My other foot flies high in the air as I land on my back and roll down the slope a few feet. Ouch. But there's no time to feel humiliated. If Zach's sisters' Korean dramas have taught me anything, it's that if you've managed to get yourself in a "possibly injured" situation, milk it for all its worth.

Sure enough, Alexandra's worried voice cuts through the yard. "Marshall, are you all right?"

I hear her running toward me and keep my eyes closed even though I know it won't work.

"Marshall!"

I peek at her. Alexandra drops onto her knees next to me and shakes my shoulder. "Marshall, can you hear me?"

She presses her hand to my cheek. It's ice-cold and forces me to draw a sharp breath.

"You faker." Alexandra tosses some snow at my face.

I jump to a sitting position, wipe off the snow with my sleeve, topple her onto her back again, and press my icy hand to her cheek just like she did a moment ago to me. Alexandra shrieks at the top of her lungs. Sweet, sweet vengeance. I brace for struggle, but she doesn't move and looks me straight in the eye.

"Thank you for making me come."

I should say something back. I'm too distracted. The light produced by the back porch lanterns barely reaches us, but I can see enough to forget to breathe. Alexandra is beautiful. Even though she's working on catching her breath, her eyes sparkle from playing in the cold, and she seems happy. The only other time I remember seeing her happy is when I signed her P Bass. It strikes me with a brutal force. Despite everything I've done, I can make her happy. I love it.

I'm in love with her.

For the sake of keeping my own heart and my friendship with CJ intact, I have to let go of her.

Alexandra's eyes roam my face. "You've got snow in your hair."

"Whose fault do you think that is?"

I lean closer even as everything inside of me screams to get up and run. But there's a big difference between knowing what you have to do and what you actually want to do. I want her all to myself. Today, tomorrow, forever. Since that's impossible, I'll indulge in one last act of insanity, a Christmas gift to myself, then I'll force a reboot on my feelings and get out of CJ's way.

Tread Carefully

Alexandra

It's a full-on mutiny. Holding Marshall is a life-threatening, all-consuming urge. My heart demands to know whether he meant anything by that kiss on Halloween night. He still hasn't said anything. Does he like me? He's been different. More approachable and more distant at the same time. How is that even possible?

What does he want right now? What does he want from me in general? Maybe nothing. Maybe he's just toying with me, taking advantage of me at my most vulnerable. Maybe that kiss didn't mean anything. Maybe I should punch him in his irresistible face, walk away, and never look at him again.

Marshall's hand is still on my cheek. It's warmer now. He's closer. I'm paralyzed by the smoldering intensity in his eyes and don't move even though I know what's coming, even though I should stop him and make him explain himself. It's all out of control.

"Alexandra."

I don't feel the same excitement from him saying my name as I have in the past. His voice comes out low. It's ominous. It's a warning.

Then I understand. I got it all wrong. He's not about to kiss me. He doesn't want me. He sees right through me, knows about my feelings, and he's telling me to cut it out.

Until he actually tells me that, I won't. I've spent all day doing who knows what just so that I wouldn't betray my feelings to others, but there's no one else here right now. I tug on the loops of his snow-covered scarf.

No fear.

Load the gun and spin the barrel. A demolition of my mind. A total eclipse. A challenge and a complete surrender. I want him. I love him. Curses, I love him.

How did it come to this? He's obnoxious.

Do I even care?

Shouldn't I care?

While I ponder that, Marshall's lips cover mine. Hard and relentless and hungry and for one long moment—perfect. I gasp for air and reach for more, but it's already over. Breathing hard, Marshall moves to get up.

His scarf is still in my hands, so I hold on to it and make him stay. "We can't have holiday make out sessions then pretend like it's nothing."

He exhales. "We won't."

His eyes flicker to my lips one more time, and my heart stops, beats like a drum in my ears, then stops again when Marshall rises to his feet in one abrupt motion and stalks away, leaving his scarf with me.

Confused and mourning the loss of his warmth, I gaze at the starless sky. He fought and fought with me, then for whatever reason changed his mind about me, then stole my heart and left me lying in the snow.

In the dark. All by myself.

✳

Fiona waits for us in the Nest's driveway when we return to Portland on the second day of January. It's been a long trip through bad weather and several clogs on the roads. Marshall barely grumbles a hello to her before he disappears inside.

I feel the same way. Christmas and New Year's Eve with the Tangs have been amazing and absolutely exhausting. I'm glad to be home.

"Did you and Marshall fight again?" Fiona helps me carry my bags to the guest house.

"No, we didn't fight. He's just…"

"He's just what?"

We get inside, dump everything on the love seat in the sitting room, and go to the kitchen. I need a drink and a moment to figure out how to explain Marshall.

While my glass fills with water from the fridge dispenser, I stare at the back of my phone. The wrapper from the minty kiss he gave me on the way to Utah rests between the device and its transparent case. I think of all the other kisses we've shared and remember his question. *What more do you want?* Back in the van I felt like he was just asking me about snacks, but now I wonder whether he was asking me about what I wanted from him. Oh, I only want all of him. Or at least not to be left wading through all of this uncertainty.

"So, Marshall?" Fiona prompts.

"I don't know. I think he's just tired."

The water's done pouring, but I stay by the fridge, smiling at everything that has happened away from the Nest. Marshall's been avoiding me like the plague after he kissed me on Christmas Day. I don't think he has said more than three sentences to me since then. That's probably not a good thing, but I can't help enjoying his struggle.

I believe he is starting to like me, only he can't accept that after being against me for so long.

Fiona's eyebrows rise. "What are you smiling about?"

"Nothing."

"Nothing? There's no way you can be smiling about 'nothing' when we're talking about Marshall Jones. You like him, don't you?" Fiona whistles, low and puzzled, and crosses her arms on her chest.

"I suppose."

"I didn't see that coming. You like them challenging then?"

Up until now, I haven't even considered Marshall as a challenge in that sense. I wanted to prove myself to him as a musician, and then...

And then...

"Tread carefully. Don't give the band another reason to get rid of you, as if they don't already have several," Fiona says.

Chilled water burns like boiling tea in my mouth.

"They're getting rid of me?"

Does she know something? Did I already fail, and the Vipers dragged me along with them to Utah to soften the blow? They can't be that cruel. Not my Vipers.

"No. Well, not that I know of. I'm sorry. I'm freaking you out." Fiona sighs. "What I meant to say is consider if you want to go any further with Marshall. If you two have a thing then end up being unable to stand each other, you're out of the band. Everyone will be extremely sorry and all, but you're the one who will have to leave. Marshall can't go. They can't afford to lose him."

The panic leaves my body with a tangible *whoosh*, and the next sip of water tastes normal again.

"Fiona, I don't think there's any worry of us having a 'thing' right now." I'm sugarcoating, of course, but not by much.

She shakes her head. "You've never had a boyfriend before, have you?"

"I was kind of busy with other things." I finish the water and try to swallow the darkness that has crept upon my mood.

Dating and relationships weren't often on my mind while I traveled before choosing the right university to attend. Later, I was too consumed with trying to figure out how to buy my next transit pass or pay my phone bill to worry about anything else.

Fiona's expression softens. "I'm just saying, be careful. It's Marshall. Attractive and emotionally overwhelming Marshall. Take your time. Keep him at a distance. I worry he'll break your heart and won't even notice, and you'll be stuck in the band, bound by the contract to watch him date some other girl."

I give her a hug. "I will be careful." I'm not entirely certain how I'm going to keep this promise.

▶ Track 22
A Master of Self-Control

Marshall

I hop the stairs two at a time and go straight for a shower. Hot water pelts my skin. I start to relax almost immediately, but it still takes a long time to unwind after being stuck with Alexandra in the minivan for almost sixteen hours, listening to her chat with CJ, Shane, and Zach about music and what it's like to tour and everything else they felt like dredging up. I sat up front with Graham and did a fantastic job taking turns between napping and scowling at the traffic. During one of our pit stops, I almost pulled her aside and said, "Listen, no more clinging to CJ, no more indulging Zach's jokes. Be mine. Just mine."

Almost. I shut off the water and clunk my forehead on the tiles. I should've just done it.

There's music coming from my bedroom. I sigh because it seems like I can't have a minute of peace even in my own room. I towel off and pull on a robe, giving myself some time to calm down before I go out there.

CJ sits at my desk and uses my laptop to scrub through our most recent recording. "Hey, what do you think— Oh. You feeling okay?"

Why in the universe does he think something is wrong? I frown so hard it actually hurts. Ah, maybe it's the frown.

"Can it wait until tomorrow?" No matter why he's here, I need to sleep and not think about anything.

"Sure." CJ rolls away from the desk. "Did you ever show Alexandra the song?"

"Yes." I point at the door.

CJ heads out but lingers in the doorway. "Did she like it?"

"She's perfect. Leave already."

"She's perfect?" CJ lifts an eyebrow.

"She said the song is perfect."

"That's not what *you* said."

I push him out and slide the door closed.

Why can't I just talk to CJ?

It's not just him. I can't talk about it with anyone else.

But I need to. I know I'm the odd one, always needing to discuss everything. I know it's a weird need for someone who fears opening up more than anything, but knowing everything to a T makes it so that I know what to do, what to expect, and what other people expect of me.

What does Alexandra expect of me after this vacation? I should probably make sure she knows nothing more can happen between us. It's better that she's sad now.

I throw on some clothes, then go outside, cross the yard, and knock on the guest house door, glancing over my shoulder like a kid who's snuck out after the curfew. I am a kid. Twenty-two and a half, vulnerable and weird and—

Alexandra opens the door. "What's up?"

"Can I come in?" I glance over my shoulder again.

"Why? To confuse me more?"

Ouch. "I won't. I promise."

Her eyes narrow. She's doubting me and my promises, which

is fair. I turn to leave, but Alexandra grabs my upper arm and pulls me in.

I shouldn't have come without a life vest. I'm already drowning. It's harder to breathe. I came to tell her we're done, but images of our kiss in the snow consume my brain cells. Again. Every time I let my guard down for one second, the memory of that frosty and hot and unbearable kiss sears through my body. I promised myself that it would be the last time, but… It was the last time. It was. It has to be.

Also, I smell heaven—butter and garlic. "What are you eating?"

She shakes her head and walks away. "Nothing."

I lock the door and follow her. One more scent hits my nose. "I smell cheese."

Alexandra bars my way. "No, you don't."

"You're having spaghetti, aren't you?" I don't know why she's hiding it from me. It's not like I'd tell on her to anyone.

"I was just so hungry, and it was quick, and I can't stand the sight of a salad right now."

It's entertaining to watch her try and justify herself to me. "Is there any left?"

"Why are you here?"

My resolution to butt out of her relationship with CJ is still there, but the words won't come out. At least not the ones I need. "Watch a movie with me," I blurt out instead.

"Okay. The TV's in there." She points down the hall.

"I know."

I get to the family room where I drop on a big, comfortable couch and fiddle with the remotes. She joins me with two bowls of spaghetti in her hands. The smell of it, still warm and rich, is enough to make me weak at the knees. We've eaten lots of great food over the holiday break, but I expect that bowl of simple pasta with cheese to hit the spot hard.

I start a streaming service. "What do you want to watch?"

"I haven't seen that yet," she says about the latest Star Wars installation.

"You like Star Wars?" Does she have to make it even harder? If a girl likes sci-fi, she's a keeper. Everybody knows that.

"What's not to like? I used to watch those from bootleg tapes when I was a kid. It was grainy, you know? I loved it."

"You had a tape player? I almost forgot what those things look like. Only one of the families I've lived with had a tape player. The rest kind of tried to keep up with modern technology."

This reminder of the "good old days" only brings more weight to the already difficult situation. Suddenly cold, I get up and flip the switch on the fireplace. Flames come to life with a soft pop.

Alexandra chokes on a mouthful of spaghetti. "Turn it off!"

I flip the switch again. The fire dies.

What is it about Alexandra and fire? She didn't want to sit around the fire pit at the Tangs'. She's downright freaked out about the fireplace right now.

Alexandra pulls the cardigan she's wearing tighter around herself and presses a hand to her forehead. "Are you cold? I'll get you a blanket."

Before I can say anything, she leaves the room but returns within a minute with a thick quilt. Her gaze darts to the fireplace once more as she forces even, slow breaths in and out of her lungs.

I sit with her again and spread the quilt over our legs. Alexandra continues staring at the fireplace, her breathing still labored.

"Alexandra?" I touch her cheek.

She blinks and looks at me like she's barely noticed me, and I struggle to understand this scene. What is going on? What happened to cause such a reaction?

"I'm sorry. It's been a long day," she says.

"Let's talk about it."

She frowns, confused. "The day? You've been with me through all of it."

"No. Tell me about you and fire."

Alexandra rubs her temples. "No."

"Why not?"

She shakes her head. "Not talking about it."

"Is it a secret?" I force myself to focus on her and not the bitterness her justified distrust plants in my chest.

"No. It's not. It's… I really *can't* talk about it."

If I ask simple but direct questions, will it help? I won't know until I try. "You really are afraid of fire, aren't you?"

"Yes." Her breathing accelerates once more.

What do I do? How can I help her? What is this that crumbles Alexandra the Fighter into a mess of a human being? It doesn't matter. Right now I've got to get her to feel calm and safe again.

"Hey, come here." I coax her into my arms. "We don't have to talk about you, but you can ask anything about me. All the girls I've dated, noses I've broken, cars I've stolen."

That last bit gets her to perk up and look at me. "You stole a car?"

"No, actually."

"But you did break someone's nose?"

"Many times." I can't help smiling at her interest in my supposedly nefarious past.

Alexandra slides her fingers up and down my forearm. "Why?"

I refuse to react to her touch. I'm a master of self-control. "Sometimes because people looked at me the wrong way or said something stupid, but mostly because of Zach. People harassed all of us, but surprisingly, he got it the worst. Everyone assumed he was stuck up and considered himself better than others because of his family's wealth and his musical ability when in reality he was just super shy. There wasn't a week in our freshman year when I didn't find him cornered by some bully."

She chews on her lower lip for a second. "I can't really picture that at all. Zach? Shy? Bullied? He's as tall as a giraffe. He can probably plow through anyone without even noticing them."

"He wasn't at fifteen, and I had a bad temper back then."

She raises a mocking eyebrow. "Had?"

This girl. So sneaky.

"Just watch a movie with me." I pull over an ottoman and we both put our feet up. Sinking into the soft comfort of the couch and her scent, clean and sweet, I start the movie and stuff a huge pile of spaghetti into my mouth. So good.

"How do you speak Russian?"

I should've known she didn't forget about that.

"I'm taking online classes toward an art history degree. One or two at a time, as much as the band business allows."

Alexandra stares at me with huge, surprised eyes. "Seriously? You're going to college? Right now?"

I nod.

"So then, you were serious about reading Tolstoy?"

I nod again.

She pats my cheek. "My condolences."

This time I laugh. "Thanks. I flunked the class."

"Flunked? As in failed? Why?"

"All I had to do was read a few books and write a few essays. But guess who hasn't been reading or writing as much as he should have. And guess why." I tap her chin with my index finger. "I completely spaced most of the assignments, so I'll have to retake it."

Alexandra offers me an apologetic smile. "I could help you next time."

"You *will* help me next time."

She smiles wider, happy.

I have to hit the brakes. I'm not here to make her happy. I'm not even here to make better friends with her.

"Why art history? Why Russian?" She grins. "Why not, right? You really don't seem like the type, though. You guys keep surprising me."

"*Ya znayu*." *I know.* It's not often that I get to practice with a native speaker, so I end up sounding nervous.

Alexandra's face lights up with delight as she gets back to her food. She loves that I can speak Russian to her. I will never do it again.

Rebels make plans, the Empire carries on with its schemes, droids beep, and lightsabers buzz. We munch on our secret late dinner. Alexandra relaxes against me, our shoulders and thighs touching, and my chest fills with content warmth I have no business enjoying.

"I'm sorry if I've been confusing," I say, preparing to tell her why I'm really here.

When she doesn't respond, I crane my head. Her eyes are closed.

"Are you asleep?"

She rests her head on my shoulder and drapes one arm over my chest. "Mmmm?"

I tuck the quilt around her and kiss the top of her head. I came to talk, but it doesn't seem to matter right now, so I choose to let it go.

Friends No Matter What

Alexandra

A sharp pain in my neck wakes me up. Hissing, I lift my head and realize I'm not in my bed. Soft light slants through the open blinds in the family room. It's going to be a sunny day. Rubbing the back of my neck, I sit up.

Marshall issues an incoherent grumble and stretches out on the couch behind me. His dark hair splays against the light fabric, revealing his entire face for once. I can't tear my eyes away from him: long, dark eyelashes, slightly parted lips, the fresh fuzz that covers his cheeks. Neither can I resist brushing his eyebrow with my fingertip. Marshall scrunches up his face and pulls a large section of the quilt under his chin. He's impossibly cute. And he's impossibly complicated.

It isn't hard to tell we're drawn to each other, but it's also easy to see that he resists it. Why? We're so comfortable in each other's presence when no one else is around.

"Let's go get breakfast somewhere," he says with his eyes still closed.

"Is it a date then?"

Please, Marshall, say something solid. Yes or no, just don't leave me hanging again. But there it is, in the tight line of his pressed lips—that conflict I can't understand. He asks me to spend time with him, but something isn't right.

He opens his eyes. "No. Just breakfast."

I thought I wanted to hear him say no. Now I realize I'd rather be left hanging.

Marshall stands and stretches. I can't help rising on my toes and kissing him on his rough cheek.

"Stop it," Marshall grumbles with a small smile. "We're just friends."

"Right." I step away, intending to go to my room and change, but Marshall catches my hand.

"I mean it."

I work my fingers out of his grip. If this is how things are going to go, he can't hold me. I won't be able to think straight if he does. "You promised to not confuse me."

He sighs. "I know I am…frustrating right now, but can I… I don't know how to say it."

"Just be honest." That's all I've ever wanted from him.

"Honest. Okay." He swallows. "Please know I'm only trying to make sure I won't hurt your feelings. And not hurt myself in the process. I like you, but, to be honest, I don't want you to have any expectations of me. Can we have this"—he motions between us—"go at its speed, without any hopes or plans? We need to learn to be friends no matter what."

I nod and push aside the part where he told me he liked me. I can't shake off the feeling that even though he's trying to be honest with me, the truth is still hidden in between the lines.

"Let's just have fun then," I say. We can be friends even after we kissed. I think.

"Still wanna get breakfast?" he asks.

"Yes."

Marshall heads out. "See you in five."

I hurry upstairs to change my clothes and to brush my teeth, and to avoid thinking of our conversation because if I do, I'll cry. It's stupid, I know, but I can't help it. Marshall likes me, but not the way I want him to.

Done getting dressed and all, I pull out my goals list and add one more box to check to the bottom—be friends with Marshall. Out of dozens of lines marking songs to master and business ropes to learn, that last one feels the most impossible to achieve.

Fair Enough

Marshall

I want to break my skull when I enter the Nest. I was supposed to tell Alexandra we're not happening. Instead I stayed at her house, slept there all night, then asked her out. Genius.

Fiona comes out of the ground floor office with a bunch of papers and a laptop in her hands. "What are you up to?"

"Nothing. You?"

She gives me some of the papers. "I sent you all an email, but here's a hard copy of what will be happening at the festival. It's going to get a little crazy soon."

"Too late for that."

"I'm told you're getting along with Alexandra a little better." Fiona sounds neutral, only I know her enough to not trust it.

I pretend to study the festival details. "Yeah, I guess."

"You guess?"

I plaster a smile onto my face. "Alexandra and I are going to be fine from now on. I'll behave."

"I know you like to be tough and handle it all on your own, but change is hard for everyone. I actually thought you'd throw a much bigger tantrum about it. Kiera had way more faith in you than I did."

I use this conversation as an opportunity to ask something I'm not supposed to. "How did Kiera find Alexandra? Why from Russia? She's great, of course, but we have plenty of local talent."

"Honestly, I don't know. One morning she went through her emails, had a couple of phone calls, then announced we had to go to the airport to pick up your new bassist."

That's random. "Just like that? No plans, no auditions, no research?"

Fiona sighs. "Marshall, I'm just an assistant. I know you think I know everything, but I don't. I'm sorry. She could've done the research and even the auditions without me. Most likely though, The Label handed her Alexandra and told her to deal with it."

"How did The Label pick her then?" I remember Alexandra getting really upset when I called her the president's pet. She said she'd never met him, but... It's not that I don't trust her. I only find it hard to believe The Label's president had nothing to do with her joining us.

"I don't know."

"Shouldn't we though?"

Fiona holds my gaze with ease. She always does. "Marshall, you're asking for trouble. You agreed to a bassist replacement with no questions asked."

"I know, but who is Alexandra? There are no records of her online, no social media presence, no Tube videos. She's obviously talented, but how did she end up with us without ever trying out for anything or performing anywhere? Or posting a single tweet about her favorite makeup? She's from Russia, not from another planet. They have computers and smartphones there. And since I agreed to ask no questions, I need someone else to do it for me."

"All right, all right. Settle down. I'll see what I can find out. I guess it's only fair you know something about her."

"Thanks."

She flicks me a semi-irritated look. "You're welcome, but don't expect me to play any spy games or snoop around. My relationship with Kiera is largely built on trust. I won't break it for you."

"Fair enough." I want to know everything about Alexandra, but I'll take anything, any crumb Fiona can find out about her.

All the Chocolate

Alexandra

The garage is open, and CJ is unloading the remaining bags out of the minivan when I approach the Nest.

"Morning," he greets me.

"Morning." I jog up to him.

At the entrance to the garage, right where the sliding door meets the ground, there's a bit of ice, which I don't realize until my foot hits it and I slip.

"Careful!" CJ leaps to steady me, and in my attempt to regain balance, I grab his arm and end up yanking a little too hard. CJ slips as well, and his forehead collides with the edge of the workbench next to the minivan.

"Are you all right?" My stomach ties itself into sharp knots while I wait for him to look up. Or pass out.

Hand on his forehead, CJ straightens. "I'm fine. Are you?" He lowers his hand and reveals a large smear of blood on his forehead and a slash across his eyebrow.

"You're bleeding!"

"So it seems." CJ dabs at the slash with his white sweatshirt sleeve, marring it with deep red.

The blood starts dripping in earnest. I pull off my new merino wool scarf, fold it, and press it to his forehead.

Marshall enters the garage from the house. "What's happening?"

"I… He's…" Overrun with guilt, I wring my hands and struggle to explain.

Marshall comes over and examines CJ's injury. "Better get you to Urgent Care." He takes CJ by the shoulder and leads him to his car.

"I'm coming with you."

"Stay home," Marshall says in a calm tone. "We'll be back soon."

How can I stay? I need to make sure CJ's injury isn't serious. "You drive, and I'll make sure he doesn't pass out?"

Marshall takes a long look at me. "Okay."

CJ checks his face in the side mirror. "Just a scratch. Don't feel so guilty, *Matryoshka*."

"I'm so sorry," I say again anyway.

"Alexandra, please stop. It was an accident." CJ sounds a bit irritated as he climbs onto the back seat.

Marshall joins in. "If he says he's not mad at you, he's not mad at you. Stop apologizing."

I keep quiet during the drive. Mostly because I was told to stop apologizing and apologies are all I've got.

Two other people sit in the small lobby of the clinic. A young receptionist mutters, "Yikes," when she sees CJ and summons a nurse immediately. CJ is taken behind the door that leads to examination rooms, and I try to follow him, but Marshall holds me by the sleeve.

"Let's wait here. They'll take good care of him, especially if we don't get in the way."

The receptionist asks Marshall whether he knows anything about CJ's insurance, and he deals with the billing stuff. I wallow in guilt.

How can I not?

Marshall asks me something, but it doesn't register.

"What?"

I expect him to be annoyed, but his facial expression is one of gentle concern instead. "Are you hurt?"

"I'm fine."

"Good."

"I feel like such a klutz." I hide my face behind my hands.

"Well, it happens to all of us now and then."

I sigh, and it's stunning how much tension and embarrassment it releases. "CJ's gonna hate me now."

Marshall offers me a comforting smile. "He's not gonna hate you over something so minor."

"It's not minor. Did you see that gash? It's definitely gonna leave a scar, smack in the middle of his eyebrow too. If you won't kick me out, then he will for sure."

"He'll be fine. If it's really ugly, he can get plastic surgery to fix it. But he won't stop liking you, and he will never kick you out." Marshall pulls me in for a hug.

Offended to the tips of my hair with his lighthearted tone, I push him away and walk outside the clinic to pace on the sidewalk.

The air is chilly and crisp, full of subtle winter scents—resting dirt and rain. Right here, right now, the world smells like home. I fill my lungs with air to capacity. Amidst my guilt and worries, the feeling of belonging hits me like a hammer, and I hold on to it.

Home. I'm home.

Visas, green card applications, fighting for my place with Project Viper, the endless torture of my soul that is Marshall, struggling to acclimate now and then, and yet, I feel at home.

Marshall joins me, hands in his jacket pockets, collar raised, his whole posture tense. "What does it matter if CJ likes you or not?"

I glare at him. "What do you mean? He's been so nice to me. Always helpful, always encouraging. I don't want him to hate me. I like him a lot, okay? I don't want to give him a reason to send me away. I don't—"

"Got it," Marshall cuts me off. "Don't worry. He won't send you away."

"But you will?" The words rush off my tongue before I fully think about them.

Marshall lifts his face to the sky before turning on his heel and going back inside. I follow him. He sits on a green, vinyl-padded chair and pulls out his phone and earbuds. His every movement is languid and easy, but a hard edge to his mouth betrays that it's all a show.

I sit next to him. "You can't just walk away without answering." When he doesn't respond, I yank out his earbuds.

Marshall bristles up. "What?"

I know exactly what I want to hear, but my motivation deflates. I won't be able to deal with vague answers this time, and I can't afford to lose hope if he says I can't stay with them. I still have time to change his mind. I changed Shane's mind, so it's not impossible. I'll cling to that.

"Nothing."

I relocate to a different set of chairs and turn my back on him. I let my guard down too much. Everything that's happened between us made me believe I'm winning him over. I've been celebrating too soon.

Eventually, CJ re-enters the waiting area, cleaned up and sporting a square bandage over his eyebrow. "I'll live," he announces with a smile.

I return it, however weak.

"*Matryoshka*, you look like you need ice cream," CJ says as he opens the door that leads outside. "I want ice cream, preferably chocolate. Lots and lots of chocolate. Chocolate ice cream, chocolate chips in it, chocolate fudge on top. All the chocolate."

Marshall puts his phone away. "Are you five years old?"

"You *sound* like you need ice cream. It's decided then."

"Don't drag me along with the two of you," Marshall grumbles as we approach his car.

"I'm gonna walk," I say, dying to get away from him. Why is it that every time the three of us are together things go sauerkraut?

"What? No," CJ protests. "I can tell the two of you argued again, and I'm happily pain-free from a shot of lidocaine. We're all getting ice cream."

"Come on, Alexandra. He won't let us be until he gets his chocolate fix." Marshall gets behind the wheel.

"Atta boy." CJ climbs onto the passenger seat with a laugh.

I give in. Going with CJ is the least I can do to make up for his bashed forehead.

Marshall drives us to an ice cream shop. I watch the proceedings from the car, refusing to come in. The clerk immediately recognizes them and smiles the whole time, bouncing in her spot now and then. Phones are brandished, pictures taken. Marshall even deigns to smile at the teen girl who scoops his ice cream. The jerk. Always smiles for the fans and hardly ever for me. What a stupid thing to be jealous of.

I watch my guys exit the ice cream shop. Both are smiling about something as they talk or maybe share a joke. Everything's great between them without me around.

They get in the car, and CJ climbs onto the back seat with me this time. "Didn't know what you wanted, so I got you a version of spumoni. Nothing beats cherry, chocolate, and pistachio together."

He hands me a cup with three neat scoops and a dainty plastic spoon. The green, dark brown, and pink spheres of ice cream look mouth-watering, but I won't eat it. CJ's happy expression cracks, his eyebrows coming together for a concerned frown, but he doesn't let it linger. He simply puts the ice cream cup onto my lap and leans on my arm.

"Come on, have a bit of mine." He scoops a generous spoonful and brings it to my lips. "Who doesn't feel better after some chocolate?"

My eyes are glued to the bandage on his eyebrow. How can he be so nice with me after what I've done to him? "I'm a vanilla girl."

"You're anything but vanilla." He leans closer and whispers, "Smile and eat to spite him."

I stare at him in shock. CJ winks, and I allow him to feed me a bit of his ice cream.

"Are you still feeling bad about this?" He points at the bandage on his forehead.

"No." I do, a lot, but my guilt is thoroughly overpowered by the clinging unease from Marshall's refusal to talk about my future with the band.

"Then what is it? Why are you so wound up?" CJ doesn't smile anymore, doesn't try to cheer me up. It seems he only wants to know what upsets me.

"I'm sorry I cause you so much trouble. I promised I'd do my best, and I bug you all the time instead. Now I broke your face. Everyone says you love me so much, but you totally won't love me anymore after this."

CJ gives me the most serious look. "I'll never stop loving you. If the cut scars, I'll keep it as proof of just how much I love you." He seals his words with a kiss on my forehead.

A choking sound comes from the driver's seat. Marshall shoves his ice cream into the cup holder, starts the car, then pulls out of the parking lot with the tires squealing.

"Careful! Invalid and *Matryoshka* in the back," CJ chides his friend and finally buckles up.

Marshall rewards him with a hard break on the first red light for that.

Do You Like Her or Something?

Marshall

"What did you two fight over this time?" CJ asks after we drop Alexandra off at the guest house.

"Why do we have to talk about Alexandra?" Every time we do, I want to punch him, and CJ doesn't deserve it. All he did was be nice to a girl when I did my best to be a mean idiot. The worst part of it is that I don't know how to stop being one, and whether I can fix anything even if I do. CJ's in love with Alexandra, and she doesn't mind his attention.

I go upstairs.

CJ follows me. "I know you hate to talk about things, but I also know how much you need to talk about things. What's happening? You're not yourself lately, and I can tell it has something to do with Alexandra."

"You're wrong." Of course I lie again. When I get to my room, I block the doorway so he doesn't get in. "It's not about her."

It is, but it has more to do with him and his reaction to her than with what Alexandra has done.

"Come on, Marsh. Do you like her or something?"

"Like her?" My tone comes off too angry, but I can't take it back.

CJ has no idea. I don't like her. I need her in order to think, to breathe, to feel like my heart is still there. I refused to see it, but now I know why I resisted the change Alexandra brought with her. It's not about the band. It's about me. She changed *me*. She proved to me that I want that kind of a relationship. I want to hold a hot-blooded, living girl, snuggle her on the couch, kiss her in the dark, be jealous when she looks at someone else. I never thought being in love would alter me so much, but it did and still does. I feel like I'm alive for the first time, and it burns like madness because the girl I crave seems to be in love with my best friend.

She totally is. Why else would Alexandra be so worried about CJ liking her?

He raises his hands in surrender. "Sorry. You sure act sometimes like you'll throttle me if I ever sit with her again. All the glaring. If you like her—"

"She's all yours." I mean it.

CJ frowns. "But—"

"Don't you love her?" I don't want to hear his response, but I know that I need to. Once more and for sure. One final nail in my coffin.

"Marsh—"

"Let's start practicing Alexandra's song tomorrow. Everyone expects us to present something new at the festival, so let's let her sing."

I close the door and hear CJ groan loudly outside. That's exactly what I want to do, but I let it go. Everything will be fine soon enough.

Another Vague Answer

Alexandra

I wake up in a much lighter mood than the night before. A new day, a new plan. Marshall is a pain, and being in love with him complicates everything, but neither of those things will stop me. I have to keep fighting for my bassist spot. My heart can wait.

I brush my teeth, get dressed for the workout in a hurry, and run to the Nest. Everyone but Zach is already in the gym, but the pianist keeps late hours and always rolls in last.

"Morning," CJ greets me the moment I step in.

"Good morning."

Yesterday he told me to act happy to spite Marshall, then kissed me. It was a very brotherly kiss, but he still did it. While he told me he'd always love me. I was too frustrated to think about it, but now that my head is clearer, I take the event apart.

Did CJ mean *love* love?

He has to know I don't feel the same way about him. I value our friendship, but there's no love. Not the same kind I feel for his best friend.

I don't get any time to corner CJ about it. Zach finally arrives, and we start the workout. At the end of it, Marshall surprises me by putting my dumbbells on the rack then saying, "I'm sorry about yesterday."

Did I hear that right? He took the first step toward making peace. I shouldn't be too surprised, though. Marshall does that all the time. Zach's sister, Nari, was right. The Vipers are good guys, or they try to be.

I open my mouth to reassure Marshall that I'm not mad at him, but he's already at the door. The O'Neals and CJ have gone ahead, and Zach lingers on the cycling machine, so I feel safe to whisper when I catch up with Marshall. "Did you already eat breakfast? I didn't. Should we go out like you wanted to yesterday?" This is also part of the new plan—keep being nice to him, pretending that he can't get to me.

"We need to practice the new song."

I take his smooth expression and lack of grumbling as a good sign. "Okay. Do you…" I hesitate, and Marshall finally faces me.

He looks so calm that it makes me stumble. His eyes lack their usual fiery glimmers. He is serene. So good.

Now's not a good time to get lost in him. I've got to stick to the plan.

"There's an opera performance of *Eugene Onegin* here in Portland in February. The troupe that's bringing it is from Russia, and they're amazing. My parents took me to see them once as part of the present for graduating from the music school. Would you…" Just say it, you scaredy cat. "Would you like to go with me?"

Marshall stops. He's going to say no.

I try to act like I don't care one way or another. I even pull out my phone and pretend to check it for messages.

"I'll think about it," he says.

It takes all of my self-control to not groan. Another vague answer. What did I expect?

"Breakfast! Breakfast!" Zach emerges from the workout room and pushes us both toward the kitchen.

I sit next to Marshall during breakfast and stay close to him throughout practice. I haven't lost yet. I can still win him over. Marshall acts completely relaxed the whole time. It's nice but weird at the same time. Like something is missing. I've gotten used to dealing with a discontented Marshall. What do I do with this one?

We practice the new song. Having listened to the demo hundreds of times, I know all the words, but I'm not certain about the style. I don't want to sing the same way Marshall recorded it and rip him off.

"What do you think? Is it right?" I ask CJ.

He shrugs. "Ask Marshall."

Marshall glares at CJ. "Don't ask me. It is *your* song."

CJ scowls and walks to the other side of the room.

For the first time, I see trouble brewing between the members of Project Viper.

I look at Shane, Graham, and Zach for clues. Graham shrugs, as he always does, and the other two shake their heads, refusing or reluctant to help me out.

CJ and Marshall at odds. It's not right.

Can't Be Together

Marshall

In the four weeks that follow, Alexandra and CJ do a great job learning and recording my song. Their song. They take turns singing the verses and do the chorus together, with Alexandra singing the bridge in her high, breathy voice. It's beautiful, but it sounds all wrong. The emotional charge is completely different from what I had in mind. I'm the only one to blame though. Had I chosen to sing it with Alexandra, we would've gotten it right. Now that I've passed all responsibility for the song to CJ, I have no right to complain.

"Got the opera tickets today," Alexandra announces one dreary evening in early February.

My initial desire is to storm off without a response, but I've been trying so hard, and succeeding, to be nice and restore the balance to the band that I can't afford to indulge my temper. Everyone seems to breathe easier since I've started "being myself" again.

Everyone but me, of course.

I want to know why Alexandra wants me to go with her. She's

always with my best friend. But we kissed and she didn't seem to mind that. Alexandra bubbles with energy and shoots me excited looks any chance she gets, but she still hangs out with CJ like her heart will never belong to anyone except him. But, but, but... Maybe Alexandra's trying to see if she and I have potential. All the same, it's clear as day she likes CJ more.

"The performance is on the twentieth at seven," she continues.

"Glad you managed to get the tickets."

Alexandra huffs. "Kiera did. She got us really good seats too. I should get her a thank you gift."

"She'd like that. I hope you enjoy the performance." I'm eager to get out of talking about the opera. I should've been honest and refused her from the get-go. Now she seems to think I'm going. I need to find a way to get out of it. I need to butt out altogether and save her from the awkwardness of having to choose between me and CJ.

Speaking of our former bassist. "Why don't you ask CJ to go with you?"

Alexandra grins. "Fiona did. We got four tickets, so I asked her if she'd like to come. She has done so much to help me feel at home. I want to treat her to a fun evening. You don't mind, do you?"

I shake my head and silently grind my teeth. There goes my easy way out.

"Formal wear, all right?" Alexandra goes on.

"About that—"

"You don't have a tuxedo or a formal suit?"

"I have many."

That's not the point!

"Great."

"Please don't make me do this," I mutter, disgusted with my lack of guts. I don't want to hurt her feelings, but is there anything I can do to avoid that now?

Alexandra pats my shoulder. "Opera sounds boring and maybe a little intimidating, but don't worry. You'll love this one."

She doesn't give up easily. I always knew that about her.

"You're not going to take no for an answer, are you, even if I mean it?"

"Of course not. Especially since you have many tuxedos." She leaves the main house, walking on air.

What a disaster. A beautiful and persistent disaster.

For the remaining time until the blasted evening, I do my best to avoid having any one-on-one time with her.

"Ready for tonight?" Alexandra pounces on my arm after the rehearsal the day of the opera, and her warm fingers on my bicep send shivers down my spine.

I free my arm. "Don't worry about me. This is something you wanted to do, so enjoy it no matter what. Deal?"

"Deal." She beams at me and hurries down the hallway to join CJ for whatever it is they're planning to do.

She's going to hate that deal, and me for it, but she has to see we can't be together.

Birthday Cake in a Cup

Alexandra

Fiona and I get dressed for the evening.

"So, let's not make a big deal out of this, okay?" I say to her. "I only want the guys to see some amazing singing techniques."

And to celebrate my birthday without anyone knowing. Both Connor and Kiera called me this week to ask what I wanted to do, but I convinced them that opera would be enough. A date with Marshall is enough. I'll find a way to get some dessert later and sing a birthday song to myself in my mind as I eat it. Although, I guess, I can't call it a date since I've been friend-zoned. Whatever. Marshall can define tonight as whatever he wants. For me, it's a date. The first one and the last one.

Fiona finishes slipping her black dress on and gives me a questioning look but refrains from commenting. I wonder if she'll unleash them later. Probably with Elise, Charlie, and Juliette present for it.

She comes over and gives my hair a final brushing and a few spritzes of hair spray. "Green is good on you," she says about my dark green velvet gown with exposed shoulders and long sleeves.

"It's so comfy." I twirl on the spot. "And! It has pockets. What kind of a formal gown has pockets?" I've worn plenty for my singing recitals. None of them were this cool.

"Yours apparently." Fiona smiles and runs a hand over her sleek hairdo. "Let's go downstairs. CJ texted me that they're coming to pick us up."

When I asked her to invite someone to complete our group, she picked CJ. I'm beyond curious why. Are they friends? Are they *very good* friends?

While we wait for our escort, Fiona goes to grab a drink from the kitchen, and I pace in the living room. That is, I take several steps around the plush gray rug, then scoff at myself for being nervous. In all fairness, I should be fully justified in my nervousness before a date with Marshall. Stormy, moody, unpredictable. So much more patient as of late. He finally acts like he's gotten used to me, but my insides still roil with anxiety.

A loud knock on the door cuts through the silence. I run my hands over my gown one last time and square my shoulders.

No fear.

Watch out, Marshall's heart. Here I come.

Fiona returns from the kitchen and gets the door. I tiptoe to the hall that leads to the entryway and peek around the corner.

"You guys look a treat," Fiona says without a drop of bashfulness. "Alexandra, you ready?"

I come into the entryway and stare at CJ and Zach dressed in fine black suits.

"*Matryoshka*, are you okay?" CJ asks.

I'm incapable of explaining the difference between my expectations and who stands in front of me. I expected CJ and Marshall, not CJ and Zach.

"I have a stomachache all of a sudden."

It's not a lie. My stomach feels as if someone punched me. Or at least I imagine that's what being punched in the gut feels like. Hands on my middle, I turn away.

Fiona guides me to a sofa in the side room. "Would some water help or are you feeling like you're going to throw up?"

"I'm sorry to say this, but her face matches the color of her dress," Zach says. "I don't think we should go."

"You were fine earlier." Fiona's tone isn't accusing, only worried.

I didn't expect to react that way. I didn't expect Marshall to bail because that's what it is. I check my phone, and there are no missed calls or voicemail notifications or texts.

"No. No need to cancel the evening because of me."

Fiona sits next to me, looking miserable. "But you're the one who wanted to do this in the first place. I'm staying with you."

"No. I'll go lay down, and you just...just go."

CJ crouches before me. "But—"

"Go and have fun. Please." Feeling sick to my core, I leave them and stumble upstairs, drop onto the top step, and hide my eyes behind my hands.

Car doors slam outside. They drive off.

My eyes sting and my lip trembles. I bite it. I will not cry like a little girl. So what if I'll miss out on something I've been looking forward to for weeks? I'm not sick enough to stay home, but I don't want to spend the evening with Zach. If I did, I would've let Kiera throw me a party.

I heave myself off the floor, go to my bedroom, and fling the top desk drawer open. The list, folded and innocent, sits in the corner. I grab it, unfold it, and cross out the bottom line, the one about being friends with Marshall, with such force I strike a long gash through the paper. The hole resembles the one in my heart too much. I crumble the paper in my fist, throw it back in the drawer, shove it closed, then return to sitting at the top of the stairs, away from the useless sheet of paper that represented all my hopes and dreams.

No matter how hard I resist, tears overcome me. They drag me to the golden, carpeted floor, oddly soft under my cheeks, and I sink into it, weak and angry with myself.

The front door opens and closes again. I listen to the sound of steps until it stops. After a minute of cutting silence, wary curiosity gets me. I push off the floor and turn around.

Hands in his trouser pockets, Zach stands at the bottom of the stairs. I've never seen such a grave expression on his face before. "Alexandra, would you please come down?"

I can only imagine the mess my makeup has become. "No."

"Please?"

Fine. I stomp downstairs, stopping on the second-to-last step so that I can be at least the same height as the tall pianist. "Did Marshall get sick?"

Zach shakes his head.

"Did something else happen?"

"No."

"He asked you to come instead of him, didn't he?"

Zach nods.

"Why did you agree?" I shout.

Sadness followed by anger is normal for me. I'm guaranteed to feel bad later, but for now Zach will have to deal with me.

He shrugs. "I figured it'd cause less damage if I went with his harebrained scheme than let him come up with something else."

I want to press myself against the wall and become one with the plaster, hide from Zach's patience and knowing eyes.

"Less damage? How considerate of you." A new wave of tears floods my eyes, but I blink it away and breathe through my nose, lips clenched tight.

Zach steps closer and wipes my cheeks with his thumbs. "I'm sorry."

"*You* have nothing to apologize for." And I won't listen to the one who does. Not again.

"Can I tell you a secret?" Zach's soft hands cup my face and hold me captive.

"Do I have a choice?"

He smiles. "Not really. And you must promise me you'll keep it between us no matter what, no matter how mad you get at Marshall."

Intriguing. "I promise." What exactly did I sign up for?

"The secret isn't quite mine, it's Marshall's, but I'll share it with you anyway."

No thanks. "I changed my mind. I don't want to know."

"But you really do." Zach leans to whisper in my ear, "His secret is that he's extremely insecure."

I snort. "Marshall? Insecure? Have you seen the guy? Handsome, confident, and knows it too."

"It's all a show, same as on the stage."

"Zach, please. Don't defend him. I'll only get mad at you too."

"You already are." He adjusts my bangs. "I'm not defending him. I'm giving you a strategic advantage against him."

I have to take a moment to process this. "There's no such thing with Marshall." No matter what I attempt, nothing works.

He still holds my face, a sly smile playing on his lips. "Just watch him. He acts put together and like he doesn't care about anything to conceal how much he struggles with change. And you have been an enormous change in all of our lives. Plus, you're awesome. You came halfway across the world to do something out of your comfort zone and endured all of his criticisms without giving up. He probably feels like he's not good enough for you or something, especially when you're with CJ."

"What does CJ have to do with anything?"

Zach douses me with a dubious look and shakes his head. "Seems like we have more than one oblivious person in the pile."

He steps away, and I suck in a deep breath. Zach sure can have a hefty effect when he wants to. Until he moved, I didn't even realize how he filled all of the space around me.

"How am I oblivious?"

"*What does CJ have to do with anything?*" Zach throws my question back at me as he takes off his tie.

"We're just friends."

"You two seem a little too close for just friends."

"Anyone can tell there's nothing between me and CJ," I grumble. "He's like a brother to me."

Zach laughs and rubs his forehead. "Alexandra, come on."

"Okay, enough. We're not talking about this anymore. I'm over Marshall's antics and him altogether."

"Are you now?" He's next to me once more, our faces inches apart. Zach's eyes are full of mischief and challenge. "Then you won't mind if I do this?" He wraps his hands around my waist and pulls me into him.

I grab his shoulders. Heat floods my face, and my breath sticks in my throat. "Zach?"

"Yes?" His nose brushes against mine.

Is he really going to kiss me? Not if I have a say in it.

"What did I tell you about touching me?" I grab his ear and tug hard.

Zach hisses and leans into my hand. "Hey, hey. Easy now."

"Even if I wasn't in love with Marshall, why are you such a pain?"

With a pleased smirk, Zach murmurs, "So you do love him."

"No!" I drop my hand and take a clumsy step up the stairs.

"Hey, it's okay." Zach heads toward the kitchen. "Your secret is safe with me."

My heart encrusts itself with panicked ice. I run after him. "Just like Marshall's secret?"

He checks my cabinets and fridge.

"Zach!"

"I'll keep your secret because I want to see Marshall squirm. He's my friend, but for goodness' sake, he deserves to suffer for ruining our *Matryoshka's* birthday."

I gasp. "Is there nothing you don't know?"

He chuckles and sets two large mugs on the countertop. "I have three older sisters who taught me, in rather tangible ways, that you don't forget about the birthdays of women in your life, no matter the relationship. I found out yours as soon as you got here."

I slump onto a bar stool next to the kitchen island. "Ugh, Fiona."

"Kiera, actually. Don't worry about it. I didn't tell anyone else because you didn't act like you wanted a party."

A canister of flour, a stick of butter, eggs, baking powder, milk and vanilla extract follow the mugs. I have no clue what Zach's doing until he mixes up something that looks like cake batter in one of the mugs and sticks it into the microwave.

"This is not the best but better than nothing," he says. "Unless, of course, you still feel like going out with me tonight."

I shake my head. "Sorry, it's not because of you."

Zach starts slicing a pear from a fruit basket on the island. "I know."

We don't say anything more until the second cake in a mug finishes cooking.

Zach tops both of them with thinly sliced fruit and sticks a fork in each. "Dig in?"

I deposit a heap of cake and pears into my mouth and exhale. It's so good despite the method of cooking. Sweet, fruity, crumbly. It hits every exhausted piece of my heart just right. "Thank you."

"You're welcome. And Marshall may be an idiot, but you don't have to be one along with him. Tell him how you feel."

I choke on the cake. "What? Never. And you can't breathe a word of this to him. You spent the evening with me. That's all he needs to know. Same as everyone else. Don't say a word about my birthday. Promise me."

Zach sighs. "Fine."

We finish the cake, and when I see him off, Zach lingers in the doorway and fishes in his jacket pocket. My eyes catch a sparkle of silver, then he stands behind me and clasps a necklace around my neck.

A small, cool to the touch pendant rests on the skin on my chest—a thin, delicate bar, with five small amethyst hearts across it.

"One for each of us. Happy birthday, Alexandra. Sorry it was such a bust." Zach plants a quick kiss on my cheek.

Now, that kiss, friendly and innocent, is more than welcome. "Not entirely a bust."

Zach smiles, back to his usual, cheerful self. "Good night."

"Good night."

The moment he steps off the porch, I disappear inside, climb upstairs, and curl up in my bed. I have no strength to think about Marshall anymore or to deal with what's left of today.

What's the Problem?

Alexandra

After a night of fitful sleep and zero messages from Marshall, I wake up with a realization that makes me scowl at myself. Marshall never agreed to go to the opera with me. The opposite, in fact.

Fiona knocks on my open bedroom door.

"Happy belated birthday. Kiera told me when she found out you couldn't attend the opera. It's from all of us—Kiera, me, Elise, Jules, and Charlie." She sets an enormous basket of goodies at the foot of my bed.

I rise from the pillows. "You didn't have to."

Fiona takes a moment to look at me. To pity me. I'm still in my green gown. The minky fabric is soft and pleasant to the touch. I looked forward to appearing in something so lush and beautiful in public, but it has become pajamas.

"Would you like to talk about it?"

"No."

"Come on. You'll feel better."

I rifle through the cookies, lotions, bath bombs, hair masks, and makeup in the basket. "I don't think I will." I don't want to feel better yet. My mind and body need to work their way through this hurt and develop a cure on their own.

Fiona sits on the bed next to me. "Why didn't you actually go?"

"Marshall was supposed to go with me, not Zach." The words spill, and I turn away, embarrassed.

"Something must've happened."

My nose prickles with building tears. "No. He told me he didn't want to go, in multiple roundabout ways, maybe even to spare my feelings. But since he never gave me an outright no, I decided he didn't want to dress up and risk a boring evening. It never occurred to me he simply didn't want to spend the evening with me."

I suck in my lower lip. I won't cry. Not again. Not about the bitter disappointment from missing out on seeing some of my favorite performers, not about breaking down in front of Zach, and not about Marshall Jones.

Especially not about him.

"Alexandra, I'm sorry." Fiona strokes my hair. "I know you don't feel this way right now, but you will be fine eventually. Sometimes things don't work out, and it's a good thing everything ended between you before... You two didn't, you know, didn't, right?"

I strain to understand what she means. "You do remember English is my second language? When you speak in riddles, it's even harder."

Fiona lets out an exasperated sigh. "You didn't sleep with him, did you?"

Yikes!

"No." Well, I did, but it wasn't like *that*. "I told you before. We barely had a thing."

"Good. This way you won't have regrets haunting you for the rest of your life."

I don't know about that. Right now I regret everything—agreeing to this madness with Project Viper, coming to the United States, talking to Fiona, and Zach, about Marshall.

"True," I say all the same.

I climb out of bed, pull off the gown, and hang it on a padded hanger in my walk-in closet. Reluctant to face the guys today, I consider returning to bed, but I hate hiding from trouble. I'm not going to now.

"Feeling better?" CJ asks when I join them for breakfast.

"Much." I feel a touch guilty for ruining his evening last night.

Marshall hasn't come down yet. Zach and CJ won't stop talking about the opera. That is, CJ does all the talking while Zach, for once, nods to the outpouring of CJ's words. He took Fiona out to dinner afterward. It looks like I ruined nothing at all.

My heart burns as I listen to him. I should've gone. I should've stuck it to Marshall and celebrated my birthday with or without him.

"I take it you had fun." Marshall enters the kitchen and goes straight for the counter with the food. He grabs a bowl, fills it with high-fiber cereal flakes, blueberries, and almond milk, and sits across from me. He stirs the cereal, runs his fingers through his bed-tousled hair, and stifles a yawn, laid back like nothing's wrong at all.

"Yeah. Fiona and CJ had a pretty good time," Zach says.

I glare at him, and he hurries to add, "Alexandra and I had a great night too."

Shane's head snaps toward me. Cereal drips off his spoon. "A great night?"

"Don't twist his words," I tell Shane and glare at Zach one more time. "And you, don't give him anything to twist."

My admonition has no effect. Zach and Shane chuckle together, as they often do, and carry on victorious.

"Did you like the opera?" Marshall digs through his breakfast with a neutral expression on his face.

I pick up my half-finished bowl of food and take it to the sink before taking off to the rehearsal room.

Breathe. Don't say a word. Don't react.

Too late. Already gave him a cold shoulder.

I chide myself for my reaction, but I've been justifying and excusing Marshall for months now. I've been putting on a patient face. No more. I don't care about the insecurities Marshall supposedly has. He will not trample over my feelings anymore. I have them even if I prefer to hide them.

In the rehearsal room, I grab my P Bass. Cord, plug, crank up the volume. Lightning strikes. Thunder roars. The rattle of the amp reverberates through my sternum and soothes like nothing else can. I grab a steel pick and unleash... I'm not even sure what I'm playing. It's just pouring out of me. Angry, biting, dark. Mournful.

The pick falls out of my fingers, causing me to mess up a few notes, but I continue without it. Releasing emotions through music has always been akin to magic to me.

"Dang." Shane manifests in the doorway as I start winding down.

I whirl around, sending the cord snapping against Graham's bass drum.

"Sorry." I rush to lower the volume on my amp.

Shane comes closer, twirling his phone in his fingers. "You sounded really good."

"No. It's awful. Offbeat and... You weren't recording that, were you?" They always record every hum, every little snippet someone comes up with.

Smiling, Shane stuffs his phone in his shorts pocket, then takes a deep breath and motions for me to do the same.

I nod and breathe. Just in time. The rest of the Vipers file into the room. Marshall comes in last.

"Let's get rolling," he says.

The rehearsal starts out well enough, but soon things come apart at the seams. Even though I'm set on not letting Marshall get to me, his very presence unsettles me. Him keeping his eyes on me isn't helping anything either.

I snap in the middle of the fifth song. "Jones, either stop glaring at me or tell me what I'm doing wrong. Again."

"You're not focused today. If you're so tired after an evening of opera and whatever followed, you should've just told us and slept in."

CJ jumps to my defense. "Alexandra didn't go."

For once, he's entirely, painfully unhelpful.

"You didn't go?" Marshall asks.

I drum my index finger against the top string, filling the room with subdued, rhythmic thumps of low E. "Zach and I decided to do something else."

Marshall rests one hand on the microphone stand. Frustration simmers in his green eyes. "Then what's the problem?"

He is mad at *me*? My disappointment over missing the performance returns, along with a massive wave of indignance. This flammable mix of emotions sets me off. "I am. I know! I'm the problem. Everything I do is wrong. Every single time. I'm sorry, okay? For being such a nuisance. For ruining your perfect life. For being alive!"

The "being alive" part sucks all air out of my lungs. The room disappears, engulfed in ethereal flames. I jam the heels of my palms into my eyes, whispering to myself, "It's not real. It's not real. I've never seen it. I'm okay, I'm okay, I'm okay. *Vsyo horosho.*"

The Vipers stare at me through the veil of super-charged silence. Speechless Marshall, wide-eyed Shane, nail-biting Zach, frowning Graham, and gaping CJ. Adding a brokenhearted, mental Alexandra to them doesn't work. Who thought it was a good idea to drop a grieving nineteen-year-old girl in the middle of five confident, strong young men?

Why did *I* think it was a good idea? It could never work.

I slide my hand across the top edge of my red bass, this symbol of how I can do anything. Can I? No. No, I can't. I can try anything, but I can't necessarily do it. I should just give up now, before I hurt myself more.

I look up at CJ.

He gives me a tentative smile and reaches for me. I fling the bass strap over my shoulder and stick the instrument into his hand. The weight of it sends his arm to the floor, and CJ barely manages to save the bass from thudding against the fancy wood planks.

"Alexandra!" he cries out in surprise.

I run out of the room.

One or the Other

Marshall

Zach launches toward the door. I follow him. I pushed Alexandra too far this time. Shane hauls us both back by our shirt collars. Him and his bench-press-powered strength.

"Give her some space to cool down," he says. "She'll claw your faces off if you go after her right now."

I exhale and rub the back of my neck. Zach drops to the floor, legs crossed, and rests his elbows on his knees.

"Zach, play something," CJ says as he secures Alexandra's bass on its stand. Playing classical piano pieces is something Zach does when tempers flare. While he plays, everyone has to shut up and listen.

Zach leans back on his hands. "Nope. I wanna see Marsh try to dig himself out of this one."

The temperature in the room drops below zero. All eyes are on me, of course. Okay, here we go then. I knew my idea with Zach would backfire, so I'm ready to face the consequences.

"What was all that?" CJ strikes first.

I'm ready, but it doesn't mean I'll make it easy for them.

"What was what?"

"Why are you always so mean to her?"

"Why are you so nice?"

"You and CJ are morons," Graham interrupts from behind his drum kit.

I gape at this veritable speech coming from a friend who is the opposite of outspoken.

"What did I do?" CJ exclaims.

"Seriously?" Graham crosses his arms on his chest. "You hug her, hold her, do everything with her. And Marshall's jealous like death but will never admit it. Just like he won't notice that while Alexandra practically hangs on you, because you probably remind her of a good friend or family member she left behind in Russia, she still orbits around him. Always watching him, always trying just a little harder to win his approval."

"But that's all there is," I protest. "And she does love CJ."

"No, she doesn't," Zach adds like he knows anything.

"She does! Always going on about CJ this, CJ that." I turn to my best friend. "You know what she was worried about the most when you slashed your face on that dumb worktable? That you wouldn't like her anymore. When did she ever care if I like her?"

"From the beginning, you dimwit!" CJ snaps.

"I won't deny she's after my approval, but that is it. It. It's not like I care either way."

The stupid lies I spew? I can't believe it. They won't either.

"Why did you kiss her then?" Graham asks.

I freeze on the spot. Did he see us? When and where? Did anyone else?

"Graham, you're full of crap," Zach says. "If he'd kissed her, he would've denied it a thousand times already. But look at him. Marshall, don't make that face. Alexandra's hot. I'd totally kiss her."

And I'd totally punch him in the mug for it, but my jealousy is not helping anything right now.

"You've all gone off the rails," CJ gives me the worst kind of a desperate look. "Alexandra doesn't love me."

Graham uses the bass drum to bring our attention back to him. "Listen you two, I don't care who gets the girl, just figure it out fast. One or the other. Take turns if you want to. It's a free country and a liberal generation. We've got work to do, and The Label has a decision to make. If our festival performance is in any way less than perfect, she's out no matter what we say. Or is that still your goal?" He stabs me with a downright evil eye, and I have no doubt he'll destroy me if I get the band in trouble. Or Alexandra.

A Glimmer of Hope

Alexandra

I run to the guest house and stumble in the middle of the stone path when I realize that if I don't belong with the Vipers, I don't belong in the guest house. Twirling around on the spot, panic rising, I try and fail to decide what to do. Where do I go? Who do I talk to?

My phone buzzes in my back pocket. I yank it out, see Connor's ID, and tap the decline button. As usual, his timing is the worst.

Connor calls again.

The phone buzzes in my hand as I stare at the answer button. Things are out of control. I might as well just tell him that the experiment with Project Viper is a complete and utter failure and that he should ship me back to Russia as soon as he can.

I settle on one of the large, flat path rocks in the lawn. It's cold and wet from the recent rain. The moisture seeps right through my jeans, sending a shiver through my whole body.

I can't go back. What do I have to go back to other than despair?

"Hi, Connor."

"Busy or tired? You sound a little flat."

"We just finished a rehearsal." A seriously botched one.

Connor chuckles. "The guys are being difficult? Well, I hear from Keira that you're doing great."

"I'm glad she thinks so." I slump backward into the wet grass. A patch of blue sky clears up above me, and a few raindrops hit my forehead. That's Portland for you. Same as my life—the moment I get a glimmer of hope, something spits in my face.

"You think you'll be ready for the festival?" Connor asks.

I wipe my forehead with my sleeve. "Probably."

"You'll be fine. And I'll make sure to come and see you then. I'm sorry I've been so busy and haven't taken any time to visit you."

"It's okay."

"Call me if you need anything. I mean it."

"Of course."

He hangs up. My back is wet, my neck is freezing, and the piece of the blue sky is growing smaller with each breath. I stand up. Hope may be a luxury I'm quickly running out of, but I still have some. And while I have a crumb of hope that I will convince the Vipers to keep me, I have to fight. I have to be able to say that I've done my absolute best until the very end.

► Track 33
Tomorrow as Usual

Marshall

I find Alexandra later in the Nest's family room. She's snuggled in an enormous bean bag chair next to the couch, under a fluffy blanket, with a bowl of popcorn, watching *Nacho Libre* with Shane and Zach, who sit on the floor in front of her. My imagination immediately likens them to two loyal hounds at the feet of their goddess.

"Either stop hovering and sit down or go away," Shane grumbles at me.

I pick the end of the couch near Alexandra. She doesn't say anything or look at me, just munches on the popcorn. I want to scoop her up and place her on my lap and cuddle with her under that blanket, but as much as my heart urges my hands into insanity, I'll stick to cutting things off between us before I hurt anyone. I don't believe Alexandra's messing around with me and CJ on purpose. I know she loves him. Or she was falling in love with him, and I mucked it up.

Zach turns to us and mouths something to Alexandra. She frowns and shakes her head. He drills her with an impatient look. She frowns harder and shakes her head again. Three slow, resolute movements—no, no, no. What does he want her to do?

Alexandra steals a sideways glance at me, then brings two fingers to her eyes and points at Zach. She's watching him. What has he done to be in trouble with her?

Eyebrow raised, Zach does the same two-finger gesture at his eyes, then points at her, then raises two fingers. He's watching her too.

Alexandra rolls her eyes.

Zach's hands form a heart that he presses to his chest, all accompanied by a cutesy tilt of his head and an adoring smile. In response, she glares and taps her ear. Zach covers his own and quickly turns away.

As amusing as it has been to watch, what the heck?

I scoop some popcorn out of an enormous bowl on the coffee table into one of the smaller ones. The crispy, salty snack helps me mull over what I can say to Alexandra that wouldn't hurt her feelings but get the message across. I'll be a villain either way though. That grave has been dug. Time to lay down and die. I'll try a text first.

> I honestly thought you'd enjoy going to the opera with Zach more than you'd enjoy going with me.

Alexandra's phone sits on the edge of the bean bag chair. When the message is delivered and the device buzzes, the vibration sends it toppling to the floor. Alexandra ignores the whole thing. I pick up her phone and hold it out to her. She continues refusing to look at me or take her phone.

"Please." I speak softly so that Zach and Shane wouldn't hear me over the movie.

Maybe too softly because it seems like she can't hear me either.

I reach and place the device in her hand, and my fingertips graze her skin.

Alexandra tenses and squeezes the phone. Lips pursed, she swipes her thumb across the screen, reads my message, then types the response.

```
Matryoshka: Noted.
```

It's enough for me. She's opened the gate for a conversation, however mad at me she is.

```
          I should've been more direct. I
               should've said I wouldn't go.
```

```
Matryoshka: That would've been nice.
```

I had all these responses and excuses, but they have all evaporated. I type without thinking.

```
          I shouldn't have kissed you. We
          can't be in a relationship. Look
          what happens to the band when we
          argue. The guys don't deserve the
          uncertainty that would come with us
                          being a package.
```

That's the best I can do right now. Please, heaven and earth, let it work.

```
Matryoshka: I understand.
```

I check her expression.

She smiles at me. "Practice tomorrow as usual?"

That smile slices my heart in two, then three, then four, until I'm pulverized. It doesn't reach her eyes at all. She's putting on a brave face, but I know without a shadow of a doubt that I've hurt her badly. She has the right to be mad at me and let the whole world know about it. Instead, she says that we can continue making music. CJ or not, I don't deserve her.

"Tomorrow as usual," I say and head out of the room.

Zach watches me with pursed, disapproving lips, Shane gives me another glare, and a strong suspicion settles over me that the next time I pull something stupid, I may be the one who gets tossed out of the band.

The Only Thing That Matters

Marshall

It's early March, and the Tangs are in town on business, so they stop by for lunch and to check on the property.

"The whole gang is here." Seo-yun greets us each with a kiss on the cheek then looks around. "Wait, where is the princess?"

CJ explains, "Alexandra's with Kiera. Whatever they're doing, she'll be gone all day, apparently."

We were not informed of their activities. Kiera dropped by in her shiny black Tesla and took Alexandra away first thing in the morning.

Seo-yun props her fists against her hips. "I bet you lot make her life impossible."

"Everyone is really nice to Alexandra." I attempt to defend the band.

Zach's mother sees right through me. "I knew it. It's you who causes her the most grief."

Shane snorts a laugh and goes into the kitchen to help prepare lunch along with Zach, his dad, CJ, and Graham. I try to follow, but Seo-yun holds me by the arm. "You've always been the troublemaker. What did that poor girl do to you?"

I hug her with one arm and try to pull her out of the entryway. "Nothing. I promise." She will never buy it.

"You listen to me, Marshall Jones," Seo-yun says in a tone that bears no arguing. "I raised four children, and then I got the four of you. I've learned a few things in the process. Young people think no one else understands them or sees what's on their minds, but trust me when I say, your feelings toward that sweetie are more obvious than you think. You spent nearly two weeks at my house during the holidays and did nothing you typically enjoy—singing, playing guitar, drinking gallons of that nasty stuff you love so much, pulling pranks on the kids. Nothing's changed with our family. The only thing that was different was Alexandra. From what I've seen, she's wonderful. So what's the problem?"

I don't need any more lectures on the matter, but I don't want to offend Seo-yun either. "There isn't a problem. Alexandra is wonderful, but—"

"But what?"

"But nothing. There's nothing between us."

Seo-yun relinquishes her grip on my arm with a sigh. "You boys think you can do whatever you want. You got the talent, the fame, the money, the looks. What I fail to see in any one of you is brains. None of you can keep a girl, except Shane, of course. When your fame is gone, you're going to be all by yourself, trying to figure out the rest of your lives. You don't think you need family because Project Viper's good enough for now. But family is the only thing that matters. And before you know it, all the good girls will move on to men who want them and who treat them right."

I nod. There's nothing I can say in my defense.

"Marshall, you worry me the most. You burn the brightest. You've got the most to lose, yet you don't have an anchor of any kind. Stop being so stubborn. Let Alexandra in."

"CJ claimed her," I mutter and almost curse.

No one's supposed to know I have...that I *had* feelings for Alexandra. Ever. Now Zach's mother won't leave me alone until she's heard the whole story. But Seo-yun is quiet for an uncomfortably long moment before she pats me on the shoulder and finally proceeds inside.

Seo-yun's words keep haunting me days after the Tangs visit. I go for a drive and end up parking on the side of the road, late in the evening, miles away from town. The night is quiet, there isn't anyone to intrude on me, and I can sort through my thoughts.

I don't think I need a family because I never had any?

That's the only thing that matters?

It's not the only thing that matters. There's friendship, loyalty, music, accomplishing hard things. Guitars, cars, trips around the world, fans. All these things make a life complete. Fulfilled. Not lonely.

Who am I kidding? I am so lonely. I hide it well because I can talk to CJ and the others about absolutely everything. They have my back. They know my quirks and accept me all the same, and I'd give my life for them.

But meeting Alexandra shifted something in my soul. All I can think of is the times her eyes glowed with hope and excitement when she looked at me. Or the times her face was shadowed by confusion and struggle. There were too many times like that. She didn't deserve any of my anger. I wish I saw what I was really doing. I wish I could take it all back and lift her up instead of indulging my insecurities.

Alexandra's distanced herself from me. She doesn't interact with me as much anymore, and when she does, I can't read her. I miss her glances that filled me with something foreign, something I've never experienced. Not with any other girl.

I understand what Seo-yun meant. I never had a family in blood, but I can always make my own family.

With Alexandra.

She'll never take me now. There's also CJ.

My phone buzzes—a text from Fiona.

> F Knight: Kiera sent me to deliver some papers to the president's office, and I asked him in an indirect manner as to how they ended up picking Alexandra. He told me to tell you to stop nosing around.

I huff.

> That's great.

> F Knight: Sorry. Maybe after the festival we'll all know more. Maybe.

> Thanks anyway.

I find the email Juliette sent me with that photo of Alexandra and me. I hesitate for a second, my thumb trembling slightly over the image icon. No. I won't open it. What can't be can't be, no matter what everyone else sees.

Too Late

Marshall

A week before the festival, CJ and I come to the rehearsal room together. Alexandra's already there, fidgeting with the knobs on her bass.

"Is something wrong?" CJ takes the bass out of her hands.

Alexandra looks at me, purses her lips, then turns away. "No. I was just trying to memorize the settings for the festival."

CJ lays the bass on top of our huge bass amp. "That's next week. You'll be great. Our fans are gonna love you."

"They're gonna hate me. I'm new and inexperienced and—"

I want to tell her that I'm not worried at all about her performing with us and that I don't mind if she stays, but CJ flashes Alexandra a flirting smile, the high-octane one that has girls swooning left and right, and I hesitate. I've never seen him smile at her like that.

Hmmm. I consider the revelation. Why does he never flirt with Alexandra the way he does with other girls? The answer is simple, of course. She's taking his place, so he needs to show her respect, but what was that just now?

"They have no choice." CJ rubs her shoulders. "They'll love you because I love you."

Alexandra's eyes widen with questions that mirror my own. What does he mean by that love?

Stealing a sideways glance at me, CJ takes another step toward her and kisses her.

I stumble backward. He kisses her here, now, with me in the room? There's no reason why not. He's serious about her. I already knew he was. That's why he didn't try any of his usual tricks on her. He wants more from Alexandra than the fleeting awe he gets from everyone else.

Alexandra slides her hands around his neck and leans into the kiss. My knuckles pop as I ball them into fists.

I wanted this. I wanted CJ to be in a relationship with Alexandra, wanted her to like him back.

I hate this.

And I did this to myself.

I clear my throat. "Don't mind me."

CJ pushes away from Alexandra and stumbles over to his guitar. That's a weird reaction to have after kissing someone you're so into.

"You two are okay?" Alexandra picks up her bass again and starts her warm up routine. "You both look kind of pale. I hope you're not getting sick or anything. There's no time for this now."

"I'm fine," CJ rasps out, looking at me with his jaw clenched hard, his expression shifting between infuriated and guilty, weirder than weird.

Alexandra's right though. We all need to pull it together and focus on the festival. On keeping her with the band.

All Areas

Alexandra

Even though The Label hasn't announced anything solid about my participation in the festival, the world knows.

It's nothing but rumors on social media about a guest performer joining Project Viper, but they're enough to rattle me. I need to learn to deal with this. If by some miracle I manage the festival, I may be staying with the guys for a long time. Things are rocky at the moment, but I'm trying to find a way to stop wreaking havoc on the band. They're still the best chance at a comfortable life I've got. Perceptive Zach, unshakable Graham, dependable Shane, thoroughly confused CJ, and...Marshall.

CJ and Marshall will be the death of me.

I avoid all Vipers outside of rehearsals after CJ kisses me. I still can't believe he'd do that to me. Did he think I wouldn't figure out what he was up to? Kissing me in front of Marshall. He's never tried to get close to me like that before, so the moment that dazzling smile came out, I knew he was up to something.

CJ doesn't want me. Then the only reason he kissed me was to prove some point. That's why I kissed him back. It's been beyond awkward to pretend like his kiss didn't affect me. It did. Foolishly, I hoped for more of a reaction from Marshall, but he said nothing. That part, his indifference, knowing that he doesn't care for me after all? That hurts. Hope dies last, and I've been hoping against all odds that I'd figure him out. It breaks my heart. Almost as much as the festival.

Not the event itself, but its date. Nineteenth of March. It's a bad day. The worst day. The anniversary of my parents' death. I'd very much like to spend the day mourning and crying and trying to convince myself that I need to move on, that I have a life ahead of me, that I will have a family again. But, of course, there's no rescheduling of our performance when everyone in Project Viper is well and the event organizers themselves aren't experiencing any significant problems.

On the morning of the festival, I wake up earlier than usual thanks to Elise texting me image after image of clothes she's bringing for me to wear on stage. We already talked about this, but I guess I wasn't decisive or convincing enough. Meanwhile, I pull on a pair of jeans, my Project Viper T-shirt that I brought with me from Russia, and a blue zip-up hoodie. The T-shirt is old, and the ink is all faded, but it feels appropriate somehow to wear it today. For good luck maybe.

A familiar queasy feeling starts brewing in my stomach, but I grab some headphones and summon all of my strength. No matter how scared I am, I won't let the Vipers down.

Headphones on, I leave the house. I need music, vicious and deafening, to stifle my old grief and new panic and to strengthen my motivation. Approaching the Nest, my feet slow down with every step. What are the guys like on serious gig days? Are they nervous too? Will I add to their stress with my own black mood?

The sun disappears behind a thick mass of clouds, and a chill wind teases several hair strands out of my high ponytail. Music pounds in my ears, setting my heart ablaze, warming my blood despite the cold.

The garage door slides open, startling me. Tapping a set of drumsticks against his thigh, Graham walks out and takes a long look at me before saying, "There's still time to eat breakfast. Zach and Shane are checking the gear one last time."

"I'm fine."

He comes closer. "Nervous?"

I'm uncertain as to why he's talking to me. Graham's never unfriendly. He just doesn't talk much in general.

"Yes." I stuff my hands in my hoodie pockets.

Graham looks up at the darkening sky. "I have horrid stage fright."

I stare at him in shock. "How do you manage to perform?"

He shrugs. "I can only do it because I don't have to be on the front lines. Once I'm behind the drums, they drown out everything else, and the fear melts away."

I can understand that. If only I didn't have to be on the front lines too.

As though sensing my apprehension, Graham says, "You managed to hold your ground with Marshall. What's a few thousand people compared to him?"

His comment coaxes a smile out of me, which fades the moment I remember that Graham hasn't told me yet if I'm good enough to stay with the band. It's so easy to relax in his presence because he's so calm and quiet, which presents a danger of becoming complacent around him.

"What do you think?" I say. There's no time left to mince words or worry about being too blunt. "Can I do this?"

Graham keeps tapping the sticks against his leg. "Do you really care for my opinion?"

"Yes. Why wouldn't I?"

He shakes his head. "I mean, do you really need my approval?"

"Yes! Everyone in the band has to agree to me staying—"

The drumsticks land on the top of my skull. The hit doesn't hurt but definitely causes me to stop talking.

"You give too much power to us and not enough to yourself. Do you want to stay? You said it yourself. Everyone in the band has to agree." He runs his hand over my hair once. "Sorry. And stay. You're a better musician than any of us were, except Zach, when we started this thing."

Four out of five. I could shout from joy and relief, and I would if it were five out of five.

Speaking of which, Marshall appears in the garage, hands full of bags with gear and my bass. He sets it upright in front of me. "Morning."

"Morning." I hold the bass close and take his gaze straight on.

It's been a torture to pretend like I don't care about him anymore. No matter what I do, no matter how many times I remind myself he's nothing but pain, my feelings for him won't go away. If only I could talk to my mama about it.

Thinking of Mama brings a dangerous sting to my eyes.

"Nervous?" Marshall asks.

Is it written on my face? I'd better get a grip before the show starts. Even if my knees quake, even if I want to puke, our listeners can never know that. They're paying for a fun performance, not seeing a green musician faint on stage.

Besides, I've already decided I'm not going to let Project Viper down, so I'm not going to faint. "I'll be fine."

The minibus arrives, towing a small trailer. Kiera emerges from the vehicle and waves at us with a bright smile on her face. When she's next to us, she hugs me. "Think you'll be okay?"

"I'll be fine," I say again and push a little more conviction into my tone.

"Alexandra Dmitrievna," CJ calls out to me with a polite version of my name as he comes out of the house. "You are not going anywhere until you eat."

"Good idea." Kiera pats him on the shoulder when CJ approaches us carrying a bowl and a tall, lidded tumbler with a flexible straw. The bowl contains scrambled eggs, cheese, bell peppers, and ham, and I suspect it's a protein shake in the tumbler.

My stomach protests at the sight of food, but CJ's unbending.

"Don't give me that look. You're eating or staying here. What if you pass out during our block?"

Grabbing the food, I glance at Marshall. Not for support, just out of some odd habit.

He grins. "Better get going."

"Thanks for the encouragement," I grumble and climb into the minibus.

I use up our entire drive to munch and sip through my breakfast. It serves as a nice distraction, actually, until we park in an underground parking structure.

This is it.

My fingers tremble and tingle as I try to undo the seatbelt.

One of the venue employees leads us to the changing rooms. I zombie-shuffle at the tail of the group, right behind Graham, and cling to our conversation and my earlier resolution to not chicken out. It doesn't work. There's little besides my drumming heartbeat that I can feel and think of.

Breathe.

No fear.

I'm going to be fine.

I grab Graham's hand, needing to hold onto something before my feet stop and reverse their direction. Graham squeezes my fingers and continues walking. I'm so grateful for his silent support.

The place smells like dust, dried up beer, sweat, and memories of past events. Kiera's matter-of-fact chatter cuts through my haze here and there, but the rest of the sounds are fuzzy. My hands grow clammy, but I don't dare to release Graham's hand. We take an elevator for a short ride, a level or two. Then we walk down a long, bare concrete hallway and into a similarly decorated room with a rack of hangers, portable mirrors, a dressing screen, and several chairs.

The support team isn't here yet, so we dump our things and grab our badges. Zach snatches a can of ginger ale from a small table stocked with snacks, then we head to oversee our gear setup and for a turn at the soundcheck. CJ carries my bass since officially he's still the Vipers' bassist. He'll participate in the soundcheck, and I get to watch from the sidelines. Thank goodness. He knows my setting preferences, and I don't want to flop while so many other musicians are watching. Not that I want to flop during the real deal performance either, but logic isn't my best friend at the moment.

Hood over my head, I stick to Graham once more as we approach the stage. Air freezes in my lungs and I stop, my eyes failing to take it all in. A different band is already having a go with their sound. Guitars shriek and lights strobe. I might have heard the song before. I hope for a few more seconds of music, but it cuts off abruptly, and the guitarist announces through the mic that he likes the sound.

I've seen plenty of what happens in the background life of a band, but this is different. There's quite the crowd in front of the stage. Fellow musicians chatter, bursts of laughter pop here and there. All of these people know each other. Once again, I'm an intruder, so I stuff my badge inside my hoodie before anyone sees it.

"Hey." Marshall comes back for me. He lowers my hood and fishes out my badge. His fingers linger on the rectangle of plastic for a few long seconds. Then he gives me a soft smile. "Don't fall behind."

I won't. I'll keep pace.

We join the rest of the Vipers in front of the stage, but I inch my way to Kiera, who stands a few steps behind them, texting. The guys wait their turn with their feet set firmly on the ground, arms crossed on their chests. Confident, irresistible, and awesome. Doing my best to be covert, probably unsuccessfully, I keep looking around. Project Viper stands in a bubble of space. Others are whispering around them, throwing a mix of curious and envious looks and paying no attention to me. Good.

While one of the bands leaves the stage and another takes their place, a slender young woman with a short, blonde ponytail and red bangs passes me from behind. "Hey, Viper Beat," she calls out as she heads for Graham.

At lightning speed, he whips around and pulls out his drumsticks from his shorts pocket. Wood clanks as the two exchange a couple of blows like they're fencing. Both laugh then clap their hands in a tight handshake.

"Well, well, well. If it ain't everyone's favorite snakes." Another newcomer appears by my side, a guy who's almost as tall as Zach. Dark hair, blazing orange highlights, black jacket, and guitar case straps hugging both of his shoulders.

Recognition turns on a light bulb in my mind. He's from Acid Churro Dreams, the band that opened for the Vipers when I first saw them live. The girl who sparred with Graham is their drummer.

Another guy joins us and stands right in front of me. ACD's singer. He's a couple of inches taller than me, and that's probably only because he's wearing a bulky beanie. I grin. Good to know I'm not the only dwarf on the local music scene.

"Hi, Kiera. Who is this?" The singer's eyes are on me, a flirty smile making an appearance.

Our manager looks up from her phone. "Oh. This is Alexandra."

"And whose little darling are you?" His eyes roam my body without any shame whatsoever.

"Who are you calling little? Or darling?" Even though what courses through my veins is mostly panic instead of blood at this point, if I don't hold my ground now, from the first encounter, I will never be able to.

The singer's jaw drops.

"Oooh, burn. Good job, Alexandra." Marshall comes to stand with me, our shoulders touching. "She's with us."

She's with us.

A wave of goosebumps rushes down my spine. I cling to my badge.

The singer notices and eyes my lanyard. "She's with Project Viper? In what capacity?"

I squeeze the badge tighter and glance at Kiera. She didn't offer that information when she introduced me. The manager looks at Marshall. So do I. He gives me a one-shoulder shrug, as though saying it's up to me how to respond. But if it is up to me, does it mean I've finally secured five out of five? I doubt it. His response must be telling me to remember my place.

"Wouldn't you like to know?" I mutter.

ACD's singer smiles, unfazed and all the more handsome for it. "You've got some nice temper. I'm Link Hart, by the way. Currently single."

Marshall snorts. "Nice try."

I can't help smiling. "Nice to meet you, Link."

It really is. I've been with the Vipers for a while, but I haven't had the chance to meet any of their friends thanks to all the secrecy that surrounds me.

"Link, let's go!" The girl with the red bangs waves at him.

Link's expression grows a bit more serious. "Good seeing you, guys. It's been a while. Rumors had it you either broke up or were working on something big."

I steal another glance at Kiera, but she's busy with her phone again.

"We're fine," Marshall says. "Good to see you too."

ACD assemble and take a turn at the soundcheck, and I continue absorbing the scene around me, trying and failing to not think about the fact that Marshall stays by my side. CJ sets my bass on the floor and rests his hands on top of it. A ping of longing singes my insides. That's *my* bass.

After ACD say hello, the bubble of space around the Vipers disappears as more and more people come over to fist bump. Kiera finds the venue manager, and we tell him our thanks for having us over. The guy nods in appreciation and gives us yet another copy of today's schedule, a different one than what the audience will have. Ours has every minute written out: who gets on and off when, how the equipment is distributed, which bands are in which green rooms, etc.

The Vipers go on stage. Kiera keeps talking to the manager's team, and I watch Zach negotiate something with one of the techs while another person clips transmitters to our guitar belts. Marshall helps a tech set up his microphones.

I'm left to stand all by myself, surrounded by many people yet alone.

What am I doing here? I've been working hard to fit in, to not let the Vipers down, but do they need me? Looking up at the dark ceiling, I press my hand to my chest and tell my doubts to beat it. They don't listen. They don't have any ears.

Graham does a check of each individual drum, then starts a punchy rhythm. The small crowd rewards him with impressed hoots, and even I, all too familiar with his drumming now, want to cheer for him. CJ, Shane, and Zach take quick turns with their equipment, then pool it together into the intro to *Don't Look Back*. Marshall joins in.

Ice-cold shivers pierce me. I've been listening to Marshall sing for half a year now. But here, hearing his voice carried by massive speakers, I remember the day I first saw him perform. He doesn't really try right now. No need. It's just a check. His voice takes me apart, piece by piece, all the same.

I look at my badge. My photo smiles back at me. It's a good one, back from that photo shoot I had with CJ and Marshall. Underneath is my status.

Alexandra Lermontova

Project Viper

All Areas

Six months I've been with Project Viper. I've signed piles of paperwork that prove I'm part of the band, at least for another couple of weeks, but this? This is the first official verification that the last six months have been real.

I lift my eyes to the stage again. CJ grooves on my P Bass, totally in his element. That bass is where it belongs, not in my hands.

Project Viper is complete. They were before I arrived. I'm in the way. I have been this whole time. And I realize now, way too late, that it's completely unfair of me to ask them to pay the price for my secure future.

I embed my memories with this vision of my Vipers and Marshall's voice. Zach bops his head in rhythm with the beat and plays with the switches on his effects board. Shane and CJ riff off together. I can't quite see Graham from behind the drums, and Marshall's busy making faces at someone in the crowd.

I could leave now and nobody would notice.

Turning around, I yank the badge off my neck and drop it to the floor. Everything blurs in front of me, but it doesn't matter where I go. Out of here, so toward the set of open doors on the side. I'm a coward. Worse. I'm a failure, bailing out at the last moment. I've wasted all of Connor's effort to bring me here. My parents would be so disappointed, but this is the right thing to do. The Vipers deserve to be free.

I pause in the doors and wipe at my eyes with both hands. When I lower them, Marshall stands in front of me.

Frowning, he hangs my dropped badge over my neck. *"Kuda eto ty sobralas'?"*

Where do you think you're going?

I'm so shocked that he's here, that he's noticed me leaving at all, that he spoke in Russian to me, I stand speechless as Graham's question from earlier comes back to me. *Do you want to stay?* I understand it now. I thought he was asking something too obvious, but I believe he wanted me to give myself permission to claim my spot with the guys and allow myself to think that I belong with them.

Marshall's focus shifts to something behind me. I turn around to discover the rest of the band coming our way. I know I almost just left, but can I stay?

Wait. That's wrong. I shouldn't be begging. I've done everything to prove I can work and learn and succeed. I will stay. I'm good enough. But if the guys don't agree, it's their right. I've done my best.

"Did we sound good?" Zach asks when the rest of the Vipers join us.

"Yeah. So, so good." My voice is pinched and heavy with emotion, and Marshall gives me a concerned look.

"Alexandra, darling, I know you're curious, but don't wander off," Kiera scolds me gently.

"I'll make sure she won't again." Marshall takes my hand.

Kiera pats his upper arm. "Good."

I reclaim my hand from Marshall the moment she turns away.

By the time we get back to the green room, Elise, Fiona, Charlie, and Juliette have arrived.

"Alexandra first," Elise declares without any hellos, an enormous roller brush in her hand. "The rest of you grab the garment bags with your names and start changing. You know the drill."

Shane and Zach pull out a dressing screen and split the room in two. I strip off my regular clothes and squeeze into the stage outfit. Fiona and Charlie stuff my feet into a pair of tight boots while Elise starts working on my hair.

"Come on, give me a smile or pull a face." Juliette hovers with her camera like a surveillance drone. Although, it's mean of me to think about her that way. She's only doing her job. I manage a limp smile.

After layers of faux lashes, mascara, eyeshadow, and everything else, Elise douses me with generous clouds of hair spray and ushers me out of the chair. "I need to deal with the guys now, but you look perfect."

Staring at the mirror, I'm struggling to find the perfection she's talking about. The green leather pants may fit me like a glove, and the white leather jacket over a black tank top may add a dash of sass to my appearance, but all I see is a lonely kid who longs for her parents. Despite the confidence that took over me a little while ago, I struggle to find balance between wanting to conquer the world and crumbling apart.

When the girls remove the dressing screen, Zach lets out a low whistle. "Sweet biscuits, Elise! You turned our already perfect *Matryoshka* into a goddess."

My cheeks burn. Fortunately, Elise has no time for his praise. "Get in the chair."

Zach obeys without another word. My attention drifts to Marshall, who stands motionless. Why are his eyes so wide and full of worry?

He gave me my badge back, but he knows I can't do it, that's why. No matter how much I've improved, I'm no bassist. I'm a singer, and I'll ruin them. He always knew it. They should have listened to him, and I'm definitely sliding to the crumbling apart side. The walls are low and tight. Suffocating. I grab my headphones and dash past everyone through the door and into the hallway.

"Alexandra!" Marshall calls after me, but I don't answer.

Outside the dressing room, security patrols the hallway and exchanges brief but excited conversations. Project Viper aren't the only big name performers hired for the day. Everyone's anticipation singes what's left of my nerves. I bolt from the door and round the corner.

Kiera catches up with me and places a hand on my shoulder. "You're a little more than nervous. Did something happen?"

"Today. It's today," I blurt out. The weight of my flaring emotions is threatening to crush me. I need to talk to someone.

"What is today?"

"My parents died a year ago today."

"Oh, sweetie." Kiera pulls me into a tight hug and rubs my back. "I am so sorry."

I swallow a sob. "I'll be fine. I can do it."

"You really can. If they could see you now, they would be so proud of you. You've grown so much in these past six months."

Papa would be the first one to agree with her. He believed that a person could do anything they wanted, even in the darkest of times. Mama just believed in me. I can't prove them wrong. I managed to come this far without them, and I won't undo it all today, no matter what it costs me.

"I can do it," I repeat, and this time, I believe it.

Courage

Marshall

"My job is done." Elise rolls up her tools. She gives Shane a quick kiss, says to Graham, "You got this," and heads for the door. Our team leaves, and Alexandra returns.

Kiera peeks in. "You have fifteen minutes. Do your thing."

She closes the door, and silence takes hold of us.

I breathe in and out and work on relaxing my muscles. Once I'm out of this room, I'll be someone else. I'll be what the crowd demands me to be, putting the real me away for a short while. I love making music, but I love this part too.

CJ, Shane, and Graham do push-ups. Neither CJ nor Shane need any time to put their minds together, but they do their best to distract Graham from freaking out.

Zach sits next to me, his back to the room, arms crossed on his chest, eyes closed. Sometimes he meditates, sometimes he prays. I don't know what it is this time.

When I release a somewhat loud breath, he looks at me, then over his shoulder at pacing Alexandra, then at me again. Zach doesn't say anything, but his eyes are pleading. I suspect he's concerned about the way things are between me and Alexandra and whether I'm still set on getting rid of her.

I squeeze his shoulder. "It'll be great. Don't worry."

Will it? Alexandra tossed her badge and walked away. I was playing with the mic when I realized I couldn't see her near Kiera anymore. In that moment, fear-fueled adrenaline surging through my chest, it felt as if someone had turned my head to show me Alexandra, the back of her hoodie. I saw her approaching the doors, and, cutting off mid-verse, slid down the ramp to the stage and ran after her.

I was sure she wanted to stay, but does she? With the band? Yes. With me? I don't want to even think about the answer to that.

To the rest of the band I say, "Are we ready?"

They nod. Ten minutes until we're expected on the stage. It's almost showtime, baby, but one more thing remains to be done.

We stand in a circle, familiar with the ritual, but Alexandra takes a moment to catch on and join us. She eyes us with a great deal of doubt.

CJ must notice it as well since he explains, "There's this little thing we say every time before we go on stage. It's nothing special. We just go clockwise and name our strengths. Mine is inspiration."

Shane's next. "Freedom." As in freedom to choose his own path.

My turn. "Fearlessness." I've always said this, and usually that is my strength, but today it feels tainted, untrue. I haven't been fearless in the past six months. I've been anything but.

Zach cuts my inner scolding short. "Loyalty."

"Inner strength," Graham says and looks at Alexandra.

She fidgets with the zipper on her jacket. "Um…" Her mouth opens and closes a couple of times, and I know exactly how impossible it feels to have to describe yourself, positively, in one word.

"Courage," I offer.

There's no better term to describe her. She's left her home to meet a bunch of strangers and to accomplish wild things, all while a certain someone made her life impossible. She stayed no matter what.

"That's definitely it," CJ agrees.

Reluctantly, she nods.

The ritual ends with a double clap on the back to the Viper next to us, then we're out the door.

Alexandra pushes her headphones back onto her ears. I walk behind her and watch her gait grow steadier and less tense as she hums. It's only at the edge of the stage that Alexandra surrenders her headphones to a stagehand. She clenches and unclenches her fists, stuffs and unstuffs them into her jacket pockets. Her skin is paler than usual, maybe due to the lighting. I sure hope she won't faint.

When she continues clenching her fingers, I take her hand. "You'll do fine. You practiced, so you got this. Right?"

I hope Alexandra will glare at me and snap back as in, "Right! I got this. Get lost. This band is mine now." She does nothing of the sort. She yanks her hand out of mine and walks on robotic legs onto the stage when the crew gives us the green light.

The crowd roars, and Alexandra jumps and presses a hand to her chest. I remember my first time in front of an ocean of people the likes of which shimmers around the stage. I couldn't believe so many would come to listen to us. I get the jitters even now, but I'm used to it as well. It's hard to describe.

"Ready to make some noise?" I shout through my mic, eliciting a new wave of cheers and squeals. "Good! Let's go!"

I sing, Zach and Graham do their thing, CJ and Shane tear the air on the guitars and stay close to Alexandra as much as they can. CJ throws her encouraging smiles, and whenever she looks at me, which doesn't happen that often, I do the same. Eventually, Alexandra loosens up and starts jiving with her bass, dancing along with her sidekicks. We sound fantastic. Project Viper at its finest, ladies and gentlemen.

During a particularly energetic chorus, I lean into Alexandra's microphone. It's a habit from when CJ had a more active backup part. Alexandra shoots me a concerned look, but, to her credit, continues playing and singing with me.

This is where my heart rips off its chain and curses me to the pits of all misery for being the idiot that I've been. She's got me with those blue eyes. I see her feelings—excitement from the gig (no one can help it once it gets going), apprehension toward me, and pain I'm probably to thank for. All I can do is put all of my love for her into my singing.

Alexandra pulls away the first chance she gets and migrates to CJ's side. I suck in a quick, deep breath for the next line and allow the disappointment to settle in. I deserve it, but I resolve to fight. I'll tell CJ the truth. I'll tell her that I love her. And whatever follows, I'll deal with it one way or another like a grown man even if I'm far from being one.

The festival is a casual affair for a bunch of bands to cheer up the masses in the middle of a dreary spring. Since it's only meant to last one day, our set list is short, so we play six of our old songs, then it's time for *Devastation, Free of Charge*. But first, I get to do some introductions.

"As you can see, we're here tonight with an updated cast." I laugh at my attempt at a joke, and the crowd roars again.

Feeling like I'm stepping on shards of glass, I walk over to Alexandra. She has one hand wrapped around the neck of her bass, silencing the strings, and taps on the red body with the fingers of the other. We never got her an electric short scale bass. I'll fix that as soon as I can.

Back to reality. I smile at our petite but tough bassist. Here goes. "Please give some love to Alexandra Lermontova, the newest Viper."

Zach sputters ginger ale all over his keyboard. The audience goes wild. The Label will kill me for this. The guys will too. Nothing's been settled, no paperwork signed, but Alexandra's become one of us, and I won't let her go.

Alexandra stares at me with absolute terror in her eyes.

I wink at her. "Show them what you got."

She bites her lower lip and plays an upbeat riff, eliciting more cheers and claps. Graham drums along, always knowing how to support. It probably helps that Alexandra leads him into our next song.

I press my fingertip to my earpiece, switching the microphone to a dedicated channel that only the band and the tech crew can hear.

"Alexandra and Graham, loop that intro a few more times. CJ, give me your guitar."

He blinks and touches his earpiece. "What?"

It's my song, and best friend or not, CJ can't have it. Not this time. I brace myself and look him straight in the eye. "I'll sing it."

CJ's face splits into the most intolerable grin. He transfers the equipment to me then performs a similar exchange with Alexandra, who looks increasingly perplexed.

"Sing it out," I tell her. "However you like. It's all yours. I'll do the backup."

Her face takes on a tortured expression. "Why?"

In the background, Shane and CJ have started adding flourishes to the intro. I've picked the worst of times to explain this to her. The venue manager will chew me out later for the delay, but no backing out now.

"I wrote this song for you. We should've just practiced it with you as the lead the whole time."

Alexandra nails me with the angriest look I've ever seen from her. When I give her the lead mic, she rips it out of my hands and kicks me in the foot.

I wait for Graham to drum to the end of the intro and begin with the lead guitar part properly, now a little nervous I'm going to screw it up since I haven't practiced it much—I never planned on playing the guitar parts myself.

Alexandra starts out quiet, her voice haunting and raw. With every line, her volume grows, her emotions spilling out in earnest. At first she doesn't move much, but as the first chorus hits, she sways and dances, and dwarfs me with her vocals. I finally understand, to my shame and awe, that she truly knew what she was talking about that one time she accused me of crummy singing. Her voice flows like a river of fire and consumes everything, and I almost forget to sing my part.

⯈ Track 38
A Galaxy of Glowing Phone Screens

Alexandra

During the bridge, I disintegrate. It's too much—having to perform and hold it together in front of such a large audience when I want to grieve, the overwhelming music, Marshall.

Marshall is the worst of all. He said he wrote that song. For me. He also went as far in pushing me away as to make me believe that CJ was the one to compose it. I don't know anything about him anymore. Worse than that, I still want to. I have to hear what in the universe is going on in his mind.

Still singing, somehow, I fall to one knee and prop my arm against it. The words pour out of me, releasing all of my angst and anger. It feels so good to let it all out. It hurts so bad.

The song wraps up, and I hold the last note for a long, long time, until I run out of breath and my vision darkens. Great. Am I going to pass out after all? If I do, it'll be the end of Project Viper experiment for me. They don't need a fainting weakling.

I force air into my lungs and rise to my feet. An arm encircles my waist—Marshall. CJ stands on my other side, his arm around my shoulders. His desire to do something different has changed my fate. Where would I be now if not for him? He saved my life by giving me this chance, and I will owe him forever, regardless of his recent stunt.

Marshall motions for the crowd to calm down. It takes a little while before he can be heard over the masses.

"Isn't she just amazing? I wish I could sing like that."

His hand is still on my waist, and he's been smiling at me the whole time we've been on stage. Of course he'd do that. It's a part of the performance. But he's sung that song with me...

The crowd goes wild again, and I'm blinded by the camera flashes next to the stage. Marshall delivers a flourished bow and signs something to Graham. That's right. We still have one more song left to sing, and they taught me all the stage gestures, but in my foggy state I can't remember what they mean.

CJ offers me my bass back. Hands trembling, I take it and find comfort in the familiar weight. He taps me on the nose with his fingertip and mouths, "You got this."

Graham launches into a barraging beat, and my mouth drops. He leads us into the intro to *All Your Broken Promises*. It wasn't on the set list. Judging by a quick exchange of looks between the rest of the Vipers, they're just as surprised as I am. I swing to face Graham, nearly tripping over a cord. He machine guns through the beat and flashes me a smile so quick I almost think I've imagined it.

This song is not for the crowd. It is for me—a Viper and a fan at once.

I tap my earpiece and squeak out, "Thank you, Graham!"

He smiles wider and nods with his chin, reminding me to play. The others can't start until the bass goes.

I whip back toward the audience.

Zach's fingers hover over the keyboard. Shane and CJ have parked themselves next to one of the amplifiers. Each has one foot resting on the rugged casing, picks hovering over the strings, ready to strike. Marshall taps out the drumbeat with his hand on his thigh. Black jeans, gray T-shirt, a white leather jacket that matches mine. When our eyes meet, he smiles and gestures with both hands for me to join him.

I give Graham a few more beats to make it an even number of measures before I jump in. *One, two, three, four.* Meanwhile, the performer part of me relinquishes control to the fangirl.

A host of blazing stage lights.

An ocean of people.

A galaxy of glowing phone screens.

My favorite song. My favorite band.

And in the center of it?

Me.

One, two, three, four.

I grab a new pick from the bass strap and lift it high.

One, two, three, four.

On the next *one*, I join Graham with a steady triplet pattern of crunchy, distorted, low Gs. Zach cues in the effects, then the guitars weave in their cunning, playful patterns. Fog floods the stage and swirls around our ankles, rising up to our knees.

Marshall sings as only Marshall can—dancing across the stage, breathing into the mic, throwing smolders left and right. He stretches on the floor until the fog engulfs him and spends the whole second verse concealed from everyone's eyes, then sits up slowly, as if rising from the dead, wisps of fog slithering down and all around him. It's a stunning visual trick, very clever. For a moment, I worry that the mosh pit girls are going to have to be airlifted to the nearest hospital en masse because they scream so hard.

I get a dramatic pause of my own when the bass drops out for a few words in the chorus, allowing me an opportunity to slide to Marshall's side and send a wave of fog at him. He twirls the mic in his fingers once before bringing it to my face, his green eyes crumbling what's left of my heart as we finish the last four lines together.

I have a vague but grateful thought along the lines of how lucky I am that the last measures on the bass are simple. I play on autopilot, then lose all control of reality when Marshall brushes his fingertips across my cheek. My knees grow weak while the front-row fans shriek at ear-splitting frequencies. Marshall grins. His touch. Was it meant to be only a part of our performance too? I don't want to know. I'll take it and keep it in the deepest corners of my soul, whatever it means.

Marshall lowers the mic. Eyes still on each other, we breathe hard. My last note, deep and long, fuses whatever's happening between us. I can't stop smiling, overflowing with adrenaline and sizzling elation. Neither can Marshall.

The rest of the guys surround us, bowing to our guests and hugging me, ruffling my hair, and doing high fives.

On jittery legs fueled solely by the remnants of the emotions buzzing through me, I leave the stage. Kiera and the girls exclaim something about our performance. I'm dying to go home, but we stay for the rest of the festival to listen to the other bands, sign people's arms, shirts, posters, and pose for what seems like a million photos. It's after we finally get to the dark and cool parking garage that I breathe out.

"We have to celebrate." CJ picks me up and gives me a whirl through the air. "You nailed it. Nailed it!"

"I can't believe it." Laughing, I hug him.

"Better believe it, *Matryoshka*." Marshall chuckles.

He hasn't used that nickname since the day he gave it to me. The other Vipers use it as an endearment, and Marshall did say I'm part of the band now...

Thinking about it all sends my heart into a fluttering fit. Cut it out, you stupid, love-stricken muscle. Stop betraying me. Just because Marshall and I clicked on stage, doesn't mean we're good in real life.

I untangle myself from CJ. The sooner we get home, the better. I need time to sleep and reset and not be around Marshall. He's too confusing. My heart takes his attention as hopeful signs, and I need to put an end to that. Trusting him has burned me more than once.

But... I managed it. I allow the thought to circulate through my mind. I didn't butcher any songs. I engaged with the band. I even did a reasonable job of the song CJ—wait, Marshall—wrote for me.

While the band loads into the minibus, I pace and nurse a bottle of water Kiera procured for me earlier. Marshall waits for me with one foot on the steps to the minibus, quiet energy in black jeans and a maroon knitted sweater.

"I meant it back on stage," he says. "You were fantastic."

He sounds so soft, almost proud. What do I say to that other than maybe thanks?

Tension drains from me, and I realize that despite tonight's success and my dreams coming true, I'm not done crying for the day. Now I'm looking forward to my bed more than ever. A couple of pillows to drench with my tears and to squeal with excitement into, then a good night's sleep.

⏵ Track 39
Tell Me Something I Don't Already Know

Marshall

"We have to re-record the song," Shane declares as the minibus drives us through the dark neighborhoods of Portland.

Kiera, who rides back to the Nest with us, and Zach lean from the front seats to watch him swipe through his phone. Alexandra sits with me in the back, but she's subdued, sipping water without commenting.

Shane manages to find a video of our new song on the Tube. Already. "You've got pipes, girl. Why were you hiding it before?"

I want to know that too.

"She hid it because she knew Marshall would be jealous and toss her out." Zach guffaws.

I throw a handful of spicy Cheetos at him from a package I started earlier even though I know not a single one of the tiny orange spears will hit him. "I totally would've gotten jealous, but I don't think I can toss her out. You all like her too much. *I* like her too much." I look at Alexandra, my heart grinding to a halt.

There, I admitted for all to hear that I like her.

Alexandra doesn't seem to hear me. Or if she does, she ignores me. She brings her feet onto the seat and buries her face in her knees. I gently touch her arm near the elbow. "Alexandra?"

She bounds toward the front of the bus. "Pull over. I'm feeling sick."

I guess the festival was a little too much. It happens. Big concerts can definitely be exhausting.

The minibus comes to an abrupt stop. Alexandra leaps out the doors and runs to the back. I follow her, but Kiera puts out her arm to block me. "Let her be. She just needs to cry by herself."

"Cry? Why?" My eyes are glued to Alexandra's silhouette outlined by the red glow of the back lights.

"Today's not the best day for a show. It's the first anniversary of her parents' death."

I feel like I got clunked in the head by a guitar. Shane did that to me multiple times throughout the years.

"Her parents' what now?" CJ jumps in while my brain fails to relay words to my mouth.

"You forgot? It's been a year since her parents died. Awful deaths. Burned in a fire." Kiera's mouth drops. "Wait. She didn't tell you?"

I wish to die on the spot. Her comment on how I should know what it's like to be an outsider, all her clinging to my bandmates, that agony I couldn't understand during her performance... I should've understood.

Instead, I made it impossible for her to trust me, and the rest of the guys as well. The grief she must've been dealing with, all by herself, in a foreign country, away from everything familiar. The painful memories today, doubled with the anxiety brought on by her first show with us. How unbearable it must've been to have to go through that and do her best regardless of her feelings.

I should've been her foremost champion and protector, someone always to rely on, like CJ. I still can be. I will be if she'll give me another chance. If I'm willing to put my friendship with CJ on the line.

I face my best friend. "You're gonna hate me."

He frowns. "I am?"

"I love her."

I love her enough to throw years of friendship away.

Well, not exactly. I simply don't think I can survive the longing anymore. I need Alexandra to know how I feel, and if she hates me, permanently, I need to know that too. Otherwise I'll be stuck in this nightmare forever.

CJ relaxes in his seat. "Tell me something I don't already know." He's mocking me, but he's not mad or threatening.

The rest of the people in the minibus stare at us in confusion. Whatever. It's not about them. This is about…

I was wrong about everything. So, so wrong.

"I'm going to tell her," I continue with CJ.

"Go for it," he says with an encouraging wave of a hand.

"Please, do." Zach pushes me to the steps. "Make this madness end."

I hop out. Alexandra stands at the tail end of the vehicle, leaning with her hand on the side and clutching her chest with the other. I close the short distance between us, wrap my arms around her, and hold her tight. "Don't cry alone," I whisper in her ear.

She shoves me away with all she's got. "I'm not crying!"

Alexandra's angry, but she really isn't crying. It seems Kiera has misinterpreted the signs. That's good—we know the truth now, but I wouldn't have tried touching Alexandra just yet if I had an accurate estimate of her mood.

We stand quiet for a few seconds, then Alexandra leans her back on the minibus. "What?"

"Are you okay?" Well, that's just brilliant. Considerate, yes, but dumb, and I'm playing it safe.

"I was until you showed up."

That is such a loaded response. "Just now or in general?" I'm crossing some dangerous lines without proper backup.

"Both," Alexandra groans, exasperated. "What am I going to do with you? Today you want me, tomorrow I'm nothing. You know what? I'm done with you. Done."

She walks along the side of the road and leaves the bus behind.

I follow her as fear, cold and acidic, spikes my blood, and blurt out, "Even if I say I love you?"

Still walking, Alexandra laughs. "You? Love me? Please! How could you love me? You've done your best to make my life a living nightmare. And you've made it abundantly clear that you have no interest in me. You let your best friend kiss me like it was nothing. *On lyubit menya.*"

He loves me.

"I do love you!" I dash to bar her way. "Please. I'm guilty of all the things you've listed, but I need to explain. *Pozhaluista.*"

Alexandra sighs and looks up at the dark sky. "Will it change anything?"

I can't say because I don't know, but I really, really hope so. I have to try to make things right between us.

She waves for me to continue, although the skeptical line of her pursed lips hints abundantly at her doubts and impatience.

"A lot of things I'm going to say will sound like I'm blaming everything on you, but I want you to know that I don't think any of it is your fault. It's been me the whole time. Completely irrational and idiotic and...and...afraid."

Unease simmers in Alexandra's eyes. She's far from convinced.

"I admit, I really disliked you at first. I was worried you'd ruin us. Later, even when I knew you could hold your own with the bass, I still resisted accepting that you belong with us. I just wanted everything the way it was. Project Viper was already perfect for me. I only agreed to try a new bassist because I thought we'd get some ugly dude, not a mind-blowing, strong-willed girl. But you? You are unbelievable. Fearless, kind, beautiful. And you scolded me for being a bully. Then Halloween changed everything."

"Changed everything how? You refused to acknowledge it ever happened."

I take a risk and wrap a lock of her hair around my index finger. I realize I can't stop myself from playing with her hair any time I get a chance. "I fell for you then."

Alexandra scoffs. "You fell in love with me, so you let your best friend kiss me."

"Let him? I didn't know he was going to do that. And if I did, what did you expect me to do? Tie him up and drop him in the desert somewhere?" I explode even though I'm on the apologizing end of things. "You and CJ are always so close, it's impossible to not assume that the two of you have something going on. He hugs you, tells you he loves you, kisses you, and you reciprocate."

Alexandra releases a deep sigh. "You thought I'm in love with CJ after all."

"Are you?" Give me a straight answer. Please.

She tilts her head and narrows her eyes. "No. Thank you for finally asking. He's like a brother I never had. That's all."

"I know the feeling," I say.

The minibus headlights shine on us. Alexandra hides her hands in her hoodie pockets and kicks at the gravel underneath our feet. The low rumble of the idling engine distracts me from figuring out how to breach this round of silence.

"I'm not asking you to forgive me, but I'll say it anyway. I'm sorry, Alexandra. I never meant to be so…absurd. I never meant to hurt you."

She will never forgive me. I might never forgive myself either.

I could've been happy. *We could've been happy.*

The silence suffocates me.

Alexandra sighs. "I wish you had just talked to me. So much nonsense could've been avoided. Don't ever do anything like this again. I won't forgive you next time. I'm not entirely sure I can this time."

Her words float through my ears like fairy dust.

Next time.

Alexandra's still mad at me, but she gives me hope. I scoop her into my arms and kiss her, fully ready for a smacking. Alexandra gasps and digs her fingers into my shoulders but doesn't try to move away. I kiss her cheeks, her eyes, her nose, her chin. Her hands find their way to my neck and urge me closer, returning every kiss with desperation that matches mine.

"*Nu ty i durak,*" she says with a giggle.

You're such a fool.

Lightheaded with euphoria, I smile back. "Fair enough. But stop clinging to CJ. Or Zach. Or anyone. You have me."

Alexandra raises a challenging eyebrow. "I'll do whatever I want, Marshall Jones. You'd better remember that. And I love you, not CJ. You'd better remember that as well."

I kiss her again and again, until we both can't breathe, then some more. She claims me, and I surrender without a moment's thought. Alexandra's lips eradicate all thoughts other than I'm happy to rip my heart out of its cushy protective envelope. It's the scariest thing I've done in years, but for her, I'm not afraid of anything, even changing.

"I love you," I say through the kisses, never moving my lips away from hers. "Love you, love you, love—"

"Okay, okay!" Zach hollers through the minibus door. "Can we get going again? Please?"

Connor Eaton

Alexandra

Marshall intertwines his arm with mine and pulls me toward the bus.

"Wait." I hold him back. "What about… How are we…"

He chuckles. "Let them get it out of their systems tonight with the I-knew-its and I-told-you-sos and finallys."

Already embarrassed, I want to run for my life, and going back into the minibus isn't going to make anything better. "You're right. Let's just get it over with."

To their credit, the guys deliver only a minimal amount of cheers and snickers.

When we're back in our seats, much closer to each other this time, CJ turns toward me. "I only kissed you to prove to Marshall that you had no feelings for me. You kissed me back. Why?"

Both CJ and Marshall watch me with entertained expressions, and I itch to punch them for it. "Next time don't go kissing a girl who, as you already know, doesn't actually like you."

CJ's mouth drops. "You owe me an apology, *Matryoshka*."

"I owe you an apology? You've lost your mind!"

"Go away." Marshall pushes CJ back into his seat, hugs my arm, and whispers in my ear, "Why did you kiss him?"

Nibbling on my all too pleasantly swollen lip, I take a second to absorb my new reality. I'm staying with the Vipers. And Marshall finally explained himself, somewhat. He loves me.

It's a challenge to process everything that's happened, and my paranoia gets the best of me. What if I'm dreaming somehow?

Marshall trails a few kisses up my jaw and over my ear, sending shivers across my skin. "Why did you kiss CJ?"

"To spite you two, of course."

"I knew it!" CJ exclaims from his seat.

Marshall pulls me into a hug. "We have so much to talk about. Your parents, for starters."

I jerk to face him and bump our foreheads. "What about my parents?"

Marshall rubs his face. "Kiera told us."

My chest constricts with panic. Oh no. No, no, no. "What did she say?"

"That they died a year ago. In a fire." Marshall squeezes me tight and kisses me on the temple. "She didn't give us any other details."

At least she didn't tell them about Connor, it seems. I breathe in and out and relax my shoulders. Marshall and I definitely have a lot to talk about when we get home.

Back at the Nest, everyone assembles in the living room.

"I think it's time to explain some things," CJ says to me. "I can't believe you withheld the truth about your family for so long. And I definitely don't understand why."

"You're one to talk," Charlie grumbles. "Do you go around telling people about your darkest, deepest fears and secrets? It's not as if we know anything about your family. So quit it. Alexandra doesn't owe anyone here her whole life story."

CJ's mouth drops. "Now, wait a minute—"

"It's okay," I say. Sitting on the ottoman while the others occupy the large sectional, I feel like a kindergartener stuck between two squabbling adults. The prospect of discussing my family threatens to turn me inside out, but I don't see a way out of this. Not when five of my favorite people sit with faces that reflect various degrees of curiosity, confusion, and hints of hurt. "I will explain."

"How about you start with why today was difficult?" Kiera suggests.

I swallow a lump in my throat.

No fear.

They won't shred me to pieces or judge. The only one who has ever judged me is Marshall, and he's already atoning for that.

I fidget with my fingers to hide that my hands are shaking. "I told you a while ago. My parents owned a smallish convenience store back in Saint Petersburg. The store was getting old and unpleasant, and they needed a loan to help with the remodeling, but all the regular banks turned them down. So, my dad borrowed from one of the local criminal leaders." I pause to steady my voice. I can do this. "Then he had trouble paying it back. He made regular payments, but they were lower than what was agreed upon, and the lender got impatient. To get his point across, they set the shop on fire. As a warning. That's what the actual culprit said in court later. To warn my parents to pay faster or else, you know? As though that made any sense. How were they supposed to pay faster if they had to borrow even more money to fix things after the fire?"

Tears start streaming down my face, and I choose to leave my pain exposed. I'm so worn out from keeping this a secret. I continue,

"My parents were inside the shop, and the man who set the place on fire knew that. He said it was a small fire and they shouldn't have had any problem getting out. But that's not how it went. There are so many flammable things in shops like these. All the merchandise, the wallpaper, the floors, the ceiling tiles. Trying to save their livelihood, my parents lost their lives when the fire got too big and cut them off from the exits. Anti-burglary bars on the windows certainly didn't help."

"Why not tell us?" Shane asks. "We kept asking you about your family, your friends. You must've felt completely alone and sad and…"

I refrained from looking at anyone during my *story*, but now I'm curious to see Marshall's reaction. He sits right in front of me, and it's easy but also so hard to look at him, at his bouncing knee and solemn frown. "I didn't want your pity."

"That is the stupidest thing I've ever heard," Graham says, creating a flurry of shocked gasps from the girls. "You knew our backgrounds. You should have known we'd understand your pain better than anyone else."

"That's exactly why I kept it to myself," I mutter, feeling more and more foolish by the second. Connor only forbade me to mention him around the Vipers and their team. He never told me to be quiet about my family. That was my own choice. "I grew up in a happy family. What right do I have to ask for anyone to feel sorry for me? Bad things happen to every—"

Marshall rises from his seat, grabs my hand, and pulls me onto his lap. "Graham's right. That is the dumbest thing I've ever heard. But really, it doesn't matter why you didn't tell us. Trust is hard, and showing your soul to strangers is even harder."

"I'm sorry." I press my nose against his neck and inhale his scent. Complicated. Remnants of body wash, smells from the festival venue, and sweat. All Marshall. All mine.

For now, though, no matter how much I'm dying to get some time alone with him, I need to say one more thing to everyone.

I slide from Marshall's lap and stand in the center of the room.

"Let's try this again. I'm Alexandra. I'm twenty, an only child, have no living grandparents, uncles, or aunts, and my parents are also gone. Because of the way they died, I'm nervous around fire even though I didn't actually witness their deaths. And until a few weeks before I came to the United States, I'd never held a bass of any kind in my life. I play a bit of guitar and love singing the most. Nice to meet you."

Zach laughs, Charlie smacks him in the head with a cushion, and the two of them engage in a round of verbal sparring. Smiling, CJ shakes his head. Graham heads for the fridge and starts tossing popsicles out of the freezer onto the marble island, at which point Shane joins him. So do I. With a mouthful of frozen strawberry juice, I search for Marshall, but he's already by my side.

"Nice to meet you too," he says with an easy smile. "And when did you turn twenty? When Kiera first brought you here, you were nineteen."

I groan on the inside. Can we not talk about this on top of everything else tonight?

The doorbell rings. Yes! I'm saved.

Zach checks our security app and scrunches up his nose. "Crap." He runs down the hallway, toward the main door. We all crane our necks and try to figure out what's going on.

Connor walks into the living room. Zach follows in his shadow, his face nothing but nerves. The girls quickly retreat back to the sectional and sit close together, out of everyone's way.

I swallow hard. Can today get any more insane? What is Connor doing here?

"Excellent," he says. "Everyone is here."

"Evening, Mr. President. To what do we owe the honor?" Shane asks. Judging by his lighthearted tone, he is joking, but I stare at Connor with my mouth open.

"President?" I ask. "Of what?"

Hands in the pockets of his gray slacks, Connor smiles. "The Label, of course. How did you think I had all those sweet connections?"

"You're The Label's president?" My tone comes off accusing, but I will not apologize for that. "You told me you had some good friends in high places!"

"And you told us you didn't know the president." Graham crosses his arms on his chest, one eyebrow raised.

I open my mouth to argue, come up with no comeback, try again, and end up saying, "I didn't know he was the president."

Connor nods. "I never told Alexandra what I did for a living. Not that it matters right now. Ladies, could you please give us the room for a bit?"

Elise pushes the rest of our support team to the door. "We'll see you later."

The girls say goodbye and leave. Kiera stays. Makes sense. She's the manager. Whatever Connor has to say, she might need to know it too.

▶ Track 41
Try to Take It Slow

Marshall

We sit around our dining table, Connor at the head, and wait for him to start. Connor takes his sweet time, taking turns to look at each one of us. Just like CJ, he likes to use silence as his weapon, to intimidate in this case.

"I assume I don't have to explain why I'm here?" he says at last.

Since I don't want to prolong this awkward meeting any longer than absolutely necessary, I say, "Because I announced Alexandra joining Project Viper without anyone's approval?"

"Does the band approve of her then?" Connor takes another look around the table. It's obvious he's invested in her success, and now I'm itching to find out why.

"We do approve," CJ says. "She's been great."

"Agreed," Zach adds.

The O'Neals nod.

"Are we signing a long-term contract then?" Connor addresses Alexandra.

She looks at me. I give her an encouraging smile.

"I'd like to stay," Alexandra says to Connor.

"Good. Then I need to see you all at the office on Monday. You too, of course." He points at Kiera. "There's a pile of paperwork to sign, lawyers to talk to. You know how it is."

Half of my friends slump against the backs of their chairs, the other half rests their upper bodies on the table. I remain sitting straight. This isn't over yet.

Alexandra squeezes my hand.

Connor squints at me and says, "Come with me."

We end up in our office.

"How do you know Alexandra?" I ask before he can say anything.

"Her dad was a good friend of mine. I'm sure she'll tell you all about it. But you and her?"

"I'll take good care of her," I promise.

"Does she want you to take care of her?" He sits on the edge of the computer desk, and his gaze turns to ice. "Don't think I haven't heard of your pigheaded attitude. And before you ask, no. I didn't hear about it from Alexandra. She never said anything. Whenever I called, she always sounded like everything was great."

"Then how?"

"I have my sources."

And I have my suspicions. Fiona. But I choose to drop the issue. I was no angel, and it won't help anything if I get defensive.

"It's different now," I say.

I wouldn't have believed six months ago that I'd fall for Alexandra with such hopelessness, but she changed the way I think about my life, about her, about Project Viper. And I love every single bit of it. I love this change. Something's wrong with me.

No. Everything's just right. Perfect, in fact.

"I saw you on stage with Alexandra." Connor brings his foot to rest on his knee. "You're in a tricky situation. Project Viper's future will largely depend on you and your ability to keep things in check with her. If the two of you have a major falling out, it's not going to end well for the band, so don't jump into a relationship with her blindly. You're mad about her today, but what about tomorrow? What about a year from today?"

"It'll be fine."

"Are you sure?"

We stare at each other. I know Connor doubts me, but I'm all in when it comes to Alexandra. He has nothing to worry about.

"One thing at a time, I suppose," he says in the end. "Just try to take it slow."

Slow? With Alexandra? I don't think either of us is capable of that.

"Of course," I say all the same, because what other choice do I have?

He leaves.

Kiera peeks into the office. "So, you like Alexandra now?"

I chuckle. "Subtle."

She gives me a gentle scolding look. "Took you long enough."

"Don't even start."

"Fine, I won't. But remember how I told you she'd be good for you?"

"You can't possibly take credit for *that*!"

Kiera laughs. "*Can't* is not a word in my vocabulary."

I scowl, but I have better things to do than stay irritated with her. It's been a long day, and normally I'd be pumped to go to bed, but there's no way I'm going to be able to sleep tonight. I've got too many apologies to repeat and too many missed kisses to make up for.

What Do You Want to Do?

Alexandra

I stand with Connor on the front porch of the Nest.

"Why didn't you tell me who you really were?" I ask him.

He checks his phone. "It had to be this way. The Vipers already gave you trouble for joining them the way you did. If they knew you were directly connected to me, do you think they'd treat you well?"

Knowing the guys as much as I do now, I believe they would. Although, Marshall did get ticked off that one time he was present for Connor's call. So I have to correct my belief to include one vital word— eventually. I nod my understanding. Connor hid his involvement for the same reasons I didn't tell the guys about my family. We both wanted me to have a place with them with as few things affecting their perception of me as possible.

"Thank you," I say. "For doing so much for me."

"You're welcome." Connor pats my head. "I'm sorry about the reasons that ultimately brought you here."

"Me too. I'm happy here though."

"Good." He heads to his car.

This is all nice and wonderful, but…

"Connor, what would have happened if I failed?"

He turns around. "I'd take care of you either way. Send you to college here or something. We'd figure it out."

There was a safety net for me all along? Connor is devious. Nice, but devious. Had I known I had nothing to worry about financially, I might've given up on Project Viper a long time ago.

After Connor drives off, I exhale and gaze at the star-dotted sky. What a day. I survived my first performance in front of thousands, and by all accounts, I was pretty good. I jump a few times in excitement. I'm a recognized singer. Heck, I'm a bassist!

Marshall comes out to the porch, and I can't help laughing. When we first met, he hated me and reminded me any time he could that I was not, in fact, a bassist. But I am now. Me! A tiny girl with tiny hands a bassist for Project Viper.

"What are you giggling about?" He wraps his arms around me.

I can't stop smiling at him. I told Connor the truth. I am happy here. My body's light enough to float, and I'm so ridiculously giddy seeing Marshall return my smile.

"So, you don't mind then that Connor forced me on you?"

"You know I did, a lot, six months ago. I didn't know you or what you could do. But not anymore." His hands slide to my waist. "It's late, but what do you want to do? Watch a movie? Go for a ride? Oh! I know."

Marshall takes my hand and leads me to the garage. "You don't mind a little outing, do you? I mean, you must be exhausted, but—"

"I don't mind."

His face is aglow with some brilliant plan, and I'm curious to find out what he came up with. Besides, I love this decisive Marshall. Such a wonderful difference from what he has been with me up to now.

We take his old BMW, although there's hardly anything old about it. The body is from the sixties or the seventies, I'm not an expert, but the paint is spotless and appears brand-new. Black with a slight pearlescent shimmer to it. And the insides are all polished to a shine, maybe replaced, including the red leather seats. It's a fun car, and I feel like I'm finally allowed into Marshall's world without having to force my way in.

Speaking of Marshall. He rubs his palms against the steering wheel and shifts in his seat every time we come to a red light.

"What are you planning that you're so squirmy?" I tease him.

"Nothing too awful." He pulls into the next parking lot.

I take in the building that gleams with bright windows in front of us. There are tables and a few people inside. "Is this a restaurant? Still open at this time?" I glance at the clock on the dashboard. It's after midnight.

"Yeah. It's not the best, but we never got that breakfast. So I figured, why not now?" He pops open the glove compartment and fishes out a black baseball cap that he pulls on low to conceal his upper face.

"You worry that the four people that are inside will recognize you?" I tease him again.

Marshall squints at me. "Fine." He takes off the cap and pushes it onto my head.

We go in, and sure enough, the bleary-eyed young woman that greets us doesn't even bother to look at our faces. She takes us to a booth, hands us utensils and laminated menus, and shuffles off after a promise to take our orders in a minute. Something tells me it's going to be quite a few minutes before she comes back. It doesn't matter. We're not here for the food exactly.

Marshall unfolds the napkin and arranges his utensils, then straightens a little glass dish with sugar packets, then aligns his paper placemat with the edge of the table. It's amusing to watch him struggle like this with…us being together?

After everything I've been through today, bravery is easy to find, so I take his hand across the table. "Marshall. Relax."

He exhales and moves his other hand away from the salt shaker. "I think I can be justified for being a little nervous with you. I've screwed up everything so far—"

"You didn't screw up *everything*."

He looks at me. We both cringe.

"You're too nice," he says.

"Well, fine." I try my best to be diplomatic. "You could've done a little better in some situations. I know you're sorry, and I don't want to spend tonight dwelling on the past. There's so much future ahead of me now. Ahead of us."

"Us." Marshall props his chin on his palm and stares at the ceiling for a second before his gaze returns to me. "Sounds good."

I shrink into my seat and clench my hands together. I felt a lot of different things with Marshall—anger, maddening frustration, desperation, curiosity, even desire. But now that we're on the same page, I'm nervous.

Oh. Okay. That's probably why he's been so fidgety.

The waitress finally comes back. She places two waters on the table and pulls out a tablet. "What can I get you?" She sounds quite a bit more energetic and smiles at Marshall. I don't exist.

He gives me a stern look.

I clear my throat and say, "I'll have the tall stack with strawberries and cream. Please."

The waitress jumps and stares at me. "Um. Of course. Anything else?" Her eyes still bounce to Marshall.

"Scrambled eggs."

"Sure. Any other items?"

"Orange juice."

"Is that it?"

I'm tempted to continue ordering more things, one by one, but I'd rather not waste my time with Marshall. I do, however, take a few more seconds to study the menu, then look at the waitress, who taps her thumb against the tablet. She smiles at me. I smile back. I don't know what's gotten into me. Must be that lingering bravery. And budding, territorial jealousy. This is *my* rock star. As soon as someone else goes through what I've gone through to be with Marshall Jones, they can have him. Scratch that. He's all mine no matter what.

She blinks, and I stifle a laugh. "Yes, that's all. Thank you."

Marshall orders eggs plus steak and hands our menus to the waitress. "Could we get the check right away please?"

The waitress heaves a suppressed sigh, but nods and leaves.

"She would've recognized you anyway," I say to Marshall as I adjust the black cap he surrendered to me. "And why did you ask for the check so early?"

"If she brings us the check, she'll have less reasons to pester us."

"Be nice."

He smirks. "I'll leave a nice tip."

We wait for our food in silence, although Marshall's feet find mine under the table and sandwich one of my feet between his. I take to spinning my phone between my fingers.

He breaks the silence. "I noticed something a while ago."

"Mmmm?"

"You have two phones, don't you?"

"Kind of." It looks like we're not done talking about my past tonight, which is okay. I pull my old Russian phone out of the pocket of my hoodie and place both devices on the table in front of me.

"This one's from home," I explain, pointing at my old smartphone. "It doesn't work here, but I don't need it to because Connor got me one that does. The old one has a bunch of photos and videos of my family. I have them all backed up to the Cloud and downloaded on several flash drives, but I still can't get myself to get rid of it. My dad got me this phone before I started my, what do you call it here, high school?"

Marshall nods. "You don't need to get rid of anything. I just wondered if you were a Russian spy."

"Seriously? Could you be any more cliché?"

"Probably."

He smiles, wide and warm. For me. All for me. The smile melts my core, and I have no clue why or how I'm still in one piece.

Our food arrives and we eat, rehashing the festival.

"I thought you would puke right before it was our turn to go on stage," Marshal says as he saws through his chicken-fried steak.

"Well, I'm sorry. Not all of us have years of experience appeasing large crowds." I steal a shred of potato from his plate.

He swallows his bite. "You did great."

"Really?" I mutter through a mouthful. They offered us plenty of food at the festival venue, but I was so dazed and drawn in every direction that I never got to eat anything properly. And now I'm starving. Pancakes hit the spot just right, even though they're a little too sweet for my taste.

"Really. It was fun."

"You think your fans liked me?" I reach for my new phone, but Marshall clamps his hand over mine.

"They're our fans," he says. "And don't check social media. It'll be a funky mix of comments for a week or so. Wait until we go more public with your addition. Even then, worry about sales more than fan reactions. There will always be disgruntled ones, and you can't please everyone anyway."

"But…"

It's easy for him to say I was great. I want to know what the public thinks. Did I really do well?

"Trust me." Marshall removes his hand and continues working on his steak. "Give it some time to circulate and settle. Don't worry about anything. Not tonight." He looks up, his gaze tender and reassuring. "You've been through a lot. Take a breather. You don't have to worry about anything right now."

I still remember what day it is. The struggle to win the Vipers over is also still fresh on my mind. So, when Marshall tells me not to worry about anything, tears rise to my eyes in less than two seconds. I bite my lip hard. Tears spill down my cheeks when I try to blink them away.

Marshall sits with me and hugs me, gently, like I'm about to break. "Should we go?"

There may be only a few people in the restaurant, but I'm still embarrassed through and through. "Yes. Is that okay?"

He pulls out his wallet. I stuff another bite of pancakes into my mouth while he deposits some cash on the table.

"Thank you," Marshall calls out to the sleepy, disappointed waitress that served us before we go out the doors.

I try to subdue the tears and sniffles all the way home. The moment we're in the driveway, Marshall helps me out of the car and hugs me again.

"It's okay. Don't fight it. You don't have to hide it anymore." He kisses me on the cheek. "You never had to."

His embrace is heaven, but the grief is so overwhelming, nothing comforts me. The only reason I'm here is because both of my parents are dead. How can I possibly enjoy what I have with that knowledge?

Then another thought cuts me. If they never died, I'd never meet the guys. I'd never have Marshall.

The warring realizations send me on my knees into the wet lawn next to the driveway. I sob, loudly, ugly, hiding my face in my elbow. Marshall's gentle but insistent hands pull me close and shield me from the world. He doesn't say anything until I calm down a bit, which, surprisingly, doesn't take long. A few late-night breezes, a hiccup, and a growing sense of numbness stop the flood.

"How did you... How did you ever survive?" I look Marshall in the eyes. "Without family? Without someone to love you, be with you, guide you?"

Yellowish light streams on us through the open car door. Marshall holds my gaze and smooths my hair. I close my eyes and relish his soothing touch.

"On a certain level, I couldn't miss what I never had. I only ever had dreams and wishes. You had something real that's been taken away from you. That is so much worse. Eventually, I found a family that was better than anything I could ever hope for. Now you're a part of it. I don't expect you to stop being sad, and no one expects you to carry on like nothing's ever happened, but I want you to remember you're not alone anymore. Talk to us. To me. Okay? Tell us everything. Ask me anything. Anything at all." Marshall stirs. "Rats. My butt is wet. I'm sorry. I was doing so well with my profound speech, but that's too cold."

Laughing, I stand up and offer him my hand. "Come on. Let's get inside." My behind is pretty wet and cold too.

He rises to his feet, closes the car door, and follows me to the guest house. "I mean it though. I'm here for you."

Bright, white lights come to life as we step onto the porch.

"Thank you. And I'm here for you too," I say and press my thumb to the fingerprint scanner attached to the door lock.

After the scanner gives me an approving beep, the lock clicks open. We step inside. The entryway lights, automatic like the porch ones, switch on. While I kick off my shoes, Marshall's hands sneak around my waist again and draw me to him.

"What was that saying?" I face him and slide my hands to the back of his neck. "Third try's the charm?"

"Perhaps." Marshall dips his head and inhales the scent of my hair. His lips brush the top of my ear, setting everything within me on fire.

"Are you going to kiss me or what?" I whisper, trying to regain control of my knees.

He chuckles and pulls slightly away. "Ladies first."

I thread my fingers through his dark, tousled curls, and bring him back. "I kissed you first to begin with. On Halloween. It's your turn."

He brushes his nose against mine. "I kissed you first on Christmas Eve. So it's your turn."

"We're counting now?" My voice refuses to rise above a whisper. Marshall's killing me. Another minute and I'll die. Would he just kiss me already?

"You're the one who started it. Also, the third try happened after the festival, on the side of the road." Marshall takes my chin with his fingers and traces the edge of my lower lip while his dark green eyes caress the rest of my face.

I rise on my toes to reach his lips, but he pulls away again.

"What now?" I groan, dropping my head back.

"I love you."

The way he says it—no playfulness, no teasing, but serious, his voice low and intense—steals all coherent thoughts from my brain. I stare at him, speechless. He said those words before, only a few hours ago, but this is different. I didn't doubt he meant it then, but now... Now his attitude is solid and committed.

"*Ya lyublyu tebya tozhe.*"

We kiss. Marshall doesn't kiss me first. Neither do I kiss him. Our lips meet halfway. Tentative and airy at first, the kiss gains slow and steady burn. My hands familiarize themselves with his shoulders, arms, and sides while Marshall kisses me on the forehead, the temple, down my jawline, on my neck. That last one steals my breath and makes me dizzy in the best kind of way.

"Marshall." I whisper his name. I just want to be closer. As close as possible.

He draws a sharp breath and steps back over the threshold. "Sleep in. I'm going to."

My body disagrees vehemently with this abrupt ending to our evening, but I'm grateful for the hit on the brakes. Not everything has to happen today.

"You think Zach will let us?" I lean in to kiss him one last time, but Marshall bursts out laughing.

"You know him well," he says once he catches his breath. "*Spi sladko, lyubov' moya.*"

Sweet dreams, my love.

I grab the front of his sweater and hold him in place until I steal that goodnight kiss. "You too."

By the Way

Marshall

4 months later

A few insane months pass after Alexandra joins the band on a permanent basis. I thought we'd make a few waves with that change, anger some fans, actually lose some popularity by breaking up the dude circle, and so on and so forth. All of that does happen. For two months after the news came out, we tanked in sales and streaming stats hardcore. Kiera and The Label got to do their magic by wiping off the summer from our calendars with a promotional tour abroad. We've never been this busy before.

Going through the gig routine is nothing new to me: pack, travel, arrive, unpack, perform, pack again, on the road again. Meetings, greetings, smiling, answering all the same dumb questions over and over again, although they're not quite the same now that Alexandra's with us.

Everyone is curious about her origins, her skills, her relationships with each of us. It's grueling work, and I worry that Alexandra will become worn out and tell us this mad lifestyle isn't worth it. She's a tough girl though and holds it together like she's been doing it for years along with us.

Then, in the middle of summer, the tables turn again. The more we're out with the masses, the more they see us perform live, the more people love our *Matryoshka*. When it's her turn to sing, the audiences join their voices with her as one. Not that I can't get the same response out of the crowd, but it's different. Alexandra's voice arrests a heart like nothing else can. She's brilliant, new, fresh. The rankings start rising, along with streaming and sales numbers, and we haven't even released a full new album yet. We do manage to record five new tracks for an EP, including an updated version of *Devastation, Free of Charge*. CJ still gives me the stink eye for the hours we wasted on that song any time he can, but I take to ignoring him. What's done is done. He'll get over it eventually.

Through all of this, I can't help thinking, cringing as I do, that I was right. Alexandra did ruin us. For a couple months. Just a little. But Kiera was right too. Alexandra is good for us. For me more than anybody else. That's why, despite the crammed schedule, I steal her for a week in Hawaii.

"Have you lost your mind?" Kiera shrieks at me, for once losing her cool, when she calls me the moment we land in Honolulu. "Come back immediately. You're performing in London in eight days. You don't have a week to waste! You couldn't wait until the end of August, until after you wrap up the European promo—"

"Kiera," I interrupt, holding Alexandra's hand as we wait for our suitcases at the luggage carousel.

She snaps a harried, "What?"

I kiss Alexandra's hand and take a few steps away. "I can't wait. Also." I glance at Alexandra, whose head turns around with energetic awe. She marvels at the world a lot, still, even though she's hit close to a dozen countries with us. I lower my voice. "It's too crazy. Alexandra will never say anything, but she should have a breather. We, she and I, need a breather as a couple. To not worry about who sees us or if we have a second to…look each other in the eyes." It's true, but I still grimace at having to explain this to our manager. "We needed to get away, okay? Don't let your blood pressure rise though. We'll make it to London on time."

I turn off the phone. There's no way I'm giving her a chance to keep harassing me into cutting this trip short.

We get to our London venue forty-six minutes late, but no one says a thing until the show is over and we're on the bus heading to our hotel.

"You were late. You were flipping late!" Sitting across the aisle, CJ throws his beanie in my face.

"And I made up for that with three extra songs." I toss the hat back at him. "What are you, Kiera's agent of vengeance now?"

"Don't be mad. We got stuck in traffic on the way from the airport." Alexandra looks at him with huge eyes and a sweet, apologizing pout.

CJ shoots her a half-hearted glare. "When did you learn to play dirty?"

"You're the one who taught me," she says.

Zach laughs at the top of his lungs from the seat up front, and the O'Neals shake their heads—Shane smiling and Graham staring at his phone.

"You two are terrible together," CJ grumbles. "No, I take that back. You were pretty awful to begin with. Only then you were fighting, and now you are…" He waves his hand as though the gesture explains us.

Alexandra hugs my arm and rests her head on my shoulder. "That was a great show."

"Yes. And we played Royal Albert Hall," I say. "Do you realize what it's like to play the same venue as some of my favorite musicians?"

She squeezes my arm a little harder. "It's like you're one of them now?"

Alexandra gets it. She gets it better than I do because I can't even begin to wrap my mind around what it would feel like to first join your favorite band, then play huge shows, following in the legends' steps.

I kiss the top of her head.

Zach wiggles his eyebrows at me over the top of his seat. "Did you propose while you were in Hawaii? Or was it a spontaneous, show-off-for-the-girlfriend trip?"

Alexandra hides her face behind her elbow, but I laugh out loud and pull out my phone, open Insta, and attach a photo of me and Alexandra. On our wedding day.

I really was planning to propose. We ended up eloping instead. She was the one who suggested it. The moment I mentioned wedding preparations and how Kiera and the girls would go to town with it, Alexandra grabbed the front of my T-shirt and said she'd only marry me if we did it immediately. To keep it ours, not the media's.

She wore a simple white gown with a wreath made with an assortment of pink, purple, and white flowers sitting on her head instead of a bouquet. I wore all white too. We got married on the beach, had thin, white gold bands for rings, and ate our wedding dinner in our hotel room. It was simple, quiet, intimate, and right.

Now it's going to be public.

I hold my breath as I watch the rest of my bandmates play with their phones. How long until—

"You did not!" Zach yells. "Not without me!"

Alexandra jumps. "Why is he so hyper all of a sudden?"

Zach disregards all safety and tumbles from his seat. He falls over my legs, the heavy giraffe that he is, and fake weeps on Alexandra's lap. "How could you do this? I was going to take you to the altar."

Alexandra pushes Zach away. "How did you know? How did he know?" She looks at me, frowning and thoroughly confused.

Graham throws his arm between the seats and shows her his phone screen and my post. I'm all cleaned up, she's breathtaking, and it's impossible to miss the rings on our fingers. I think it's my message that accompanies the photo that takes the cake though.

By the way.

The End

Thank you for reading!

Enjoyed this book? If you have a minute, please leave a review on Amazon, Goodreads, BookBub, or a reader's platform of your choice. Other than buying a book, reviews are the next best thing to help authors support their careers.

You can also post a review on sotical media and tag #projectviper to spread the word.

RELUCTANT
HEARTBREAKERS
& SWEET
TROUBLEMAKERS

unREASONable (vol. 1 - Marshall - vocals)

unBREAKable (vol. 2 - CJ - lead guitar)

unSUSTAINable (vol. 3 - Shane - rhythm guitar)

unBEATable (vol. 4 - Graham - drums)

unSPEAKable (vol. 5 - Zach - keyboard)

Acknowledgments

It may take a village to raise a child, but it takes just as many people to help authors maintain confidence and troubleshoot rebellious spots of their novels. It's incredible, really.

There is the creative support crew—other writers and eager readers (Sarah C, Jessica F, Briana N, Sari C, Charity W, Robin K, Tanya H, Paige U, and Jennifer H).

There's that sweet friend and neighbor who gave us writing time by making us meals when we were sick and watched our kids (Sara P).

There's the editor who staved off the anxiety that the book is garbage and should never see the light of day (Kelsy T).

There are all the musicians that provided soundtracks to the writing process and made scenes come to life, too many to name, but all of them forever etched in the soul and every line of the story and the authors' minds.

We also must thank the inventors of caffeine. We know we don't need it to fuel our "brilliant ideas," but we like to have it all the same. Especially on Fridays, at midnight. Who needs sleep? (Just kidding. We do. We really need more sleep.)

And of course, of course, it's the people closest to the madness, in our home and those we're tied to by blood or marriage. They deserve some cool awards for bearing with us while we agonize over adverbs and botched up motivations.

The readers take a special place. Always. We write these things for them, for you, and hope to give a few chuckles, gasps, tears, pouts and "awww" moments.

Until the next time,

~ Arya

About the Author

Arya Matthews is a husband-and-wife creative duo that codes web applications by day and molds their snippets of imagination into stories by night.

We chase two kids, play guitars, can't pass up a bag of Sweet Chili and Sour Cream chips at the supermarket, and dream of Tokyo ever since we went on a vacation there three years ago.

Website and newsletter: www.aryamatthews.com
Instagram: @arya_matthews_author
Facebook: www.facebook.com/amatthewsrockstarromance
Say "hello" or questions: hello@aryamatthews.com

Playlist

Plain White T's "Rhythm Of Love"

Hypnogaja "Static"

Muse "New Born"

Boys Like Girls "Heart Heart Heartbreak"

The Ready Set "Killer"

The Unlikely Candidates "Call My Name"

Plain White T's "Hate (I Really Don't Like You)"

the mother hips "Time We Had"

My Chemical Romance "The Sharpest Lives"

Blue October "Into The Ocean"

Nothing But Thieves "Trip Switch"

Thousand Foot Krutch "War of Change"

Tokio Hotel "Darkside Of The Sun"

Train "Angel in Blue Jeans"

Artist Vs Poet "So Much I Never Said"

The Ready Set "A Little More"

One Direction "I Want" AFI "Snow Cats"

All Time Low "A Love Like War" (feat. Vic Fuentes)

Jimmy Eat World "Pain"

Tokio Hotel "Monsoon"

Boys Like Girls "Five Minutes to Midnight"

Muse "Bliss"

My Chemical Romance "Sleep"

The Red Jumpsuit Apparatus "It Was You"

Fireal "Ariel"

Lovex "Take A Shot"

Sia "Never Give Up"

Black Veil Brides "In The End"

Sia "Alive"

Fall Out Boy "The Phoenix"

Broken Iris "We're Not Alone"

David Garret "The 5th"

Zach's Cake in a Mug

2 Tbsp BUTTER 2.5 Tbsp SUGAR
¼ tsp SALT
½ tsp VANILLA EXTRACT
1 EGG (large)
2 Tbsp MILK/CREAM
1 Tbsp APPLESAUCE
6 Tbsp FLOUR
½ tsp BAKING POWDER

Optional

½ Tbsp LEMON JUICE or
½ tsp ALMOND EXTRACT (Almond extract makes it superb. We promise!)

Toppings

Sliced fruit, chocolate syrup, a ball of your favorite ice cream, whipping cream, frosting, sprinkles, whatever else your heart desires and your pantry accommodates

Steps

1. Melt butter in a large mug. A short, round mug that can hold at least 12oz is ideal.

2. Add sugar to the melted butter. Stir well.

3. Add salt and vanilla extract. If using almond extract or any other flavoring that's not sour, add them now too. Stir.

4. Add egg, milk, and applesauce. Mix very well.

5. Add flour and baking powder. You guessed it. Mix until there are no clumps. But do be kind and gentle to your batter. Give it some loving.

6. Microwave for 2 minutes on high (1100 watts). You might need to experiment with lower power microwaves or settings. Altitude may come into play too, so keep an eye on your cake. ;)

Made in the USA
Coppell, TX
02 July 2022